BLEEDING SEA

K.A. KIRTLAND

Black Rose Writing | Texas

The author grants the final approval for this literary material.

First printing

ISBN: 978-1-68513-483-9
LIBRARY OF CONGRESS CONTROL NUMBER:2024935844
PUBLISHED BY BLACK ROSE WRITING
www.blackrosewriting.com

Printed in the United States of America
Suggested Retail Price (SRP) $23.95

Bleeding Sea is printed in Minion Pro

*As a planet-friendly publisher, Black Rose Writing does its best to eliminate unnecessary waste to reduce paper usage and energy costs, while never compromising the reading experience. As a result, the final word count vs. page count may not meet common expectations.

For Anna, Isaac, and Michael, who illuminate my life
with a love more beautiful than a shiny sea.

BLEEDING SEA

CHAPTER 1

March 8

Two friends, Bo and Henry, shielded from the rain in yellow slickers, stood on a pier a few miles from Pensacola, Florida and watched their fishing lines. Bo glanced at the weather radar on his phone and scrolled to the local news showing aerial images of the shoreline covered in bright red slime with sprawling slivers of crimson-colored algae that looked like gnarled, bloody fingers pointing toward the sea. Still, the reporter gave her brightest smile. "Local authorities say the harmful algal bloom should disappear in a few weeks. Today we get a break from yesterday's slow-moving thunderstorms."

A few feet away from them, a boy of nine or so slouched next to a man transfixed by a line attached to an orange balloon bobbing in the water. Near the pier, a gray-haired man on the beach tossed a cast net into the surf.

Henry squinted at the overcast sky. "I thought fish were active and willing to take chances when it's cloudy."

Bo chuckled. "Maybe you should get bait a fish would be interested in."

"You know I'm so poor, I can't even pay attention."

"The only disadvantage you have is an inability to hook a decent fish."

The men, who had worked most of their lives as deckhands on commercial fishing boats, laughed at each other. "At least I don't tell stories about catching a six-foot snook." Henry nudged Bo's arm.

"Remember that whopper you told when we come back from the Caribbean on the *Beeracuda*."

Bo grinned. "Got a big laugh from everyone on the dock."

"Except for your niece. I can still see freckle-nosed Diane, no bigger than a minute, searching all over for that fish."

"Hell, she's probably still lookin' for it, and that was twenty years ago."

Bo spotted a little girl tiptoeing in the frothy water and reminisced about his niece at that age. Next to him, the boy shouted, "We got one!"

The man, who was with the boy, reeled in a two-foot grouper that wasn't putting up a fight. The boy jumped up and down. "Dad, you're the greatest fisherman."

The father unhooked the fish and gave it to his son, then turned to Bo and offered his phone. "Would you mind taking our picture?"

Bo nodded with a wide grin. "Whadda catch!" He aimed the camera at the smiling pair and noticed their trophy had a couple of faint pinkish-red spots and a small bloodred gash. After he took the picture and returned the phone, he pointed out the flaws. "I'm not sure that's a keeper. Looks sickly."

The father examined the half-inch injury and snickered. "I'll just cut that part out." He clapped his son on the shoulder. "Let's quit while we're ahead." He grabbed their fishing gear while the boy clutched the large motionless fish with both arms.

Bo watched the cheerful duo walk down the pier toward the beach. "Reminds me of the times I'd bring Diane."

"Isn't she graduating soon?"

"Yeah. Gettin' her PhD. She wants to get a job with some fancy foundation in Fort Lauderdale. I'd like her to move close to home."

Henry reeled in his line and replaced the bait with a smelly chunk of fish. "The problem is you still think of her as a little girl. Hell, you raised her. To keep up with you, that poor thing had to learn to swim before she could walk."

The big smile on Diane's tiny face when he had taught her to doggie paddle was etched in Bo's memory. "I don't mind her at sea or swimming with big fish. What aches my fifty-year-old bones is the thought of land sharks of the male persuasion circling her."

"Can't keep her from gettin' a broken heart."

A sudden gust of wind and rain pelted Bo's face. He blinked to clear his vision, shook his head, and put up his hood. Perhaps it was time to loosen his grip on protecting her.

Sudden movement behind Henry got Bo's attention. The boy's father was kneeling at the end of the pier next to the boy, who was on his knees and frantically rubbing his arms. The fish was lying behind them. "I'm going over there to make sure they're okay," Bo said and quickened his pace when he heard the boy cry. He was maybe twenty feet from them when he yelled, "Everything alright?"

The father didn't answer. The boy grimaced and kept digging at his skin. When Bo reached them, the boy, whose arms were swollen with red blotches, looked up, his eyes watery, and choked out, "I can't breathe."

His father picked him up, his voice on the verge of panic. "It's like he's having some kind of reaction to that damn fish."

Bo reached for his phone. "I'll call 9-1-1."

The man shook his head. "We'll get to the ER faster." He jostled the boy in his arms and set off running toward the parking lot.

Suddenly, someone screamed.

Bo swiveled to see an elderly woman pointing at a man who had collapsed into a cast net that was floating around him. A couple of men bounded into the water and started dragging his limp body to shore.

Shouts had Bo turning his head in the opposite direction. A few yards away, a young couple knelt beside the little girl he'd noticed earlier. She was clawing her feet and wailing.

Something was *very* wrong.

Bo shivered in the warm rain. An odd stench caused him to glance back at the father's discarded fish, now lying on the wood planks. The lesions on its lifeless body were now a fiery red.

Lugging poles and a tackle box, Henry joined Bo. "What the hell's going . . . ?" He froze after spotting the crimson-colored grouper.

The men exchanged worried glances. Bo put on his fishing gloves, picked up the carcass, then hurled it into the sea. The dead animal floated to the surface, a bright reddish sheen surrounding it, reminding him of the fire algae he'd just seen on the news. According to the experts, the bloom would disappear in a few weeks. Red tides were hell on fish, but they always went away, eventually.

CHAPTER 2

June 3

Today was the big day: the interview. Diane rushed out of her apartment into the midday Florida sun, then stopped in her tracks. She got a whiff of a foul smell that turned her stomach. Her eyes started watering, and her nostrils were stinging from it. Though she was running late, she couldn't help herself; she followed the stench to a nearby harbor along Hollywood Beach.

Decaying fish and a dead manatee, thick flesh peeling away and covered in red slime, floated in the water. Bright red algae with sprawling, stringlike, velvety tentacles scattered across the harbor and floated up and down the swells of the Atlantic Ocean. Diane was familiar with the foul smells of overgrown algae and rotting fish, but this was gut-wrenching. She covered her mouth and nose with her hands and stared at the carnage.

The toxic bloom had first appeared along the Pensacola coast after record-breaking rainfalls across the Southeast that had begun in early March. Though the rains had slowed and the floodwaters were receding, the red algae continued to spread, turning the Gulf of Mexico's natural dark blue water into worrisome bloodred cascades. Over the past few weeks, the bloom had spread into the Atlantic. The number of floating carcasses was doubling each day. Movement on the water brought Diane back to the present.

A single vessel trolled the otherwise busy shipping lanes. The Coast Guard prevented boats from leaving the harbor. Toxin levels had become unsafe for seafarers. The only ships allowed access to the sea belonged to the Ocean Science and Climatology Foundation, or OSCF (pronounced *oh-sif*). Led by Dr. Shaun Jenson and Dr. Susan Landry, OSCF had the resources and support of the federal government to continue its exploration of the deadly bloom.

Diane headed back to her car. Her interview was for a postdoctoral position with OSCF. Her research into the microorganisms causing the growing infestation made her a highly desirable candidate. Dinoflagellates were causing the red tides, and she was an expert in their biology. A few months ago, she'd presented findings from her doctoral study at a national conference where Dr. Jenson had been the virtual keynote speaker. With charismatic charm, Jenson had given a riveting speech about the impacts of global warming, ending his talk with "If anyone says you're only one person who can't make a difference, then you do everything in your power to bring about change." Those words had stayed with Diane. Becoming a marine biologist at the foundation had always been her career goal, and this position would open many doors. She glanced down at the time on her phone and jumped into her old Jeep Wrangler.

Thirty minutes later, she arrived at OSCF's campus. A white-block, three-story building with a sign that read "Center for Atmospheric and Marine Sciences" was surrounded by smaller buildings, a private beach, and a dock flanked by mangroves. From the Jeep, Diane looked out at the campus and took a few deep breaths to calm her nerves.

The sun was out, but a few raindrops hit her windshield. Gazing at the Atlantic, she was reminded of diving in the Gulf one day when a sun-shower seemed to come out of nowhere. She had floated right below the water's surface and watched the raindrops create orbs, making a soft, garbled noise that reminded her of distant, muted wind chimes. Remembering the underwater images and sounds soothed her. She whispered to her reflection in the rearview mirror, "You can do this." After combing her hair and applying lipstick, she stepped out of the Jeep and straightened her dress, an almond color that matched the shade of her hair.

The station guard watched her approach and grinned. "Your first visit?"

That obvious? "I have an appointment with Dr. Jane Bennett."

The guard confirmed her appointment, then handed her a visitor's badge and showed her a map of the building.

"Relax, they won't bite," he said, revealing a wide, toothy smile. "Not on your first visit."

While walking to the main entry, she noticed what looked like reporters hanging around. Her knees felt a bit wobbly when the next security guard glanced at her badge and waved her inside. She was used to entering buildings on a college campus with little to no security.

In the large foyer, a huge flat-screen TV displayed satellite pictures of the bright red Gulf Coast. An anchorman reported, "It looks like the sea is bleeding." Diane had grown up near the shores of Pensacola. Watching the Gulf Coast become a blanket of crimson was like watching a cherished treasure go up in flames.

The reporter cut to a shot of a woman in Panama Beach. Her swollen, tear-filled eyes appeared confused. Her voice trembled. "My four-year-old got out of her bath last night covered in hives and hyperventilated." She sobbed as someone rubbed her shoulder. "Amy stopped breathing on the way to the hospital." She crumpled into the arms of the man standing near her.

The man holding the weeping mother gazed into the camera. "Our little girl died. She had no prior health problems." He lowered his head and, hauntingly, added, "All she did was take a bath."

Diane pressed a heavy hand to her chest as the anchorwoman read off a teleprompter. "Medical experts believe their daughter died from exposure to toxins caused by the algal bloom. If you live near the Gulf, we urge you to use filtered or bottled water for drinking and bathing."

"What a nightmare," Diane muttered.

A receptionist led Diane into Dr. Bennett's office, where she settled in a chair opposite a massive oak desk adorned with science journals, waiting for the director of biological research. Diane was young, only twenty-five, and a recent graduate of the University of Miami. She bit her nails and told herself, *You were top of your class; your research is a perfect fit,* but she worried it might not be enough to compete with older, more experienced candidates.

After a few minutes, Dr. Bennett, a distinguished woman in her late fifties with dark hair speckled with gray, walked into the room and extended her hand. “You must be Dr. Nelson.”

The director sat behind her desk and reviewed her notes before taking off her reading glasses and focusing on Diane. “We generally keep postdocs for at least three years, and it’s possible it could lead to a permanent position. Your research would be useful in understanding the conditions causing the toxic bloom in the Gulf.” She pointed at papers bound with a clip on her desk. “We received this report from the Florida Department of Environmental Protection that shows toxins in some rivers and lakes.”

Wanting to verify the news report, Diane leaned toward the desk. “Are neurotoxins infiltrating the public water system?”

Dr. Bennett placed the documents in an expandable folder. “Yes, and medical experts believe the toxins in the water system are causing paralysis of the respiratory system. There have been fatalities. Some are making national headlines today.” She hesitated, seeming to consider her words. “Our last postdoc suffered a nervous breakdown. He was incredibly smart and hardworking, but he couldn’t handle the stress.”

“Was he a marine biologist working on the bloom?”

“He’s a chemist and an engineer. Most of his work was in the application of technology to reduce greenhouse gas emissions. When the floods began and the bloom became a problem, like others, his interest changed to investigating conditions that led to the outbreak in the Panhandle.”

“What did he find?”

Dr. Bennett glanced away, as if not wanting to share what she knew. “A question with no easy answer.” She returned her attention to Diane, studying her. “I’ve spoken to your research advisor. He says you’re extremely driven. As you can see, OSCF is in the national spotlight. The problem in the Gulf is getting worse. Right now, it’s the states along the

Gulf Coast that are most affected. But that could change." She scanned her notes. "I'm interviewing more candidates today, but if offered the position, you'll need to sign a nondisclosure agreement. You cannot talk to the media or post information related to our research on the internet. Any data you collect is immediately shared with me. No writings of any kind are submitted to journals or other media without approval."

Diane wasn't concerned about confidentiality rules. Scientists didn't publicize findings until their results were peer-reviewed. It seemed odd that she would have to share her work immediately, though. Maybe OSCF was nervous about public access to information given an employee's recent mental breakdown. She wanted to present herself as a team player, so despite her hesitation, she said, "I understand."

"You have wonderful recommendations attesting to your strong work ethic. Your knowledge and laboratory skills would benefit us, but I have two questions for you." Bennett folded her arms. "This would be your first job. We've got an environmental catastrophe, and everyone is looking to us for answers. Do you believe you can handle a twenty-four-hour workload and, at a moment's notice, be pulled onto research vessels heading out to sea for weeks at a time?"

Diane didn't hesitate. "You don't have to worry about me. The challenges of research and experimentation are what drive me. Marine science is my passion."

She thought it was a great response, but Bennett didn't smile or even acknowledge the answer. Her palms were sweaty while Bennett wrote on a pad.

Finally, Bennett looked up at her. "Why did you become a marine biologist?"

Diane had prepared for every question related to the position description, but for some reason, she was not ready for this one. Her heart pounded as every answer that raced into her mind felt contrived. Many people had probably sat in this chair and said something like

"Because I love the ocean." To get this job, she had to avoid quick responses that sounded rehearsed. She went with the truth.

"When I was eleven years old, my uncle took me on a fishing trip in the Gulf. We found an oil slick about a quarter-mile long. I wondered why the people who'd left it there didn't clean it up. If gasoline spilled in their house, they'd have it professionally cleaned. If their pet stepped into a noxious chemical, they'd scrub their paws until spotless and rush to the vet. I think marine life, because it's not easily seen, is dismissed." She paused, watched Bennett lean forward with a small grin, and then continued. "People swerve to miss squirrels sprinting across the road, but boaters run over slow-moving manatees." She glanced down at her clammy hands folded on her lap, then met Bennett's gaze. "I became a marine biologist to find ways to protect sea organisms and their home."

Save them from us.

CHAPTER 3

Diane received the offer from OSCF the next day. It included a modest postdoctoral salary, and she accepted with enthusiasm. As she'd told Dr. Bennett, this was what she had dreamed of since she was eleven. Uncle Bo was the first person she called to share her news.

"I knew you'd get it," he said. "Can they teach you to fish better than me?"

She giggled. "Hey, I caught more fish than you last summer."

"Oh hell, I forgot about that."

They had kept a couple of foot-long yellowtail snappers and returned the rest of their catch to the Gulf. Uncle Bo had always told her, "Whenever you take treasures from the sea, gotta give somethin' back to her."

Her uncle was like a father to her. When Diane was born, he moved in with her mom and helped raise her. He had been the breadwinner, and now that the persistent bloom had devastated fisheries, he was out of work. Her mom's meager preschool teacher salary was their only source of income. Though Diane barely had a hundred dollars in her checking account, she offered support. "When I get my first paycheck, I'll send money."

"Don't fret about us. We'll make ends meet as long as nobody moves those ends."

• • •

Two days later, she arrived early for her first day on the job. She parked next to a truck with an OSCF employee sticker on the windshield and noticed a young man with shoulder-length hair sitting behind the wheel. He gazed at a preserved orange starfish on his dashboard. *Odd*, she thought. He looked up at her with no expression. Just a blank stare. Instinctually she waved at him. He didn't acknowledge her.

She respected his need for space and walked toward the building to find several local news trucks already lined up. Reporters crowded the walkway, all talking at once into their phones. The sound of waves crashing onto the nearby beach was gentle compared to their chortling.

Inside, the building was quiet. A TV hanging on one wall was tuned to a cable news station. The sound was muted, but the red chyron streaming below the blond anchor left little doubt about what was being discussed. "Red Tide Threatens Life in the Gulf of Mexico." Across the room, a technician carried a case labeled "Barometers" and walked into one of the many laboratories. Before the lab door closed behind the woman, Diane got a glimpse of shelves loaded with supplies and instruments stacked on long tables.

Bennett approached with a big smile. "Welcome to your first day. You're in luck. Dr. Jenson is in the bio-lab. You'll get to meet him."

Butterflies fluttered in Diane's stomach as she followed Bennett down the corridor and into the bio-lab. She paused and looked around as the door closed behind her. Three women wearing lab coats were speaking with Jenson, who, with his stubbly beard and chiseled jawline, looked even more handsome than he did on television.

She searched for the right words to say to the man who'd inspired her to pursue this dream, but she wouldn't get to use them—not then.

They were only steps away from Jenson when a loud bang followed by screams echoed throughout the building. Fast, thunderous booms got louder as the sound got closer to the lab. Diane looked at the closed door, half expecting it to explode. Bennett looked pale. The other women appeared confused, but Jenson was a whirlwind of action. He pushed everyone near a bench with front and side panels and whispered, "Get under there. Stay quiet. Don't move. That's gunfire."

The five women ducked under the bench, everyone piled on top of one another. Diane was at the bottom of the heap, her body pressed against the floor, heart pounding. The space seemed to shrink as she struggled to catch her breath. When she inhaled, a stench of deodorant mixed with cheap-smelling perfume assaulted her sinuses. She inched closer to a small space between the worktable legs for air. She could see a little of the lab from that position. A door opened, and Diane's heart clenched in her chest.

Someone had entered the lab.

She listened, holding her breath as she heard footsteps heading away from their hiding place. Someone wearing a pair of dirty, worn sneakers stepped toward the back of the room. A young woman, hands in prayer position, was pressed up against her.

Is the shooter the odd guy from the truck?

A loud explosion rang out. Glass shattered. Wood in the rear of the lab cracked and crashed to the ground. Warm air rushed over her. Sudden pressure in her ears caused sharp pain, and Diane gritted her teeth to keep from crying. Someone let out a wail. Others shushed the crier, who became silent. Nearby, three more shots exploded.

Diane's heart raced. She shivered as she tried to take a quick, quiet breath. The dirty sneakers crept toward the bench. She froze and thought of her mom and uncle in a small brick house on the Panhandle. *Will they be okay if something happens to me?*

Tears welled in her eyes as the sneakers came even closer.

Suddenly, she saw brown leather shoes rushing toward the worn sneakers.

Loud grunts, movement, a struggle.

A man whimpered, "I'm so sorry." Then a single gunshot. Something heavy hit the floor mere feet from where Diane crouched. Still shaking, she looked up. His head was tilted in her direction. It was the man from the truck. What used to be an eye was now a bloody cavity, and the remaining eye jerked uncontrollably. His body relaxed, and the eye twitched more slowly until it froze into a glassy stare.

Holy shit! Is he dead? Was that guy the shooter?

Screams and cries filled the room. The leather shoes walked past the young man lying on the floor.

Diane didn't know how long they'd been under attack. It felt like seconds, but it had to have been longer because sirens were blaring outside the building. Fast-moving footsteps entered the lab. Someone yelled, "Police! Stay where you are!" She strained to hear what they were saying but couldn't make out their words over the shrieking cries.

From behind her, Jenson's deep voice resonated. "It's safe to come out now."

People moved out from under the bench in halting, slow movements, looking stunned and afraid. Something tasted bitter. She touched her mouth with trembling fingers. *Blood. His? No. I bit my lip.* Strong hands wrapped around her waist, pulled her from underneath the bench, and lifted her onto her feet. She wobbled a bit, then turned to find Jenson splattered with blood. He grabbed a box of Kimwipes off a nearby table, handed them to her, and pointed at his mouth. "Your lip."

"Thank you," she stammered and pressed the wipe to her mouth. While looking down at the blood-stained tissue, she noticed his brown leather shoes.

He walked with the police officers to the shooter's body as firefighters worked to put out a small fire in the back. Broken bottles were strewn around the lab, and a strong pickle-like odor permeated the air. Diane recognized it as formalin, used to preserve fish. Investigators in police jackets and gloves picked up items around the room. First responders forced everyone to leave the building.

She found herself at the back of the group being hustled out of the bio-lab. Jenson spoke to an officer. "I snuck around the bench. When he turned his head, I went for the gun. In the struggle, he aimed it at himself, said something about being sorry, then shot himself."

She took one last look at the young man lying on the floor. Blood trickled from his face into his hair. He wore a bright orange T-shirt with a laughing emoji. A policeman knelt near the dead body, taking pictures while paramedics unfolded a black body bag.

Everyone seemed to move toward the building exit in a slow, awkward motion. Teardrops flowed while people whispered, "An amazing chemist," "The bio-lab fired him," and "He always looked skittish."

The shooter was most likely the postdoc who had a nervous breakdown.

What am I getting myself into?

Diane made it outside the building and, though still a bit dazed, provided a statement to a middle-aged police officer. She stepped away from him, trying to find space to breathe. The reporters who had crowded the walkway were now confined to an area ten yards away from the building. Their numbers had doubled. One of them, a young woman, was watching her. Diane glanced over at the reporter, who gave her a quick wave. Diane's senses were too numb to engage with someone searching for a headline. She turned back to the officer and asked, "Was anyone else hurt?"

"No one except the shooter. Majority of damage was in the lab where you were. Could've been much worse."

"He sounded sad when he said he was sorry."

The officer nodded, offering his card. "Murderers say they're sorry, but the only thing they regret is getting caught. If you need to speak to anyone for support, call the number on the card."

CHAPTER 4

Now a crime scene, the OSCF building remained closed for a week. Diane spent most of that time in the cramped, one-bedroom apartment she shared with stacks of science journals. When she wasn't scouring the internet for news about the shooting, she played Minecraft, an online game where the goal was to collect materials used to build structures while surviving a generated world of monsters. She had played Minecraft with an online group of friends since high school. Listening to slow reverb pop songs on YouTube while mining for diamonds helped distract her from memories of the attack.

Because she knew her mom Vera and Uncle Bo would learn about the assault on TV, she had called them soon after the incident. She remembered the worry and strain in her mom's voice. "Maybe you should get a postdoc at a university."

"It's okay. OSCF is increasing security. I can't give up my dream job." Mom had begun to wheeze, followed by a puff from an inhaler.

Diane waited a few seconds, then said, "I'm worried about you. You're asthmatic and live only a mile away from the Pensacola coast, near where the bloom started. You're at ground zero, and it's getting worse. Please go stay with our cousins in Atlanta."

Her mother's response was quick and resolute. "I'm not leaving our home. The preschool is already understaffed. People here need to work and someone to care for their children."

"Mom . . ."

"I'll be fine. I'll know when it's time for me to go." Her mom muffled a cough away from the phone.

"That would be now," Diane said in a stern voice.

"Well, I need to go. Please be careful. Good luck in your new job."

Diane thought about calling her mom again to convince her to leave the Panhandle, but she knew it would be futile. Instead, she logged in to her OSCF account for the third in a series of mandatory online meetings regarding the attack. The speaker today was the physics lab director.

His demeanor and tone were business as usual. "OSCF has implemented new systems to ensure your return to a safe workplace on Monday. We've installed additional protocols to promote a secure work environment. Please contact the list of grief counselors we've provided."

Throughout the week, OSCF sent out several emails with lists of therapists and online courses. Diane discovered a link to training on what to do in an active shooter event. The course had a "Run, Hide, Fight" logo. *I got the second one down.* She was thankful Jenson had confronted the danger, but the attacker's death saddened her.

The local chief of police was on TV. She shut her laptop, grabbed the remote, and turned up the volume on the television. "We've identified the shooter and bomber as Matthew Toft from Akers, Kentucky. Though this is an ongoing investigation, preliminary evidence suggests he was a disgruntled worker." The chief described reports of Matthew's mental state after being fired, damage to the main building, and the struggle that ended with the shooter turning the gun on himself.

They cut to a shot of Jenson, who appeared distraught. "It's heartbreaking. This was a person who used to work for our foundation. Everyone's lives were at risk."

"Why was he terminated?" the male reporter asked.

"HR policy won't let me comment on that."

Diane turned to different news channels and found more of the same, with reporters focusing on Jenson's heroic actions. Matthew

Toft's last words kept reverberating in her head. *Why did he say he was sorry?*

Over the next few days, news about the shooting became scarce. Reporters returned their attention to the red Gulf water and dead sea life littering the coastline. On the news, a Florida congressman said, "The government plans to distribute carbon filters for faucets and showerheads, as well as extra bottled water, to the most impacted residents of the bloom."

Media outlets ran several headlines about the toxic bloom, but the one Diane couldn't forget was an online interview titled "Red Tide Changes Plans for Summer Vacationers" that was held with timeshare condominium owners. She was disgusted to think that thousands of animals were dying from contamination seemingly relentless in its spread, and those people were focused on losing money.

• • •

When OSCF employees were allowed back into the building, Diane saw that the number of reporters gathered at the entrance had doubled again, appearing more like an invading army. The young journalist who had watched Diane give a statement to the police stepped toward her and said, with a Cuban accent, "My name is Isabelle Corzo. I'm with the *Miami Herald*, and I have some questions about the bloom."

Diane glanced up at the security camera. "I'm sorry, I can't comment."

Isabelle followed her gaze. "I know about the NDA." She turned at an angle, blocking the camera's view of her taking out a business card. "I'm getting zero information from your bosses. My papa always said when you're getting nowhere, change direction. If you ever feel the need to talk, Dr. Nelson, please call me."

"How did you know my na—"

"I do my research."

Diane looked at the card but didn't take it. "Ms. Corzo, I'm sure the foundation leaders will answer your questions soon."

As Diane turned to leave, the woman touched her arm. The reporter's brown eyes were filling with tears while she fidgeted with a small pearl ring on her right hand. "Lita—that's my grandmother—lived near Miami. She gave me this ring. She died last week from respiratory failure."

"I'm sorry to hear—"

"Doctors blamed it on her age. But my Lita was healthy and could walk for miles in the surf every day. I believe the poisoned waters killed her. For me, this is more than a story. Your identity will not be revealed if you can tell me anything about how this bloom started and why it's not going away."

Diane took the card and shoved it in her pocket, knowing she couldn't tell the media about OSCF's research. "I'm truly sorry for your loss."

Isabelle's expression softened, and her voice became childlike. "I don't want to lose my mom. She's all I have. We live only a few miles from where Lita lived, and I'm scared."

Diane felt the same way about her family. If anything happened to her mom or uncle, she'd be alone. "I won't stop working on this problem until I know how the bloom started and how to stop it."

Isabelle smiled sadly and walked away with her chin lowered to her chest.

She doesn't think I can figure this out.

Diane entered the building. The butterflies were back, but this time the queasiness she felt was not brought on by a chance encounter with an idol but by the memory of gunfire and the sightless eye of the disturbed young man who had died an arm's length from where she had cowered. She took a deep breath and replaced thoughts of the attack with her family living in the Panhandle and with Isabelle losing her grandmother. The spreading bloom needed her undivided attention.

The foyer, empty of furniture and the TV that had been riddled with bullet holes, seemed larger. Workers repaired drywall and painted sections of the shot-up wall.

She stopped in front of the closed door leading to the bio-lab. A small sliver of yellow crime tape remained. Her hands trembled as she recalled the fear and confusion when the shooter walked into the lab. The whole thing had been surreal.

Diane found her way to a temporary lab and recognized the woman who had been praying while pressed against her during the attack. She appeared younger than Diane.

"I'm Nicole, the lab tech." Her sunken green eyes seemed unfocused, as if she hadn't slept for a few days. "You were in the bio-lab when all hell broke loose."

"Yes. I'm Diane, the new postdoc. I've heard about first-day-on-the-job horror stories but nothing like that."

Nicole rubbed her eyes. "Did you see the news?"

Diane nodded.

"Matt was such a kind, smart person." Nicole's eyes watered as she spoke, the sadness evident. "He must've snapped." She seemed to want to say more and fought to hold back tears.

Unsure what to say and recalling Bennett's account of his nervous breakdown, Diane managed, "I'm sorry you lost a friend."

Nicole stared at a spot on the floor between them, a teardrop on the verge of falling. "Toward the end of his employment, he was nervous, especially after his meeting with Dr. Jenson and Dr. Landry." She twirled a strand of her blond hair. "I asked him a few times what was wrong, but he would change the subject. Before he was fired, he became obsessed with the algal bloom." She looked up at Diane. "That's your expertise, right?"

"Yes, my doctoral study was on dinoflagellates causing red tides."

Nicole lowered her eyes again. "Sorry you had to start with this horrific tragedy. I'm still in shock."

Diane shifted her feet. "It's a relief that he didn't shoot anyone." She studied Nicole's tear-filled eyes and added, "Except himself. Why do you think he did it?"

"No idea." Nicole's eyes returned to the spot on the floor, and then she looked up with a slight smile. "You'll meet Todd and Brandon today. They work in the lab. Todd's an oceanographer, and Brandon's a computer engineer. They're returning from resetting and deploying underwater bots in the Gulf and the Atlantic. They'll have plenty of samples."

Diane had read articles about OSCF's new autonomous underwater vehicles, labeled interchangeably as imaging drones, or underwater robots or "bots" used to identify species and concentrations of sea organisms. Despite the trauma of her first day, she was excited to view the data they'd collected.

Nicole gave Diane a tour of the laboratory and the walk-in chambers used for growing cultures. It was filled with tissue grinders, tons of glassware, centrifuges, heaters, burners, liquid nitrogen canisters, and chemicals. Matt's bomb and bullets had done substantial damage to the main lab, but plenty of equipment and supplies were still available to support any research program.

"I guess none of the lab's cultured bloom samples survived the explosion," Diane said.

Nicole scrunched her nose. "We didn't have any."

Diane's eyes widened. "You don't maintain algal cells from the bloom for tests and observations?"

"We always get buckets of it." Nicole shrugged her shoulders. "I was told there's no need to culture an organism that's always available. We can start growing it in the lab."

"Let's put that at the top of our to-do list."

In order to destroy the parasite, they needed a constant supply of it in a controlled environment to evaluate its strengths and weaknesses. She couldn't understand how a reputable foundation spearheading the investigation of a persistent lethal bloom was not maintaining samples of it. Diane would make sure they didn't make that mistake again.

CHAPTER 5

Diane heard banter between two men grow louder in the corridor outside the laboratory. A tall, lanky blond man with glasses and a beard walked into the lab, carrying a large cooler. "Is everyone okay?" he asked while setting it down.

"Todd, it was awful," Nicole said in rushed words that Diane barely heard because Brandon had entered the room.

As he lugged stacked containers behind him, Brandon paused and did a double take at Diane, probably because she was staring at him. She couldn't look away from his dark eyes that glistened under the fluorescent lights. Something stirred within Diane as soon as their eyes met, an unusual but excitable energy that momentarily had her unmoored until Todd extended his hand to her.

"You must be Diane," Todd said. "Don't get the wrong impression of us. Bulletproof vests are needed only on Mondays."

Nicole swatted Todd on the shoulder. Diane took a step back, her focus returning in a snap by the disturbing joke. She had watched Matt die. Perhaps Todd handled stress through humor. She glanced at Brandon, who was shaking his head.

Todd grinned at Diane. "Too soon? Just trying to lighten the mood. I'm glad everyone's okay. Especially glad you're here. A lot of work to do." He peeled off the tape that secured the cooler's lid. "On the ride back from Miami, we heard the state health department extended the water advisory for all of Florida. We stopped at a Walmart and couldn't find bottled water. If you smell something funky, it'll probably be me."

"There are pallets of bottled water in storage available to us," said Nicole. "Start taking sponge baths."

Diane, tuning out of the conversation, glanced at Brandon unpacking electronics. He was looking at her, his eyes twinkling in a way that made her blush, until he stumbled over some cords. He caught himself, then looked at her and smiled.

Amazing smile.

"I'm Brandon. Computer nerd learning to walk." His eyes lit up as Diane giggled at his blunder.

"Nice to meet you both."

Todd patted Brandon on the shoulder. "Smooth moves. Brandon's our bot expert."

Brandon moved closer to Diane. "Bot data with coordinates should come in later. Our bots move vertically from the surface to the ocean floor, measuring total concentration of the red dinoflagellates in real time."

"How do you get so many bots out to sea? Aren't they the size of a small car?" Diane asked.

Brandon's smile widened. "I redesigned them. Mine are about four feet tall and only three feet in diameter. Compact, a bit heavy, but easier to handle."

She smiled. "Incredible." *He's brilliant!*

Todd pointed to the cooler. "Water samples from the Gulf. Lots of red algae."

Diane reached for the samples to begin her work and realized this was the first time since the attack that she felt relaxed and excited about her job.

Brandon backed away from her and went to his computer. "I never met Matt's family, but he said they were real down-to-earth people. They must be devastated."

Todd shook his head. "Matt was a gifted chemist. What the hell was he thinking?"

The room got quiet. Diane prepared the microscope, then noticed Nicole standing near her. "Having a hard time concentrating today," Nicole whispered. "Okay if I hang out with you?"

"Always good to have another pair of eyes."

Diane peered into the microscope and found numerous bright red dinoflagellates gliding and swimming in a whirling pattern using flagella, which looked like strings of fine hair. The elongated red body had a clear, dense exterior covered in spikes. "I've seen spiny armored plates and two posterior horns on dinos, but this cell has multiple horns and a thick translucent barbed shell."

Nicole looked through the microscope. "Kinda looks like a red mite with thick antennae, a tail, and a big orange spot."

Diane agreed. "Some believe the spot on dinos evolved as an eye to help them detect light and even locate prey."

Nicole kept staring into the scope. "A single-celled organism that can see. What's next?"

From across the room, Brandon chimed in. "If they can see, they may start listening in on our conversations. They'll figure out world domination and wonder how they ended up at the bottom of the food chain."

Todd snickered. "Dude, haven't you seen the Gulf Coast? They're not at the bottom."

Diane placed small fish, snails, krill from the in-lab aquarium, and copepods that ate plankton into a large bucket of salt water and added a sample of red dinos.

• • •

Two hours later, everything was dead from the toxin. Dead fish and krill floated in the murky red water that smelled like rotting eggs. She took a sample of the water from the bucket and placed it into the petri dish. Under the microscope, the dinos spun around each other, locating and feeding on dead tissue. Diane narrowed her eyes. "Let's find out what kills them."

Nicole revealed a wicked grin. "Good."

Diane placed frigid fresh water into the petri dish. The dinos slowed their movement for only a few seconds. She put on a lab mask, grabbed a handheld ozone generator, then zapped the mixture with the colorless gas. The parasites moved in a strange zigzag. Seconds later, Diane gasped when the organisms started swimming around as if nothing had changed. Each time she introduced a novelty altering the environment, the crimson-colored pests became sluggish but eventually recovered.

Diane walked away feeling defeated and said to Brandon, "What you said about dinos overhearing our conversations to rule the world? I think they're listening."

CHAPTER 6

The next day in the lab, Todd showed Diane a graphic of the red dino's DNA they'd collected from the bots. "It's a new species."

Diane studied the charts. "I think the thick spiny shell is protecting it from changes in water quality."

"I must've napped through the plankton lectures in grad school." Todd gave her a small grin.

Diane shook her head. "I've always been fascinated by dinos. They grow like a plant and can move around with flagella like an animal. You know, they don't just cause harmful blooms. We wouldn't have many types of coral reefs without them."

Todd's smile widened. "Wow, you must've gotten a degree in algae."

It was interesting how most people dismissed microscopic life. According to some researchers, there were five nonillion—five followed by thirty zeros—bacteria on earth. If people thought about unicellular forms at all, it was the viruses and bacteria that caused them to get sick. As soon as a vaccine or antibiotic was found, they forgot about them. Studying protists like algae might never be considered sexy, but understanding these organisms, which she believed were the root of life, fascinated her.

Todd opened a geographic information system to display a static map showing different colored dots across the Gulf of Mexico. "Since our pest doesn't rely solely on sunlight for food, chlorophyll maps and satellite images weren't good enough to obtain true concentrations. Our bots provide the most accurate measurement of the infestation." He pointed to the map. "Measurements of the dinos taken a month ago. Red dots show the highest concentrations off the Panhandle, extending into deeper waters. White and yellow dots scattered along the rest of the Gulf Coast are lower counts. No dots in the southern part of the Gulf means no dinos."

Nicole squinted at the map legend. "The color of the little circles represents the number of dinos, but what does it really mean?"

Diane pointed to a red dot. "If you dropped a glass beaker into the ocean, then brought it back up to the surface, the water inside would be red because of so many dinos. For the yellow dots, less red algae would be in your glass of water, but the color would be pink and cloudy. White dots would be clear water, algae still present but not enough to discolor the water."

"Are the waters with the white dots deadly?" asked Nicole.

Diane recalled Uncle Bo telling her about a large grouper with lesions pulled out of clear-looking waters off a pier near Pensacola. "This dino is reproducing and emitting toxins at a rapid rate. If you jumped into waters with only a few of them, you could suffer anaphylaxis."

Nicole's jaw dropped. "An invisible sea monster."

"More like a relentless predator. Most red tides kill fish due to a lack of oxygen. This one does the same and also devours them."

Bennett entered the lab, checking her phone in one hand and reviewing documents in the other.

"Dr. Bennett, heads up!" Brandon yelled.

"Watch out!" Todd shouted.

Bennett looked up in time to avoid a run-in with a table.

Nicole and Diane paused and giggled. Nicole leaned close to Diane and whispered, "I have a lot to learn. I'm glad you're here."

Diane replied in a soft voice, "With this parasite, we're all learning."

Brandon called out from his computer, "Hey, guys, come look."

Everyone huddled around a large, curved monitor to watch a little circle that kept going round and round. Standing so close to Brandon, Diane could feel the heat of his skin and felt her body growing warmer. She felt nervous and self-conscious.

Brandon looked at Diane. "The image Todd showed you took less than an hour to upload. In addition to the bots we have in the Gulf, we've placed bots in the Atlantic as far out as one hundred nautical miles."

Fixated on the monitor with its spinning circle, they waited until the image emerged on the screen. No one was prepared for what they saw next: a scattering of red, yellow, and white dots along the Atlantic Coast extending up to Virginia, an immense mass of red circles throughout most of the Gulf.

Nicole gaped at the display. "Holy shit. So many of them."

Bennett rubbed her temples. "We have only a few bots in waters north of Virginia. We need to deploy more."

Brandon pointed at the cluster of red dots off the Carolinas. "Gulf Stream is doing a hell of a job moving the infestation into the North Atlantic."

Diane studied the pattern of dots. "It seems to have plenty of food, and no predator has neutralized its toxin to consume it. At this rate . . ." She paused before completing her thought, not wanting to make an overzealous prediction.

Todd pointed at the monitor. "You're thinking everything blue on the map will turn red."

Bennett stood silent for a few seconds. "Send the image to Jenson and Landry. I'm going to call them right now." She left them gawking at the computer screen.

Brandon turned to Diane. "Any thoughts on next steps?"

"I've got one. Don't eat sushi," said Todd.

Nicole rolled her eyes. "Bruh."

Diane walked back to the microscope. Brandon followed her and asked, "Do you really believe this could cover the entire ocean? Don't blooms eventually disappear?"

Diane sighed and ran a hand through her hair. Since early morning, she'd been conducting experiments, attempting to decrease the number of dinos. Instead, the dinos had quadrupled in count through asexual cell division, where the cell splits to create a copy of itself. The sample in the petri dish appeared more like blood than water.

"You're right. Blooms go away because the number of algal cells returns to normal concentrations. That happens because of changes in the environment, less food, predators, or competition from other organisms." Diane glanced at each of her colleagues before continuing. "As of right now, nothing poses a threat to this dino."

• • •

Hours later, Diane left to grab a quick snack from the break room. Jenson spotted her in the hallway. "Aren't you the new postdoc who studied red tides in the Gulf of Mexico?"

For a moment, Diane froze before looking behind her to see if Jenson was speaking to someone else. Realizing they were alone, she finally answered, "Yes. I'm Diane Nelson."

I'm talking to Shaun Jenson!

"Walk with me."

It was easy to understand why cable news reporters always sought Jenson out for interviews. He was not only articulate, but with his perpetual stubble and Dior suits, he also looked like a GQ cover model. He had intelligent eyes and an easy smile that ended in deep dimples. In interviews, he had admitted to passing up an opportunity to play professional football, and his muscular build from his college days remained. He had a slight hint of gray near his temples, revealing he was probably in his late forties.

As they walked out of the building, Diane felt that only a few hours had passed since she'd entered the lab, but the sky was dark. A whole day had come and gone.

Jenson's cell phone rang. He glanced at the screen before silencing it. "You've worked with the algal species that thrives in warm waters and grows faster with high levels of carbon dioxide?"

"Yes, but this is a different species. It doesn't behave the same way. Most dinoflagellates, like the one I studied, use photosynthesis for energy. For them, sunlight and higher temperatures increase reproduction and cause blooms. This one isn't solely dependent on light."

They were heading to a BMW in the parking lot when he stopped walking. "There's a lot more work to do in understanding this parasite. We know what has been found for other blooms."

She thought he wanted her to say global warming could be part of the problem. "I think treating this organism like the others could be a mistake." His publications on how marine ecosystems were affected by climate change were well known. He worked with many politicians on policies to reduce greenhouse gas emissions.

Jenson looked toward the Atlantic, then at Diane, then back at the ocean. She wasn't sure if he was agitated or already bored with their exchange.

He sighed. "We're receiving government support to investigate the bloom. The best use of this funding is to evaluate greenhouse gases as the potential cause of the bloom. Runoff of fertilizers from farmland or golf courses that could jump-start a red tide is probably not the avenue we should take in studying this anomaly."

She couldn't understand how anything that would start an algal bloom under these conditions wouldn't be considered. "The bots measured high cell concentrations offshore. I wonder if this dinoflagellate originated from the deeper part of the Gulf. Do you think the foundation could acquire machines to sample the ocean basin? It could provide clues regarding its weaknesses."

"Deep sea exploration is expensive. Our current funds are already tied up in other projects."

"I would think the government would support it, especially given the Gulf's current conditions. This is a huge crisis."

"I'm constantly fighting to get additional funding. A few months ago, the government awarded several huge grants for engineering and technological innovations, including space exploration."

Diane tried to hide the irritation from her voice. "We've got a deadly toxic bloom infiltrating our waters. Over 80 percent of our oceans haven't been mapped or explored. But everyone wants to go to Mars."

He cocked his head and studied her. "If this bloom continues to spread, conditions on Mars may be better than here. Dr. Landry and I will meet tomorrow to discuss the next steps."

Diane glanced down and noticed that Jenson was wearing dark leather shoes similar to those he'd worn on the day Matt had stormed the building. She hesitated, then said, "The postdoc . . . blew up most of his work in the bio-lab. Was any of his research backed up?"

Jenson's posture stiffened. "I didn't keep track of his work."

Before she could inquire further, he said goodbye, got into his BMW, and drove away.

Diane watched him drive away, remembering a picture she'd seen of a younger Jenson dressed in a dirty T-shirt and tattered jeans, standing beside a mud-covered truck loaded with meteorologic equipment. His contributions to understanding climate change and its effect on oceanic systems were admirable. However, his dismissal of Matt's work was bothersome. Matt could have discovered a crucial detail of the dino that everyone was missing. He would have backed up his work, and she wanted to find it.

CHAPTER 7

Past midnight, with the rain pouring outside, Diane sat on her bed with a laptop and used a people search engine to find Matthew Toft from Akers, Kentucky. She wrote his relatives' names—Fred and Carla Toft—their phone number, email, and address. She guessed his family would get his belongings from the lab after the investigation was complete. Once she finished her research on his family, she found a news thread: "Harmful Algal Bloom Responsible for Thousands of Dead Marine Life along the Gulf of Mexico." She clicked the link and found pictures of dead sea life and birds scattered throughout the Gulf waters and along beaches. The article noted, "Along the Gulf Coast, twenty-one people have died. Emergency rooms have reported an increased number of persons admitted with stomach pains, difficulty breathing, and burning sensation in the eyes and sinuses."

The news reports made her even more worried about her mother, but it was too late to call.

Diane heard music coming from a truck parked across the street. Noisy teenagers jumped out of the vehicle and ran toward the beach. Three cars drove up with more teenagers, who did the same.

Tired but curious, she put on her rain jacket and walked to the beach. Glistening sparks of light danced in the water. Certain kinds of algae illuminated when disturbed, causing a glowing effect referred to by oceanographers as *sea sparkle.*

Teenagers splashed in the glittering waves. Their bodies glistened in the shimmering pink foam as the song "I Feel It Coming" by The Weeknd boomed out of a Bluetooth speaker.

Don't they listen to the news?

She yelled, "It's not safe! Get out of the water!"

Most ignored her. Some laughed. No one got out.

Frustrated, she pointed in their direction and screamed, "Shark!"

They ran into each other, scrambling to escape.

• • •

When Diane arrived at OSCF the next morning, reporters were still camped outside the building. She spotted Isabelle in a row of journalists with microphones shoved in front of Jenson. Dr. Susan Landry and people in business suits whom she guessed were government officials stood behind him.

Landry wore a navy suit that accentuated her hourglass figure and brought out the silky auburn highlights of her wavy hair. She was likely close to Jenson's age, though she appeared many years younger.

Isabelle asked Jenson, "From what you've learned about this bloom, do you believe it will continue to spread throughout the Atlantic?"

"We're still analyzing data and cannot make any definitive statements on the extent of the spread."

Diane didn't believe that was true.

Another reporter shoved a microphone in Jenson's face and asked, "Where did the bloom come from, and how long will it last?"

"A talented team of scientists is working day and night to answer those questions. A team of experts from different parts of the country will go out to the Gulf today. I'm hopeful we'll find information about the origins of this new species. We'll keep you posted with any news."

Isabelle threw up both hands as if frustrated by Jenson's answers. Reporters mumbled while backing away from Jenson and Landry, who were now entering the building. Closely following Landry were a couple of men in business suits, grinning and opening doors for her.

Diane was heading toward the entrance when Bennett exited and walked up to her. "Dr. Jenson wants you, Brandon, Todd, and Nicole on the ship heading out to the Gulf today. It's stationed in Tampa Bay and scheduled to leave in six hours. Top research teams have flown in to participate with Dr. Jenson on the expedition. All our vehicles are out in the field. Do you know how to get to our vessel?"

Diane nodded with a wide smile. "Head west through the Florida Everglades." She knew all the Gulf harbors and was excited about getting aboard an OSCF vessel. Collecting on-site specimens while observing conditions was the best part of her job.

A clean-shaven Brandon appeared. He greeted everyone, but to Diane, he seemed to save his brightest smile for her. His eyes lit up, especially when he smiled at her, and she'd been looking forward to seeing that smile all morning. Diane glanced around, making sure no one was paying attention, because she was sure she was glowing. She couldn't remember the last time a man had looked at her like that, as if seeing her had made his entire day. There had been Adam from college, but they'd both been so young. Brandon was probably in his early thirties.

Diane returned Brandon's smile, then realized Bennett had said something. A little embarrassed, she asked, "Sorry, what did you say?"

"It's okay for you to go ahead. Brandon and I need to discuss recalibrating the bots."

Brandon flashed a big grin. "Maybe I should recalculate algal concentrations using *algae*-bra."

He winked at Diane, and she smiled, shaking her head. *Corny but cute.*

As she turned to walk away, he said, "See you on the boat."

• • •

After frequent stops to pour coolant into her old Jeep's radiator, Diane arrived at the dock five hours later. A sulfuric odor mixed with the stench of decaying fish caused her eyes to water. She blinked hard, then spotted the OSCF ship. Brandon and Todd were hauling large plastic bins filled with equipment and large bungee cords onto the deck. Nicole had on safety glasses. She stood on the dock waving at Diane.

When Diane walked up, Nicole handed her a pair of goggles and pointed to the crimson swamp-like harbor. "This crap makes my eyes burn."

Diane put the goggles on and examined the packed equipment. "Wow, this is a lot of gear," she said, poking through the bins.

"Belongs to the celebrity researchers. They had it shipped overnight, and we're the grunts who get to load it."

"Where are they?"

"Probably with Jenson."

As Diane carried bins on board, she felt the gentle sway of the vessel. At night, the rocking motion would lull her to sleep while others were hurling their dinner into the toilet or overboard.

"There are no filtered showerheads," Nicole said, then paused to catch her breath. "The good news is a water truck delivered filtered water. The bad news is there's only enough to shower every couple of days. I'll smell worse than the floating carcasses."

"We should keep a bar of soap on deck. If it rains, we can let nature wash us off."

Nicole pointed toward the beach on the north side of the dock. "I'm not sure who has it worse, us or them."

A team of at least forty workers in full-body suits with hoods and gloves were moving along the shoreline, picking up decayed sea life.

Diane guessed their job was to dispose of the smelly remains baking in the summer sun.

Everyone swatted at flies while moving equipment on board. Lugging heavy crates in the humid ninety-five-degree heat caused beads of sweat to run down her neck. At least she had the sea breeze. She couldn't imagine what it was like for the beach workers covered in thick protective gear and swarming flies.

Most of the equipment was on board when a group of researchers walked up the ramp, followed by Jenson. Dressed in shorts and a T-shirt, the OSCF head looked like one of the crew, a dramatic change from his usual designer business attire.

Enough online information about Jenson existed to know he was no stranger to research cruises. He had led expeditions to measure the effects of climate change on coral reefs in the Caribbean Sea. Before that, he had endured horrific storms to obtain meteorological data in the North Atlantic. Though his current work employed mathematical models, his past revealed a man who could endure rough weather and seas.

The captain, an older, tough-looking man wearing a filtered mask, came out to meet Jenson. The air over the Gulf waters was acrid, causing a burning sensation in the sinuses. Diane brought masks in case it became too uncomfortable.

After the captain, Jenson, and the researchers walked past them, Nicole smirked. "Not a 'hi' or a 'gee, thanks for loading all our equipment.' Let's make sure they unload their crap at the end of the cruise."

Diane moved along the deck, securing equipment as the ship trawled through decaying remains in the harbor and headed into the Gulf. Jenson and a team of scientists were on the starboard side, scrutinizing a bulky machine that stood at least nine feet high on eight steel legs. She moved closer to overhear them.

A researcher pointed at a tube nestled between the steel legs. "Our redesigned multicorer can be sent down to the deepest part of the ocean to retrieve tubes of water and sediment. The sample needs to be brought quickly to the on-ship laboratory with a controlled temperature." He flipped open the tube to demonstrate its easy release. "Dr. Jenson believes if we find where the red dinoflagellate originated, the sediment could provide valuable information in understanding what it needs to survive."

Didn't I say that?

She was relieved they were sailing to the basin. Maybe the large steel-legged contraption would unearth the answers they needed to end this nightmare.

CHAPTER 8

Diane had finished setting up her microscope in the ship's small lab when she found Jenson surrounded by researchers on deck.

He smiled as she approached. "This is our new postdoc, Dr. Nelson."

She lowered her mask, greeted each researcher, then faced Jenson. "I don't want to lose a plankton net in the thick algae. Can we send down the rosette before we reach deeper waters?"

Because Jenson was eager to get to the basin, he seemed reluctant to respond. Finally he answered, "I'll ask the captain to stop here."

The rosette sampler was a round instrument almost five feet tall with thirty-six sampling containers clustered around a central cylinder used to collect samples at different depths. Twenty minutes after Jenson gave the okay, the ship's engine slowed to a murmur, and momentum trailed off. The winch operator lowered the rosette into the water and then a half hour later returned it to the surface. Diane's job was to hoist it back onto the ship. Wearing elbow-length waterproof gloves, she leaned over the water with her torso against a chain and grabbed its metal rim.

An animal thrashed back and forth below her, struggling on the ocean's surface in red sludge too thick for her to identify the creature. After heaving the rosette onto the ship, she helped Brandon and Todd secure it, then rushed to the chain to locate the struggling animal. The ship had started moving again. The animal was gone.

Diane and Nicole worked until dark preparing rosette water samples for analyses. Nicole took off her goggles, mask, and gloves and then rubbed her eyes. “I’m heading to the galley. You coming?”

“I’ll finish these last few samples, then call it quits.”

Diane yawned, launched the Minecraft app on her phone, and sent a message to her gamer friends: *Working late. Can’t join game.*

Brandon walked in and noticed the game on her screen. He laughed. “You play Minecraft?” Diane grabbed her phone, flush creeping across her cheeks.

He squinted as if in deep thought. “Gosh, I can’t remember the last time I played it.”

She took off her goggles and lowered her mask. “I guess I never grew up. Still trying to build a diamond fortress.”

“What’s your gamer tag?”

She squirmed on her stool, muscles tightening, preparing to watch him laugh at her. “Dino Diva,” she said softly.

For a long moment, Brandon was still. Diane waited for the mocking she was sure would follow. Instead, Brandon beamed at her. He moved closer, his eyes locking with hers. Diane’s breathing slowed, her wistful look melting into a smile. For a moment, the bloom and the panic it was creating were forgotten. Gazing up at him, she felt what she could only describe as a connection with him, one she wasn’t expecting but was definitely relishing.

Brandon folded his arms across his chest, his smile growing impossibly wider. “Dino Diva doesn’t stop to eat? Are all postdocs this driven? Matt never took breaks either.” Suddenly, his smile disappeared, and he took a step backward. “Sorry, I didn’t mean to compare you to Matt. What happened with him was horrible.”

Disappointed that his mood had so quickly changed, she was quiet for a moment before asking, “Was there a memorial for Matt?”

Brandon shook his head. “If there was, none of us were invited.”

"Did he talk to you about what he found in the bloom?"

"No. His primary focus was the development of chemical technology to reduce gas emissions, which thrilled Jenson."

"I was told he changed after a meeting with the cofounders. Did he get along with them?"

Brandon took a couple of awkward steps toward the doorway. "Matt thought of Jenson as a god. He was quite fond of Landry too."

"Do you know if he kept a log or a backup of his work? Doesn't the foundation have a server that backs up files?"

"His data were stored in software created for his computer in the bio-lab. He blew it up. Destroyed his files."

She watched Brandon for a few seconds, but whatever they'd shared moments ago had passed, so Diane returned to the work at hand. She poured out the contents of a rosette sample collected near the water surface. Grasshoppers covered in red algae floated out of the bottle. "If we were closer to the Panhandle, the insects wouldn't be surprising. The volume of water coming from a flooding Mississippi River would carry them into the northern Gulf." She looked up at Brandon. "These guys are a long way from there."

He moved closer to examine the floating remains. "You've heard of the hundred-year flood. I think we've experienced something like a thousand-year flood. Very abnormal."

Like the red dino.

She didn't know if it was the insects, the odd smells from the samples, or what, but an unexpected wave of nausea hit her, and she began taking shorter breaths.

Brandon rested a hand on her arm. "You don't look so good," he said, his tone gentle but firm. "You should go to the med bay."

She shook her head, backing away from the watery mixture of dead insects just as a loud thud and the sound of crashing glass came from outside the lab. Brandon glanced quickly at her before hurrying out.

Before she realized what she was doing, Diane rushed to the far corner and crouched behind a tall crate. Sounds of glass shattering, gunfire, and an image of Matt's twitching eye flooded her mind.

Within seconds, Brandon reappeared. "Someone dropped a box. Glass beakers broke." He froze when he saw her peering around her hiding place. "Are you okay?"

She rushed to the microscope, her hands trembling. "Other than the police, I haven't told anyone that I saw Matt on the day of the attack. He was sitting in his truck. Minutes later, I watched him die."

A wide-eyed Brandon went to her side. "I'm sorry you went through that."

"What bothers me is I'm not sure why he brought the gun. He shot at walls and furniture. Before he died, he said he was sorry. He sounded tormented."

Brandon sat on the stool next to her and touched her arm. "I thought everyone in the lab was under the bench during the attack. I didn't know you saw him. That's a lot to deal with."

"I was pressed against the floor and could see through the space between the bench's legs." She paused, taking a deep breath. "What did you think of Matt?"

"He was in the lab for about a year. A gifted chemist and engineer." Brandon's warm, kind tone had changed. His voice sounded detached. "Mostly kept to himself." He leaned close to her and stared at the wall. "I've been with OSCF for five years. I've never seen anyone as on edge as Matt, especially toward the end. Sometimes people just snap." His big, dark eyes found her again. "There are professionals who help people with PTSD. But if you're comfortable talking with me . . . I'd like that."

"Thanks." She gave him a weary grin. "I'm not traumatized; I'm concerned. Right now I'm exhausted."

She said good night, went below deck, and washed off with a rag and bottled water before lying on her bunk. Covering her eyes with her arm, she thought back to the connection she'd felt with Brandon in the lab . . . before she'd pulled away emotionally.

I should've stayed and talked to him! I hounded him too much about Matt.

Her thoughts returned to Matt's last request for forgiveness. Empty words from a man who had lost touch with reality? Matt's bloody face morphed into the frantic creature under the crimson sludge. Soon the rocking of the ship lulled her into a deep sleep, but images of a terrified animal struggling to free itself from the red waters haunted her.

CHAPTER 9

Diane went to the galley the next morning, hoping to find Brandon. Perhaps she could revive whatever it was that had started growing yesterday. Jenson caught up with her first.

The skin below his eyes was darker than usual. His tone was softer. "I'd like you to be in the cold lab to help analyze the sample." He gave her a big-dimpled smile, and the dark circles seemed to fade. "In a few minutes, we'll be over the deepest part of the basin to send down the multicorer."

"I'll head to the cold lab now. Thank you."

"I know this isn't a full exploration of the ocean floor, but maybe we'll discover something."

"Can't wait to see what we find."

She headed towards the temperature-controlled laboratory and found seven technicians, with Brandon, Todd, and Nicole guiding the steel-legged multicorer to the edge of the stern. Todd shouted, "Check the cables. We've got only a few minutes before reaching the drop-in."

Suddenly, the engines stopped for no reason. Everyone on deck exchanged confused glances. Jenson rushed to the bridge, leaving the crew wondering what to do next. He returned with the captain a few minutes later.

The captain removed his mask and caught his breath. "The ship's onboard system indicates a problem with the propeller. Waiting for help will take at least a day."

The crew groaned and shook their heads.

The captain used the back of his hand to wipe sweat from his forehead. "We could send divers down to check. If there's any debris, they could remove it, and we should be able to get moving again."

Everyone gathered around Jenson on the stern. He waited until everyone stopped mumbling before he spoke. "We have many divers on the ship. We also have specialized dry suits with built-in gloves and waterproof footies that will fit inside flippers."

A technician brought out a dry suit. She handed Jenson a full-faced mask with a built-in regulator. He held it up and pointed at the inner seal. "To keep out water, this fits tight around the face and under the suit's hood. Make sure masks are snug." He stopped and looked at each of them. "Who's comfortable diving?"

A few people murmured anxiously; others exchanged concerned glances. Nine people, including Diane and Todd, raised their hands. Going underwater was dangerous, but she was eager to observe the subsurface infestation. Jenson handed the mask to her. "Your body will stay dry with this gear. If you have any reaction, quickly get back on board."

• • •

Diane, wearing a dry suit and a full-face mask with a headlamp, picked up an air cylinder. Thunderous sounds rattled the port side of the ship. The great force of continual thumps caused the craft to shift.

People started shouting. "What's happening?" "Did we hit something?"

Holding onto the rail, Diane and a couple of technicians saw a pod of orcas ramming into the hull. A few hundred killer whales resided in the deepest part of the Gulf basin. About ten feet from the pod, a baby orca showed no movement, suspended in a thick layer of red slime. The animals bumping into the ship seemed desperate and confused. After a few seconds, the pod descended under the ship into deeper waters.

Nicole and a couple of researchers used long-handled nets to scrub the algae off the abandoned calf. A technician pointed at his stored nets. "We could retrieve it with the larger mesh."

Another researcher nodded. "It could fit in the container below. Fill it with filtered seawater. Scrub off the algae, give it a chance to survive."

Diane watched the baby sink. *The Gulf's becoming a graveyard.*

Someone said, "It looks dead. Probably why it was left behind."

Suggestions for a rescue stopped. A feeling of tremendous sadness for the loss of the orca's life overcame Diane. She took a long breath and joined the other divers for a safety check on equipment, including a harness that kept them tethered to the ship.

The deep blue waters were normally clear on calm days. Today the sun was out and the winds were nonexistent, but when Diane entered the waters, she found nothing but floating strings of red algae. It felt like diving in freshwater, where silt is suspended, allowing only a few inches of visibility.

She turned on her headlamp, feeling the familiar buoyancy of salt water. Todd, the designated leader, guided them to the bottom of the ship. They passed the sinking calf with long, velvety strands of algae floating around it, and Diane's heart sank again. No sign of the other orcas.

Secured with the tether, she went a little farther down from the group, searching for any life. She swam near a massive cloud of red algae. The light from her headlamp shone into the slits of crimson, illuminating numerous small and large dorsal fins. More than one animal with decayed flesh were entombed.

She felt a tug on her line and quickly rejoined the divers who had gathered near the propeller. Todd pointed to large sections of blubber encrusted with red algae lodged between the blades. A couple of divers pulled on the blubber to remove it but were unsuccessful.

She guessed it was from a large mammal such as an orca but was surprised it could affect the propeller. Most ships with giant propellers could cut through whale skin.

Divers grabbed hold of different sections of the blubber and exerted enough force to pull out the largest piece. When the piece dislodged, four divers crashed into each other and in the mayhem displaced their masks.

No, no, no!

Diane watched in horror as water sloshed inside their masks. One diver squeezed the purge valve under her nose to clear the mask of water, then shuddered. Two others frantically flapped their arms and jerked their legs as the toxic water entered their mouths.

One diver wasn't moving at all, and Diane quickly swam to him. He was shivering. His eyes tightly closed, water covered his nose.

The toxin is hitting him hard.

Diane whipped around, scanning the waters, hoping to locate another diver who could help. The others were frantically kicking toward the surface. Her heart pounded against her chest like a bomb ready to explode. She shook the diver's shoulders until his red-streaked eyes opened. Pointing upward, she grabbed his arm and helped him ascend.

His body started convulsing. He stopped moving about five feet below the surface.

He'll die if I don't get him out.

Trying not to panic, she kept him with her and swam upward. A sense of relief washed over her as they got closer to the surface. Just then, the diver's arm rammed into her face hard enough to loosen her mask. Water trickled into her mask, stinging her face. Within seconds, her limbs felt weak and shaky. An image of herself drowning in the contaminant flashed through her mind.

Get out!

Only a few feet of water remained above them.

Push him! He'll break the surface.

His whole body shook as she approached him from underneath. She swam up in a burst of adrenaline, reached out, and pushed him upwards. His flippers struck her mask forcefully, breaking the seal and causing water to pool. Her face and eyes burned.

No! Shit!

She kept her eyes shut and ascended, water flooding her mask.

Her mouth burned. Her breathing slowed. No air from the regulator.

Why can't I breathe?!

Lunging upward, she broke the surface, flung off the mask, and opened her mouth. Nothing. Her throat was swollen, blocking her airway.

Scream!

Spray from red-stained waves splashed into her mouth. "Help!" came out in a choking rasp. Suddenly, her body went numb.

CHAPTER 10

"Diane?"

Her eyelids felt heavy, but she forced them open, wide enough to see Nicole standing over her. Diane was lying on a bunk. No strength to speak. *How did I get here?*

"How you feeling?" Nicole asked, moving closer, studying her.

Todd appeared, his face covered with hives. "You had a really bad reaction to the algae. You're lucky."

This is lucky?

She wanted to ask about the others and if the diver she had helped was okay, but she couldn't keep her eyes open.

Hours later, Diane awoke to a dark, empty room. Her chest felt heavy, and her rib cage hurt as she crawled out of bed. Feeling lightheaded and wobbly, she balanced herself against the bulkhead. She wasn't sure how she'd gotten into her pajamas and wasn't able to locate her bag of clothing. It had been critical to get her out of the dry suit covered with toxins, but she wondered who had stripped and redressed her.

Gripping the banister, she hobbled up the narrow steps to the deck. It was empty under the night sky. Distant lights from buildings indicated they were returning to the coast.

"Hello?" she said in a cracked voice.

No one answered.

She held onto the ship's rail and inched toward the small lab. Nicole's bottles of algae were strapped into a crate. One container was labeled "Red Algae on Baby Orca." Using a pipette, she placed a drop of its crimson goo contents onto a slide. When she looked through the lens, the brightness of the scope light caused a stabbing sensation in her swollen eyes. She closed and rubbed them for a second. Squinting enough to endure the pain, she returned to the lens and discovered the dinos had developed a chain of interconnecting cells in numbers too high to count—a strategic move to engulf large prey.

Footsteps approached. She gasped at the sight of Brandon in the doorway. His face was swollen with hives, his skin covered in welts. Instinctively, she slid off the stool, reaching out to touch his face. She stopped at the last second, realizing contact might hurt him.

"What happened to you?" she asked, unable to hide her emotions at seeing his beautiful face and smile hidden behind the nettle rash.

Brandon tried to show the smile he seemed to always save just for her. The pain was too much. His smile didn't quite reach his eyes. "You go first."

"I was helping another diver." She hesitated a moment and took a deep breath. "Water got into my mask. I couldn't breathe. I can't remember how I got back to the ship."

"It wasn't easy. We had divers heaving, convulsing, tangled up in crossed tethers. The crew unhooked the twisted ropes to reduce tension on the lines, then dragged the divers to the stern. Some were vomiting and shaking so much, it took several tries to get them on board."

"I was pulled in?"

He shook his head. "In the commotion, the unattached tethers fell overboard, a jumbled mess floating out to sea. We found you on the other side of the ship." Brandon paused again, an anguished look on his face. "You . . . looked lifeless."

Errors occurred when people panicked, but letting go of a diver's lifeline to the ship was egregious.

He touched a patch of red bumps on his cheek. "Jenson and the crew were struggling with the lines to lower the lifeboat." He gazed into the distance as if he were seeing it again. "I watched you drift with the current . . . slipping away." He looked everywhere but at her. "I didn't really think it through."

She waited for him to continue, but he was quiet. "How did I get on the ship?"

He met her eyes and stammered, "I jumped in, pulled you out."

Unable to restrain herself, she hugged him, feeling a dull pain in her bruised sternum. "Thank you."

Brandon winced under the embrace.

She gasped and quickly let go. "I'm sorry. Did I hurt you?"

He shook his head. "Only my skin was affected. Doc gave me antihistamines and lotion to apply. Your reaction was life-threatening. He gave you an epinephrine shot and administered CPR."

"That explains why it feels like an elephant's been sitting on my chest."

"We've been taking turns checking on you. When I saw you weren't in bed, I figured you'd be near a microscope."

Diane was moved that he had looked for her. When she spoke, her voice cracked with emotion. "How are the other divers?"

Brandon lowered his eyes. "Do you remember Louise? She was one of the engineers who designed the multicorer."

Diane nodded, remembering Louise doing a safety check on her air tank.

"Louise never surfaced. Todd and three other divers came back with hives. Three suffered severe reactions. All responded to treatment except one diver who passed away minutes after she was brought onto the ship."

"Shit! We lost *two* divers?"

Her first week at OSCF and three people, including Matt, were dead. *This is one crazy dangerous job!*

"It's terrible. Thankfully, you and Todd are okay."

She thought of her family, who had depended on these waters for their livelihood. Her home would be among the first to turn into a toxic wasteland if they couldn't figure out how to stop the bloom. They were losing the battle.

Brandon rubbed his hives and then made his hands into fists as if to stop scratching. "In the morning, I'll pack the sediment samples in the cold lab, then help Jenson get the researchers on departing flights."

"They sent down the multicorer instead of searching for the missing diver?"

"Jenson didn't believe it was safe enough."

Both got quiet. Classical music played somewhere on the ship.

"Sounds like it's coming from the deck. I enjoy playing Beethoven on the piano," Brandon said, rubbing the back of his arm and obviously trying to switch from the uncomfortable topic.

They went to the deck, closer to the melancholy harmonies of "Moonlight Sonata." "I'd like to hear you play."

"I didn't say I was good at it."

They sat down on a small bench bolted to the deck and watched the luminance of red dinos displaced by the moving ship. She glanced at Brandon. Even with the hives, he was still so handsome. It wasn't lost on her that he could have died trying to save her. He'd risked his life for her. Other than her mom and uncle, she had never thought anyone would go out of their way for her, much less sacrifice their well-being. She looked at him with what she hoped was the utmost sincerity. "Thank you for jumping in after me."

Brandon reached for her and gently touched her hand. A fluttery sensation filled her chest, replacing the pain that had been there. He leaned close to her, his warm breath tickling her ear. "Your being here next to me is thanks enough," he whispered, revealing a sweet grin. His eyes shone almost as brightly as the sparkling sea, competing with the starry sky above them.

CHAPTER 11

Diane followed the doctor's orders and took it easy in her apartment over the weekend. She grabbed a box of chocolate-covered raisins, turned on her laptop, and logged onto Minecraft. She was immediately bombarded with instant messages from her friends.

How did you do that?

Wow!

Her online wooden shack, vulnerable to mob-like creatures, was inches from a bridge leading to an almost impenetrable purplish-blue castle made of diamonds and obsidian crystals.

She jumped up, catching her laptop and dropping the raisins.

Every player jumped into the water-filled moat surrounding the radiant palace and collected gems out of the sunken treasure chests. No one knew how the castle or jewels magically appeared.

She remembered Brandon looking at the game on her phone and hearing her wish for a diamond fortress. *Did he do this?*

• • •

Diane was eager to be back in the lab on Monday. She was calibrating the mass spectrometer to run samples collected from the rosette when Nicole entered, suppressing a yawn. "You're here early. How you feeling?"

She smiled. "Happy to get back to work and analyze these samples."

A few minutes later, Brandon and Todd walked in, followed by Bennett.

Brandon shyly smiled at her. His hives were almost gone, and his face was no longer swollen. She started toward him, then stopped when Jenson and Landry entered the lab. Her uncle would have described the cofounders as "grinning like a couple of possums."

Jenson motioned to Landry, indicating she could have the floor.

Landry spoke with a soft, charming southern accent. "The amounts of nitrogen and phosphorus in the basin sediment were extremely high. We think the basin is the point of origin for the red dinoflagellate."

Bennett studied a spreadsheet. "Not too surprising due to record flooding of the Mississippi pushing nutrients to deeper waters."

Landry nodded. "The abnormally high runoffs into the Gulf have stopped. We hope that as nutrients continue to decrease, so will the red algae." Landry glanced back at Jenson, then added, "We believe the bloom is related to the rise of greenhouse gases."

Diane had heard enough. "Sorry, how do we know the basin sediment is the point of origin? Were there dinos sharing the same DNA found in the basin?"

Jenson answered. "We're working on a DNA profile. The amount of nitrogen and phosphorus is a red flag. We start with what we know and build upon existing research of previous blooms. There is a connection of increased nutrients flowing from waters that have risen by a degree from gas emissions."

Her thoughts went to the dead divers and her Gulf home suffocated by a relentless bloom. "We've lost people, animals, and probably an entire ecosystem. This isn't occurring a degree at a time over decades. It's happening now. You've done a lot to educate people about global warming, but why are you talking about greenhouse gases when our waters are turning red?"

The room became silent. Landry's jaw slacked. Jenson's eyes widened. Bennett stared at the floor. No one moved except a wide-eyed Brandon, peeking over a computer screen.

"How long have you been in your field of study?" asked Jenson, moving toward her. "How many papers have you published?"

"Do you have any senior collaborators?" Landry smirked, folding her arms.

Diane clenched her teeth. *Don't say another word.*

They let her stay in that unpleasant place of silence for what seemed like forever. Finally Jenson said, "If you don't like the way we think through problems, you're free to leave." He paused for a moment, then after a heavy sigh added, "But I hope you stay."

He walked away, and once the door closed behind him, Landry whispered something to Bennett, who glanced at Diane with a worried look. Bennett followed Landry out of the lab.

Diane mumbled to herself, "Why can't I keep my damn trap shut?" Sensing her labmates watching her, she kept her head down, wishing she could crawl into a hole.

Think before opening mouth, dumbass.

Moving to the mass spec, she tried to forget what had happened and concentrated on interpreting the results. Others spoke to her. She nodded but didn't hear them.

The molecular results were strange for the red dino. She rechecked the sample to find a partially dissolved grasshopper leg. After the long hours she'd spent in the ship's lab to rid the samples of insects, part of one remained. Diane sighed. While studying the mushed prickly leg, she thought of the Mississippi that had breached its banks months ago. Many had lost their homes to the overflowing river. What an enormous force that had to have been to send a cascade of insects into the deepest part of the Gulf.

What if the red dino wasn't from the ocean? Was it possible that a freshwater dinoflagellate could grow and flourish in salt water?

Consumed by her ideas, she jumped when Bennett approached. Diane said in a low voice, "Sorry, I didn't hear you come in. I apologize for earlier."

Everyone in the lab moved farther away from her and Bennett. Dark bags under the director's eyes were reminiscent of Jenson's wearied look on the cruise.

Bennett closed her eyes for a second and exhaled. "I cannot watch another postdoc lose grip on reality and self-implode. Plenty of academic institutions would hire you."

The thought of getting fired from her job caused Diane's heart to race. "I overreacted. I'm okay. Just a little shaken from the cruise."

Bennett tilted her head back, briefly closing her eyes, then looked at Diane. "Please talk to me if things get too difficult. And consider what I said."

Diane's thoughts returned to the insects. "Matt's work from the Panhandle was destroyed. Would it be okay if I went there to collect samples? My family lives near Pensacola. I could stay with them while working. OSCF wouldn't need to provide a stipend."

Bennett considered it for a moment. "It should be okay. Do you need someone from the lab to assist you?"

Diane wanted to recommend Brandon, but he specialized in machines, not organisms. "What about Nicole? She's good at sampling and culturing."

"That should work. How long do you plan to stay there?"

"I'd like to survey the area first; Nicole could join me later. Probably only a couple of weeks. Nicole's welcome to stay at my house if that's okay with her."

Diane wanted to check on her mom and uncle. Her mom's health was getting worse. Anytime they spoke on the phone, Mom would start wheezing, but no one could convince her to leave their home for a place with cleaner air.

"I'll let Dr. Jenson know your plan to work in the Panhandle," Bennett said. "It's the hardest hit by the bloom. I don't think he or Dr. Landry will have a problem with it."

Bennett left with Todd and Brandon for a seminar, where Brandon was scheduled to give a presentation on robotics. Diane, still reeling from the cofounders' beatdown, had missed her chance to talk to Brandon.

Nicole crept toward her, revealing a huge smile. "You challenged Jenson. What nerves of steel."

Diane pretended to share her amusement, but the truth was she wanted Jenson on her side. Repeated sampling of the red waters was getting them nowhere. Investigating river organisms was not part of OSCF's mission. Charging the foundation for working on a freshwater experiment could mean losing her job.

CHAPTER 12

The next day, Diane and Nicole packed chemicals, supplies, equipment, and crates of bottled water from OSCF's storage building and then loaded Diane's Jeep. When they left the building carrying packed boxes, Diane noticed Brandon talking with Jenson and Landry in the parking lot.

"Looks like Brandon's back from the seminar," Nicole said.

"Wonder what they're talking about."

Nicole shrugged. "I'm sure they're discussing how to make Brandon the future CEO of OSCF."

"What?"

"Just kidding." Nicole smiled and placed the last box in the Jeep. "They really like him. That guy can make any kind of robot. He's even working on a drone with microinstruments to travel near hurricanes and funnel clouds. On top of that, he helps the IT division maintain OSCF's network and systems." She leaned in close to Diane. "I call him a computer wizard."

"He's amazing." Diane couldn't keep the awe out of her voice.

Nicole tilted her head. "Jumping into the water to save you—that's pretty romantic."

Diane's cheeks grew warm.

Nicole grinned. "My guess is they're discussing how his presentation went."

• • •

Eerily empty streets and beaches greeted Diane as she drove to her apartment. The sense of panic in the neighborhood was growing daily; even the local newscasters appeared anxious and sounded jittery. Nearly every house, building, and business had a "For Sale" sign out front. Diane felt as if she were the only person left in Hollywood Beach in some weird sci-fi horror film.

Over the past weekend, she had watched adults with crying children pile into cars and had even helped her neighbor, an elderly man, move out of his apartment. "Will you return?" she had asked him.

The man shook his head. "I filter water for everything. If I find bottled water, it's too expensive. I used to be healthy for my age. Now I'm always sick to my stomach. Each day it gets more difficult to breathe." He leaned against his car, shoulders drooping. "I've heard rumors that major highways may close or that they might establish a curfew. I need to get out before that happens and head to the Midwest." He shook his head before adding, "I won't be back."

Diane logged onto Minecraft on her phone. Her virtual world with a diamond castle was better than this place. A mob spawned near her and blew up the drawbridge. *Damn creepers!*

She logged off the game and scanned newsfeeds. Satellite pictures showed the bloom spreading to northeastern shores. Emergency rooms were becoming more inundated with people having severe allergic reactions, paralysis of the nervous system, gastric problems, and respiratory issues.

Breaking news from public health officials showed evidence that the waterborne contaminant was aerosolizing. A female official said, "Currently, there are trace amounts of the neurotoxin in the air. It's not a huge threat at this time, but remember, this isn't a virus like COVID-19. It's poison. You cannot develop immunity to it. Preliminary tests reveal a mask with activated carbon will help to neutralize it. An N95 or surgical mask will not protect you."

She clicked on a live feed of people pilfering stores, looking for bottled water or carbon filters. Another live feed showed people who had escaped Florida now in other states with no place to go, living in their cars.

Jenson and Landry were pictured in several reports with the headline “Greenhouse Gases May Contribute to Toxic Bloom.”

OSCF was far from ridding the waters of the parasite. It was going to get worse.

CHAPTER 13

A few miles west of Pensacola, Diane's Jeep sputtered onto a gravel driveway that led up to a small brick house. The place appeared empty.

"Uncle Bo! Mom!" she yelled.

No response.

The tomato plants beside the house were droopy with two tomatoes speckled with black spots. The swing on the front porch swayed in the breeze coming off the Gulf, which was only a mile away. Every so often, she got a whiff of rotting tissue. The air felt heavy, saltier than usual, and tasted acrid. Peering through the screen door, she was relieved to find cases of bottled water on the table.

She walked to the back of the house and found a pair of legs sticking out from under a pickup truck. Bo, who couldn't carry a tune, was belting out the lyrics to "Forever and Ever, Amen" playing on the truck's radio.

She lightly kicked his feet. "Excuse me, is your name Randy Travis?"

He hollered and scooted out from under the truck. He threw his arms around her, then lifted her off the ground. "Why, it's Little Miss Know-Nothin'!"

She'd endured the nickname since childhood. Most weekends, when she was around eight years old, Bo would take her swimming at the coast—with Catie, his yellow Labrador retriever mix. Other times, they'd go on day trips to the marshes to fish and kayak. Many days ended with Bo having a few-too-many drinks. They would return home, having missed curfew but unscathed.

Mom had always asked if Bo had been drinking. Mimicking his tutorial on how to tell a fib, Diane always responded, “I know nothin’.” So came the nickname Little Miss Know-Nothin’, and it had stuck.

A short, slender man, her uncle was fifteen years younger than her mom, Vera. He’d had many girlfriends but hadn’t settled down. He had stayed with his sister and helped raise Diane. She had never known her father, whom Bo described as “a no-account, lazy, backstabbing coward.” That portrayal was the nice version.

Vera had been deeply in love with Diane’s father, and when anyone alluded to his absence, she would get teary-eyed. He didn’t want to know Diane and felt no love for them.

Bo’s favorite story was when her elementary school friend visited and asked, “Do you have a dad?”

A young Diane replied, “I got better than a dad. I got Uncle Bo!”

He had spent most of his life in the fishery business, going offshore for weeks at a time, but in their backyard, he had maintained large saltwater tanks to breed snapper, turning a hobby into a business. She frequently told her uncle, “I didn’t sign up for aquaculture classes. I learned everything I needed to know from your hatchery.” Every time he heard it, Bo beamed with pride.

Diane and Bo walked around the house, where she met her mom carrying a grocery bag and walking down the gravel driveway. They hugged for some time before letting go. “I stopped at the market,” Mom said. “Got your favorites for dinn—” She began to cough and wheeze.

Diane pulled out a box of masks with filters from her bag. “Since I can’t convince you to move to a safer place, promise me you’ll wear a mask.”

Mom glanced at Bo, then put on the mask.

Unlike Bo, her mom was fragile. Vera had been a sickly child who suffered from asthma and had never gained much confidence in herself. Now in her sixties, she appeared frailer. Though Diane and Bo tried to talk Vera into retirement, she refused, saying they needed the money and she'd miss teaching.

After everyone went into the house, Diane helped her mom prepare and put dinner on the small, round kitchen table. In the adjacent living room, Bo watched a small TV showing images of the National Guard and FEMA workers clad in biohazard suits and stationed throughout the Gulf and the Eastern Seaboard.

"Would you turn that thing off?" said Mom. "Let's eat."

Diane wondered how they remained calm while their world was collapsing. Whatever the reason, she was relieved, wanting to forget everything going on and enjoy Mom's home-cooked meal.

Bo turned down the volume and joined them.

"I saw Rita Stone at the store last week," Mom said while pouring tea.

Rita had been Diane's best friend in high school. After graduation, Diane went to college, and Rita got married. Over time, their connection went from check-in texts to once-a-year birthday cards.

"Rita's a hairdresser now. Has her own shop in town. Pregnant with her third child."

"That's great, Mom. I'm happy for her."

Diane had wanted friends in college, but she'd made more time for studies than social media or gatherings. Her B+ grade in calculus had sent her into a mild depression. She'd visited an on-campus mental health counselor, who'd said, "I wonder if your need for perfection is connected to your father's abandonment. If you're flawless, then you'd be more worthy of love."

Diane had jumped out of her chair. "That's the dumbest thing I've ever heard." After bolting out of the counselor's office, she never returned, but those words replayed in her head more often than she liked. Even now, she wondered if her desire to end the bloom was related to her need for love and acceptance.

Bo scooped up a spoonful of fried okra. "I don't want to know about people cutting hair and poppin' out babies. I wanna know about my Diane and her job."

Mom glared at Bo, then grinned at Diane. "I do too."

"Hope they ramped up security after the attack," he said, loading his plate with mashed potatoes.

Diane nodded. "Yes, cameras and more security guards."

Mom put a hand over her heart. "It's a blessing the shooter didn't hurt anyone. We've been so worried about you."

Bo pointed at the thirty-two-inch tube showing images of dead animals piled along the Eastern Seaboard. "Have you figured out what's causin' the bloom to spread so quickly?"

"It's a dino like the one I told you about in my research. But it has an odd shell around it."

"Is that bad?" asked Mom.

"Yes. The casing allows the cell to get nutrients while protecting it against changes in the environment that would normally kill it. There are millions of them forming chains in the Gulf, able to emit enough toxin in the water to cause respiratory failure in any animal."

Not wanting to add to their worries, she didn't share her near-death experience on the Gulf cruise. She guessed any news story about divers dying on an OSCF vessel were quashed by the national coverage of politicians debating over what to do about the mess of people fleeing the coast.

Bo finished a bite of cornbread. "Some folks on the news said toxins could get worse, spreadin' to more animals."

She adored how her uncle always tried to make sense of the news. "Let's say a shrimp has ten micrograms of toxin and a fish eats ten shrimp."

"That fish must be on a diet," Bo said, coughing on his mashed potatoes.

"Okay, then let's say a fish eats a hundred shrimp. Now it has a thousand micrograms of toxin. As bigger fish feed, the toxin accumulates in the tissue, causing death to bigger animals. Tissue from each carcass provides food for the dinos to feed on, giving rise to more dinos and toxins."

His grimace deepened. "They've been showin' pictures of the bloom floating off Canada. Are you saying nothin' can stop it?"

Knowing that he was too smart for any story other than the truth, she said nothing.

He patted her hand. "It'll be fine. This thing really took off during all the rains we've had. Our marshlands were becomin' an extension of the Gulf. The rains have stopped, and the waters have gone down. Even if science can't understand it, Mother Nature will rid herself of these vermin."

Her uncle and a few scientists she'd read about on social media wanted to believe that nature would take care of the problem. The trouble with their logic was that this unusual organism was a part of the environment.

Diane hadn't noticed before, but her mom's eyes were a little swollen. She wondered if the toxins were irritating them. "What's going on with your eyes, Mom?"

"Pink eye's going around the preschool. Eyes are a little irritated."

Her mom had been recently examined by a pulmonologist. "Anything happening with your health I should know about?" she asked.

"Shitfire," Bo said, chuckling. "She's got a lot. Arthritis, short-term memory loss, poor vision, she's shrinking . . ."

Mom tossed a napkin at him. "That's enough."

Diane turned to Bo. "You're no spring chicken. You should probably wear a full-face respirator that keeps out beer," she said with a wide grin.

His eyes got big. In an exaggerated nasal southern drawl, he said, "Well, bless my soul."

They laughed at each other and seemed to be in good spirits, but she knew they were hurting. Bo missed his job, his fish. Mom's small salary was inadequate, and Diane's salary wasn't much better.

Mom tired early, and Bo helped her to the bedroom.

A few minutes later, Bo returned. Diane asked, "Do you think we can find a fishing boat with a dredge to sail the Gulf into the Mississippi River?"

He rubbed his chin. "Everything's shut down. Coast Guard won't let boats through."

"I have a special permit from OSCF. I'd like to get sediment samples from the Mississippi and maybe the Gulf . . . if it's safe."

"We don't have any of the fancy equipment you're used to, but Henry has his big boat and a dredge."

She winced, recalling Henry's boat. "You're talking about the boat that plays the 'Mississippi Queen' song by Mountain?"

Bo and Henry would come back from fishing trips blasting the song. Everyone within a mile of the harbor knew when they returned. They called it the *Mississippi Queen* boat.

"It's a catchy tune," Bo said, laughing. "Henry's brother from Gulfport borrowed the boat before the harbors shut down. They couldn't get it back here, so we'll have to drive to Mississippi. Maybe we can get the boat back to Pensacola with your fancy permit. That'll thrill Henry."

"That's a two-hour drive."

"More like a four-hour drive. Highway 10 is open for emergency vehicles only. We'll have to take an alternative route and leave before dawn if you want to make good time on the water."

Diane leaned forward in her chair. "Do you think Mom will be okay if we're out for a few days? She seems weaker. Is there anything else going on?"

"Doctors tested her for COPD. Came back sayin' everything's okay. Like the rest of us, she's gettin' old. I'll let the preschool know I'm out of town. That's what I usually do if I have to go somewhere. She has many friends who'll check on her."

"I've tried to convince her to leave, give her body a break. She likes our cousins in Atlanta."

"She's as stubborn as a damn mule."

They couldn't force Vera to leave. Diane worried about how much longer her mom could survive an increasingly toxic environment.

CHAPTER 14

In the predawn darkness of the next morning, Diane went to the kitchen to pack food for the trip while Mom paced the floor and grumbled, “Going out to the Gulf is no different from walking into a burning house.”

Diane put her arms around her mom. “We’re sailing the Gulf to get to the Mississippi River. We’re not getting in the water, and we have masks and gloves. I’m more concerned about you.”

Mom, wearing a mask, pointed to it. “I’m fine. I’m not sailing on top of toxins. Before the Coast Guard closed it off, people died out there. It’s only gotten worse.”

Diane couldn’t think of another way to get sediment than being above it. The best place to do that was off the Panhandle where the concentrations of the red dinos were the greatest. Levels of toxins would be dangerous, but the potential to learn more about the parasite made the effort worthwhile. “I want to sample the river and hopefully get samples from where it flows into the Gulf of Mexico.”

“Why?”

“The Mississippi forms a blanket over the Gulf, and when there are a lot of nutrients, it can spur algal growth. It has to be covered with red algae. People call it the Dead Zone because the blooms reduce oxygen and kill slow-moving animals.”

“Ah, that makes me feel better,” Mom said, slumping her shoulders. “You’re going to a place called the Dead Zone.”

Diane stopped packing and watched Mom drum her fingers on the counter. Her mom let out a long sigh. "I don't have a good feeling about this. You shouldn't go."

"Kind of like my feeling about you staying here. It's not safe for you."

Mom closed her eyes for a second. When she looked up, she was blinking back tears. "I still don't understand why my only child wants to explore waters that kill."

"Try not to worry. As I said, the Dead Zo—"

"Please don't throw a bunch of science at me."

Diane realized her mom would not let her off easily. "You're a preschool teacher because you love children. They are innocent and need protection, someone to care for them. Isn't that how you feel?"

Mom nodded. "Of course."

"That's how I feel about marine life. I need to examine every possibility that's causing their pain and destruction—and ultimately ours. If I can find what started the bloom, then maybe there's hope for ending it."

"Don't you need a team of researchers? Extra help?"

Jenson's motivational words from his speech at a conference came back to her: one person with a remarkable idea or discovery could make a difference. "I'm not by myself. I've got Uncle Bo."

Diane couldn't think of another person more reliable and seaworthy than her uncle.

• • •

Bo and Diane arrived at the heavily guarded shipyard in Gulfport, Mississippi, six hours later. Getting to the harbor proved tedious because the guards were not familiar with OSCF's open-water research permit. After several calls back and forth with supervisors, Diane and her uncle were allowed entry.

The drive toward the harbor was excruciating, with gut-wrenching smells of death. Carcasses were scattered along the beach, making it impossible to see the sand. She grabbed filtered masks, bandanas, and goggles. After putting on the eye shield and placing two bandanas over her mask, she handed the others to Bo, who did the same.

"Where are the beach workers?" she asked, trying to catch her breath.

"Four days ago, a worker in Texas got ill after pickin' up remains. Someone said she took the hood off to get relief from the heat. She died on the way to the hospital. Gulf states are tryin' to figure out what to do about the beaches since it's considered too dangerous for the workers."

She shook her head. "Not only is the air and water polluted with toxins, but our beaches are contaminated with bacteria. I thought by now there would be mandatory evacuations."

Bo shrugged. "How can people evacuate when states are closing highways? If we were to leave for Atlanta right now, it would take us at least two days to get there. I'm not sure the rest of the country can house everyone from Florida and the coastlines."

"They issue evacuations for hurricanes, and those kill fewer people."

"Hurricane evacuations are over in a day or two and don't involve as many people."

Diane recalled images on social media of people who had left Florida and the coast living in their cars. "I heard on the news about meetings between governors and the president. Some talk about using sports stadiums as shelters."

"Gotta be at least sixteen million people living on the Gulf Coast and millions more living near the Atlantic. I'm no expert, but I'd guess if you opened up every stadium, school, and church, it wouldn't be enough."

Both fell silent, staring at the beach littered with remains. Uncle Bo cracked a small smile. "Maybe we should float over to England and see if they'll take us back."

"If it crosses the Atlantic, they'll be in the same shape," she said while turning on the radio.

A reporter said, "Officials advise those using water filters to replace the filter every twelve hours. The public water system is compromised by the constant influx of toxins into estuarine and freshwater systems. The National Guard from at least forty states is working with FEMA to send large tankers of filtered water to affected areas."

She looked up carbon water filters on her phone. Every store in a fifty-mile radius was out of stock. Though relieved to hear about the tankers, she was thankful they had plenty of bottled water.

They arrived at the dock and found the *Mississippi Queen*, which looked older than Bo. Under the hot midday sun, they loaded supplies and then set sail into the Gulf toward the Mississippi River. Bo played country music on the boat's radio while Diane investigated the dredge. The boat had a large old diesel engine that could be heard for miles. The thick smell of diesel permeated everything on the ship and provided some relief from the rancid odor of decomposition.

They made the long haul into the outskirts of the Dead Zone, where the water was covered in dark greens mixed with brownish-black ooze and thick reddish-brown slime. It looked like primordial sludge, and through her bandana-covered mask, she got a whiff of something that smelled like old sweaty socks. The foul-smelling stench caused Diane's eyes to burn and water. She blinked hard to clear her vision.

Suddenly, Bo's breathing changed to gasps for air. His forehead became a chalky color.

Before Diane could react to what was happening with her uncle, a tingling sensation started in her nostrils, followed by a tight dryness in her throat. She took shorter, more frequent breaths, then pointed in the river's direction. "Get out of here! Quick!"

Bo steered the boat full steam out of the Dead Zone and navigated to the mouth of the river, where red algae caked up on the shores. Motoring farther up the river, they found miles of torn vegetation and damaged structures where the banks had been compromised during the spring flood.

As they moved out of the brackish waters, the red algae disappeared, their breathing returned to normal, and a healthy color returned to Bo's forehead.

Bo yelled through his mask, "What the hell's happening?"

Still feeling lightheaded, Diane shrugged. She didn't fully understand what had occurred. The Dead Zone looked more like primordial soup than seawater.

They dredged the river bottom. Diane typed "River 1" into her GPS unit, which could store information about the location of the sample and had better mapping functions than the ones on phones. Unlike the multicorer with its sophisticated process of collecting a tube of intact sediment, a dredge went down and scooped up a lot of mud with water draining from it.

She had bottles ready to collect mud samples. Working into the night, they dredged up large sections of the riverbed as they sailed up the Mississippi. When next she looked at Bo, he was leaning slightly with his eyes closed. She glanced at her phone. *Three in the morning.*

They found a place to dock near New Orleans and bedded down in sleeping bags. Bo's snoring couldn't drown out the music coming from the city. It seemed odd that people were celebrating in a city that had reported high levels of toxins in the drinking water. She recalled an article about people in a war-torn country struggling to maintain a normal routine. Perhaps loud jazz music was the way New Orleans society clung to normalcy.

• • •

The next morning, Diane studied an elevation map to identify points upstream that would allow for significant runoff of nutrients: food for dinos.

Bo appeared with his eyes half-opened. She showed him the map marked by black *X*'s. "We'll dredge these spots."

His grayish-blue eyes narrowed. "How do you think a red tide came from the river?"

She told him about the insects in the Gulf. "I know it's a shot in the dark, but I can't keep pulling samples from the ocean and expect something different from what we already know."

They dredged the next two days, stopping for bathroom breaks and PB&J sandwiches. Sometimes Bo would play the boat's CD, which was a constant loop of the song "Mississippi Queen." He had a funny way of moving his hands and jerking his hips to the raunchy beat. Sometimes, she joined him in the funny jig as they pulled mud from the river.

Near Vicksburg, Mississippi, Diane took the last sample and saved it as "River 54" on her GPS. Bo glanced at the peanut butter jar. He pointed at a green marker posted on the dock that read, "Waffle House Index = Green." He laughed. "Hey, green means go. But where's the restaurant?"

She giggled. "FEMA uses that to determine the level of a disaster. I'm not sure if it's related to water advisories."

"Well, I need real food. We'll ask the restaurant if it's safe. See if there's a Denny's DEFCON."

After they returned from eating, Diane secured the sediment samples and forced herself not to get out the microscope to dig for clues. Instead, she sat with her uncle, enjoying the dark beauty of the river. She thought of rivers and lakes as places where animals lived above the softest mud and lurked in the darkest shadows. Under the water's surface, daylight appeared as a prism through drifting silt.

Bo used to tell ghost stories about lakes near their Gulf home. A part of her believed dark waters held mysterious secrets, unlike the oceans with rays of sunlight streaming through the surface as if inviting exploration. The thought of the seas turning into murky bloodred waters was painful. She'd spent years studying the type of organism now suffocating the ocean; she should have felt emboldened. Instead, she felt helpless.

CHAPTER 15

A few days later, Diane and Bo returned home. Mom waved from the porch swing as they approached.

Diane's smile disappeared when she got close to her mom. "Your eyes are swollen and red-streaked. Didn't you get eye drops to treat the pink eye?"

"I was using lubricating drops and switched to allergy drops this morning."

Diane remembered how the Gulf's toxic waters had been trapped in her dive mask, causing her eyes to sting. Her eyes had been red and swollen but had improved in a day. Mom looked a lot worse. "You may be having a reaction to toxins in the air," she said while googling full-face respirators on her phone. She showed Mom a picture of one. "I'm ordering this for you. It'll protect your eyes and airways."

Mom shook her head. "I don't want to wear that. I'd scare everyone at the school."

"Take really deep breaths and say you're Darth Vader," Diane quipped.

Bo studied the picture. "Hey, I want one of those." His tone became serious. "You need to wear it, Vera."

Mom rubbed her forehead as if she had a headache. "Dr. Bennett from your work left a number for you. She tried calling your cell."

Diane checked her phone. No missed calls. "Sailing too far from cell towers."

She called Bennett, who answered right away. "How's work going in the Panhandle?" Papers rustled in the background.

"Made it out to the Gulf's Dead Zone. Some difficulty breathing, so I sampled nearby areas." She didn't mention dredging river sediment. Her gut feeling was to not give away that information yet.

"That's fine. The technical report of your findings can wait until you return. Also, Dr. Jenson reported that DNA collected from the basin samples did not match the red dinoflagellate. Some researchers say OSCF should've covered more area and sampled deeper into the basin. Jenson believes it's too dangerous to go back out to the Gulf."

"Maybe we should've dropped a huge forklift and pulled up the entire basin," Diane joked, disappointed by the news but not surprised.

"I doubt that would've satisfied the armchair quarterbacks. I wanted to let you know that Nicole's heading your way. Not sure of her schedule. She may arrive sometime tomorrow."

Diane prepared her bedroom for Nicole, changing the sheets and neatening up. She planned to sleep on the couch, although most of her time would be spent collecting data.

She walked to the shed to help Bo set up containers for the experiment. A large orange tabby cat sat outside the door. "You got a cat?" she called out to her uncle.

"That's Wily. He's a community cat. Comes around every so often. Likes watching me work."

When she reached to pet the cat, Bo stopped her. "I've seen people rub him and leave with scratches. If he likes you, he'll ask you to pet him. If not, best leave him alone."

Taking Bo's advice, she walked away and investigated the shed. "Just like old times. Instead of my helping you grow snapper, you'll help me grow a parasite . . . if we're lucky."

Bo chuckled. "This should be easy. What's tough is keeping algae down to healthy levels in fish tanks. Shit grows like weeds."

The shed was equipped with a temperature control unit and many electrical outlets that Bo had installed for his snapper hatchery. She set up her equipment and filled the containers with bottled water purchased by OSCF. Filtered water delivered by government tankers might have contained impurities, ruining the experiment.

Diane and Bo separated the sediment sample from the fifty-four locations into containers identified as control or experimental. Because each sample was split, they now had fifty-four control containers and fifty-four experimental containers. Each container was fitted with air stones and pumps to aerate the water.

"What are you looking for?" Bo asked, peering over her shoulder.

"I'm hoping one of these containers has a resting cyst of the red dino. It's a sleeping stage of its life cycle that occurs when it doesn't have what it needs to survive. They can sleep for hundreds of years in sediment." She glanced at her uncle. "My research advisor revived a dino from a resting cyst dated over a hundred years old."

Bo let out a low whistle. "A prehistoric dino. Are you plannin' to turn my shed into *Jurassic Park*?"

"Ah, wait and see," she said with a mischievous grin and patted his shoulder. "Don't worry. It's a species we've never seen. I think the floods unearthed it along with tons of sediment carrying nutrients like farm and lawn fertilizers."

"A new organism. Nothing scary about that," Bo mumbled.

"We're going to mimic conditions a sleeping dino would encounter on its way from the Mississippi to the Gulf. Control containers will be maintained for temperature and pH of the river. Experimental containers will be treated daily with fertilizer, which is the dino's food, while slowly adjusting pH, temperature, and salinity to match the Gulf waters. If a red dino is found in an experimental container, we'll know what conditions woke it up and where it came from."

This was day one of the experiment. Small amounts of salt and fertilizer were added to each experimental container. Leaving the shed with her uncle, Diane smelled rotting tissue from nearby beaches mixed with the aroma of home-cooked vegetables coming from the house. It felt like two worlds colliding. One carried death, and the other nurtured life.

At the dinner table, Bo always made fun of how she gobbled down food whenever she returned home. "You're like a bear eatin' up everything before hibernation."

Mom shook her head at his silliness. "Oh, I forgot you had a call from Dr. Jenson while you were on the river. I told him you were hard at work on the Gulf and the Mississippi."

With each word, Diane's heart nearly burst out of her chest.

Her mom didn't notice her reaction. "He seemed very interested. Said he was in New Orleans on business and was familiar with Pensacola. Asked if he could come by."

Her appetite was gone. "Mom, tell me you didn't—"

"I gave him our address and said he was more than welcome."

Diane put her hands over her head and sat there for a few seconds.

Jenson could show up at any time.

Bo poked her arm. "Is he the guy on the news? Used to play wide receiver years ago. Great athlete. Passed up the opportunity to play professionally. What an idiot."

Diane sighed. "If he shows up, don't tell him what's in the shed or about dredging the Mississippi. I'm unsure how he'd feel about my testing a fresh-water-to-salt-water theory. OSCF focuses on marine ecosystems."

"I don't understand," Mom said, wrinkling her nose.

Diane strained to stay calm. "I know you were being nice to my boss, and that's a good thing. But I don't want him to know what I'm working on—at least not right now. All he knows is what you told him. We went up the river to visit New Orleans after sampling in the Gulf. That's the story."

Mom looked taken aback. "Why?"

She let out another heavy sigh.

Bo winked at her mom, then nudged Diane. "I'll tell him we went up the Mississippi because you like to barhop on the bayou. And then I'll tell him he's an idiot for not playing professional football."

Her mom and uncle laughed out loud as someone knocked at the door. Bo's eyes got big, and his mouth formed an *O*.

Mom left to answer the door. Diane shrugged and gawked at Bo, who was enjoying this too much.

When a young woman's voice came from the foyer, Diane exhaled and scrambled away from the table.

Nicole stood at the door with an awkward smile. "I came this evening instead of waiting until tomorrow. I had everything ready and thought you'd want to get an early start."

Diane peered around the door, half expecting to see Jenson. "Glad you're here. This is my mom and Uncle Bo."

"Come on in and have some dinner," Mom said.

Nicole's stiff posture loosened as she followed them to the table.

"Do you like fine dining, Nicole?" Bo asked.

Nicole nodded and smiled. "Sounds good."

Bo grinned. "Well, you won't be gettin' any of that here."

Mom yelped, "Hey!"

"Uh-oh." He chuckled and jumped, pretending to be startled, and beamed with a wide-eyed grin.

Nicole covered her mouth, giggling.

Working on the river had taken a toll on Bo. He went to bed soon after dinner. Mom wasn't far behind him.

Diane updated Nicole on the fresh-water-to-salt-water experiment.

Nicole beamed. "That's a great idea. If that dino's there, I'll grow it."

"We may get a visit from Jenson. He called while I was out. Mom gave him our address with an open invitation." Nicole's smile disappeared. "Yep. She told him I was working on the river."

"Sounds like he wants to see firsthand what you're up to. I haven't heard of any freshwater experiments at OSCF. I think he'd make this an exception. We're in a crisis."

"He could fire me. I really want to keep my job."

They sat quietly for a minute. Nicole rubbed her forehead. "I don't think he'll fire you, but let's say I'm helping you with culturing samples collected off the coast. You can mention that you collected river samples near the Dead Zone, but your focus is on the saltwater samples."

Diane nodded with some hesitance. “I guess that’ll work.”

“If we grow the dino, we’ll give a report that will knock his socks off. If we don’t then we’ll make up a report and take the truth to our graves.”

“Good plan.” Diane tilted her head back and grinned. “We make a good team.”

She wasn’t sure if the plan would work and figured if Jenson showed up, she would be in trouble.

CHAPTER 16

By the time Diane woke up the next morning, her mom had already gone to work at the preschool, and Nicole and Bo were in the shed.

Diane dressed quickly and was making her way to the shed when a BMW pulled into the driveway.

Oh no!

Her pulse raced when the car parked and the engine stopped.

Bo and Nicole exited the shed, but when Diane nodded at Nicole, she went back into the shed and closed the door. Bo stood near Diane.

Jenson got out of the car, took off his sunglasses, then, scowling, looked around the property. The downturned corners of his mouth rose to a large, dimpled smile when he saw Diane. He said hello, then extended his hand to Bo and introduced himself.

"Didn't you play football in college?" Bo asked.

Diane loved her uncle, but he could not keep his thoughts to himself. Perhaps the tendency to blurt out her feelings was something she'd picked up from him.

Jenson smiled, looking back at her. "Yes, wide receiver. Enjoyed being a student athlete. Turns out I was more studious than athletic."

"Well, if I could catch and run like you, I would've traded in the books for a bigger paycheck."

"Uncle Bo," Diane said quietly, pleading with her eyes for him to quit.

"It's okay," Jenson said. "I'm thankful I had choices. For me, science was more interesting than outrunning a bunch of guys trying to knock my head off each week. I'd much rather work with innovative, brilliant minds." He motioned at Diane. "Like Dr. Nelson."

Bo winked at her. "Yep. Runs in the family." He returned to the shed but remained outside, meandering around the building, fooling with a garden hose.

Jenson surveyed the shed with a blank expression. "I tried calling your cell. Your mom said you were on the Mississippi."

She remembered the plan she devised with Nicole, but when she began to speak, he interrupted her. "Before you tell me about working on the river, I wanted to let you know that a team of well-known biologists is preparing an Atlantic expedition. I'd like you to join them. The ship leaves out of Port Everglades this weekend."

If she had to prepare for a cruise, there wouldn't be enough time to train Nicole and Bo to carry out the test. Interpreting results and modifying methods to keep the experiment on track were her responsibility.

Jenson watched her as she tried to think of a good reason to stay. He crossed his arms. "I thought you'd be jumping at this opportunity."

Maybe she could say she was scared. Last time she was on the water, she'd had a severe allergic reaction. That would probably get her fired more quickly than making up a lie.

You can't be a coward and a steward of the ocean.

If she went on the cruise, the results of her experiment would be questionable. It was too important to leave behind. A chance to salvage the experiment left her with few alternatives.

She froze, forgetting about her and Nicole's scheme. After taking a deep breath, she said, "I'm working on an experiment to observe and measure the development of freshwater dinoflagellates while adding nutrients and salt to match the Gulf."

Jenson stood statue still, his stare wide-eyed. "Okayyy," he said, dragging out the word as if he were still processing the information.

"I believe our parasite came out of the river."

"Show me what you've done."

Bo's eyebrows rose in surprise when Diane and Jenson approached the shed. When Jenson entered the building, Nicole's mouth dropped open, and a box of pipettes slipped out of her hands. The skinny plastic tubes made a clattering sound on the concrete floor.

Diane looked at Nicole and mouthed the words, "I'm sorry." Then she turned to Jenson and told him about dredging the river before showing him the sampled locations saved on the GPS. He strolled around, peering into the containers while she described her methods.

Half expecting a swift firing, Diane braced herself for criticism when he walked back to her and said, "OSCF doesn't support ridiculous fresh-water-to-salt-water theories." Then he gave her a friendly smile. "However, this is interesting. I like it."

Nicole looked at her with an "I told you so" expression.

Glancing back at the containers, Jenson said, "I'll ask Dr. Bennett to join the Atlantic cruise. In her absence, you'll send a report of your findings to me." He looked her in the eye. "To me, *only*."

Diane felt her body relax. He understood what she was trying to achieve and was supportive.

After Jenson said goodbye to Nicole and Bo, Diane walked him to his car and thanked him for letting her continue to work.

"Your ideas are creative, different," he said and gave her a small grin. "Maybe you'll find the red dino." He didn't sound too convinced.

"Any more updates on the bloom in the Atlantic?"

"Satellite data shows it spreading throughout the Caribbean and up to Canadian shores, reaching over a hundred miles off the coast. We've ordered more bots to cover the affected areas. Unfortunately, until they arrive, we won't have an accurate way of measuring the infestation."

"What about your mathematical models?" Diane asked.

"Two of them predict a slow decrease of the bloom in the North Atlantic, but most are showing it crossing the Atlantic."

"And the Gulf of Mexico?"

"Only one model predicts a decrease. Others suggest it could become the new normal."

Horrified, Diane swayed slightly before steadying herself. “Unbelievable,” she said in a low, shaky voice.

Wily rubbed against Jenson’s leg. Before she could say anything, he bent down to pet the cat. Wily purred at first, then clawed his hand.

“Oh gosh. I’m so sorry. He’s a stray.” It felt odd to excuse the behavior of a wandering cat.

Jenson flicked his hand while getting into his car.

“Do you need anything?” she asked, noticing the lines of blood on his hand. “We have bandages, Neosporin.”

“Don’t worry. I grew up in a place that had lots of stray cats.” He grabbed a napkin from the glove compartment and used it to cover the scratches. Jenson looked at her before closing the car door. “Glad I got out of there.”

Nicole gave a thumbs-up from the shed as Jenson drove away.

Bo walked toward Diane. “I was wrong to say he should’ve gone with the pros. That Rolex, his fancy clothes. He doesn’t need to play football to make a lot of money.”

She frowned. “Science is the pursuit of truth, not profit.”

“Well, he’s profiting somehow.”

Though scientists didn’t normally get rich, she gave little thought to Jenson’s display of wealth. He’d invested so much of himself in the scientific community, he deserved to be happy and live well.

Diane left Bo and went to the shed. She took samples from the control and experimental containers to study under the microscope. Nicole added increased amounts of fertilizer and salt in the experimental containers, leaving the controls alone for comparison. Bo checked in often, ready to help. He was smiling more since they’d started working in the shed.

The team had no remarkable discovery on day two of the experiment.

Later that evening, Diane and Nicole went to the bedroom and sat on top of the bed to unwind. Nicole nodded toward the voices of Diane’s mom and uncle. “They really love you. Must be nice to be an only child.”

Diane wasn't sure if she agreed. "You have brothers and sisters?"

Nicole sighed heavily. "Three sisters and a brother. Whenever I go home, I'm excited to tell them about my work, but I never get a chance. My sisters are all married with children. They're always talking about their kids. No one wants to hear about what I do."

"You don't think any of them are interested in your job?"

Nicole tilted her head, looking as if she'd been asked to solve a difficult math problem. "The only one who cares about what I do is my aunt. She's a scientist. I like my brother, but . . ."

"But what?"

Nicole shrugged. "He has a girlfriend now. She works in nutrition at schools and calls herself a woman of science. My aunt flipped out when I told her that. She said, 'A person of science employs the scientific method to develop theories. His girlfriend plans school lunches and tells kids to eat fruits and vegetables.'"

Diane's eye widened. "Who is your aunt?"

Nicole paused, twirling a long strand of hair. "She's a biochemist. Nancy Weaver."

Diane furrowed her eyebrows in thought. "Hmm. I'm not familiar with her work."

They sat in silence for a few seconds before Nicole spoke. "You remind me of Matt before he lost it. He was a genius."

"What do you think happened to him?"

"Most of the time, he was in the field working on a chemical process to reduce greenhouse gas emissions. Many called him cutting edge. It's weird. When he became interested in the bloom, he was let go. He didn't seem the type to become violent. Guess you never really know the inner workings of a person." Nicole suppressed a yawn. "Switching subjects to something fun . . . Brandon jumped into toxic water to save you!"

Diane blushed. "He's nice. Super cute. And he saved me. I don't know what else to say."

Nicole scooted closer to Diane then looked her in the eye. "Do you like him?"

Diane stood up, moving away from the bed. "Yeah, but I don't have good luck with men," she said, touching a bracelet in an open jewelry box on her dresser, a gift from Adam, who had broken her heart in college. She no longer held feelings for him, but the betrayal still stung.

"Guys can burn ya. I know that," Nicole said, stretching out on the bed. "But how often does someone like Brandon come along? Isn't he worth the risk?"

Diane looked at Nicole sprawled on the bed, eyes closed. "You're exhausted. I'm going to the shed to check a few more samples before I call it a day. See you in the morning."

Nicole peeked at her through one eye. "Matt was obsessed with work before he was fired. You have his work ethic. Don't get lost in it, like he did."

Already halfway out the door before Nicole finished her sentence, Diane thought of Jenson placing his trust in her to figure out if a red parasite had found its way into the sea. This was an opportunity to win his approval and solidify her place with OSCF.

CHAPTER 17

On day three of the experiment, Diane, Nicole, and Bo started work early. They adjusted pH, added fertilizer and salt, and documented every detail. Diane took a sample from an experimental container labeled "River 10," which was located between an industrial lot and low-income housing forty miles upstream from New Orleans. She looked through the microscope lens and found the usual freshwater plankton. Several cysts had a small red mass, but one looked different. It had a large bright orange mass, reminding her of the orange eyespot on the red dino.

At that moment, Bo's cell phone rang. When he left the shed to answer it, Diane motioned Nicole over.

Nicole looked through the lens. "Nothing out of the ordinary."

"What?" Diane jumped behind the microscope, searching for the cyst with the orange accumulation. She moved the petri dish around. It was gone.

Diane shook her head. Hours spent at the microscope had strained her eyes. Maybe her vision had deceived her.

Suddenly, Bo rushed into the shed. "Your mom's in the hospital. We need to go."

Diane jumped up, dropping her pencil and knocking over a beaker. "What happened?" she asked, grabbing the overturned container only to watch it slip through her shaky hands.

"The school said she had a seizure. They called an ambulance. She's on her way to the hospital."

Nicole nudged Diane toward the door. "Don't worry about this. Go to your mom."

After thirty minutes in the ER waiting area, they discovered Mom had been admitted. When they got to her room, a physician stopped examining his notes and greeted them. "Her convulsions have subsided. Breathing is back to normal. In the past couple of weeks, we've had many older adults with her symptoms. We believe these are due to either contaminated water or air."

Diane watched her mom, who seemed to be in a deep sleep. A periodic hitch in her breathing made Diane worried and frustrated. *She should've left when I told her to!*

"Her trachea was swollen to where air couldn't get to the lungs," continued the doctor. "Her asthma exacerbates the symptoms, but she has responded to medication. Swelling has decreased, but her O2 saturation is low. She'll need to stay overnight."

Diane moved closer to her mom, whose breathing now sounded labored. Gently, she rested her head against Mom's shoulder. Her mom's hands twitched a little.

An hour later, while leaving the hospital, she looked at Bo. "Mom has to leave the coast. I wish I could go, but I can't because of my job. You'll need to go with her."

He nodded, rubbing his temples. "Will we be able to come back?"

She used to seek his advice with the same type of questions. She remembered asking him if she'd be able to go to college. He said it would be a sin if someone as smart as she didn't get all the education she could. When she'd asked if she would ever meet someone special, he'd assured her the boys would line up outside the door, and he'd planned to whittle the line down to the handful of suitors he approved of. This was the first time he had genuinely looked to her for an answer. She refused to accept Jenson's mathematical models predicting the Gulf would stay in the clutches of the suffocating bloom.

She hugged him. "It'll get better. In the meantime, you and Mom need to be in a safe place."

"What about you? Staying here puts you in harm's way."

Diane shook her head. "I use bottled water and keep my mask on when I'm outside and working with samples. I'm careful not to get toxic water on me." Despite her assurances to her uncle, she was concerned. She didn't want to lie to Bo but needed him to not worry.

• • •

Later that evening, Bo searched online for places to rent near Atlanta. People fleeing the coastline had left no vacancies. Places further away from the Gulf were reporting issues regarding the airborne toxin but nothing like the effects on persons living near the coast.

Diane headed out to the shed. Nicole waved as she entered. "How's your mom?"

"She's still in the hospital. Her asthma makes her more vulnerable. Uncle Bo can't find a hotel or a rental around Atlanta, so they're going to stay at my cousin's house near the city."

Nicole touched Diane's shoulder. "I'm sorry. She'll feel better once she gets away from here."

Diane glanced at the microscope. "Did you find anything?"

"No. What did you see?"

Diane rubbed the back of her neck. "Thought I saw a resting cyst with an orange mass. Reminded me of the eyespot on the red dino."

"What about the contents of the petri dish? Should we place it in a separate container? Keep it on schedule with the experiment?"

Diane didn't think the sample was viable. It had been left under the microscope for too long. She decided to keep the petri dish contents on track with the rest of the experiment.

There were no more large containers, so Nicole placed the contents of the petri dish into a smaller container she found in the back of the shed.

Bo had gone to bed early, so it was just Nicole and Diane in the shed. Nicole watched Diane run calculations from the experiment on her laptop in between rebuilding her Minecraft house. The mob had blown up her diamond castle and wooden shack. She switched to Minecraft's Betweenlands, a dark, swampy realm. Her mouth dropped open when the mossy world appeared on her screen.

"Shit," Nicole blurted out. "Why would someone do that?"

A hacker had changed the game's green algae to bloodred. Everything in the Betweenlands was dead.

CHAPTER 18

On day four, Diane got up extra early to work. She was reaching for the River 10 sample when Nicole came in. "Wow, I knew you'd get up early to get to River 10. That's determination," Nicole said and began making notes. Her phone beeped, and she read the text. "I have news for you," she said with a wide grin. Nicole moved closer to show Diane a text from Todd.

Jenson asked me to assist with Diane's experiment. Brandon said he wanted to help. We'll be there tomorrow. Have address. We'll look for a hotel nearby.

Nicole pursed her lips, waiting for Diane to say something.

"Maybe they could stay here," Diane said, unsure of what Nicole was expecting her to say. "Uncle Bo's made plans to travel to Atlanta after Mom gets discharged from the hospital. Tomorrow night, we'll have two open beds."

"You don't get it." Nicole placed a hand on her forehead and shook her head. "Brandon, the computer guru, never works with biological experiments. He *volunteered* himself."

Diane knew Nicole wanted her to be excited about Brandon. "Great. Can't wait to see both of them." She liked Brandon but hesitated to let herself get carried away about something that could be more imagined than real. Perhaps he didn't like her as much as she liked him. Or maybe she didn't want to get her hopes up.

Back inside the house, Diane helped Bo pack for the trip to Atlanta. The day passed without any new discovery.

• • •

Day five began with Diane following Bo to the hospital. She would miss his irreplaceable way of lightening the mood.

Mom appeared pale but relieved to get out of the hospital. Diane pushed her in a wheelchair to Bo's truck.

"Dreamed of you last night. I rarely remember details, but this one"—her mom paused, seemingly hesitant to reveal her memory, then looked up at Diane—"you were in a building on fire. The inferno was a brilliant purple. Flames raced through every corner, consuming the building. I'm not sure if you got out."

Bo shook his head in disbelief. "How many drugs they got you on?"

When they reached the truck, Diane stopped pushing the wheelchair and crouched next to Mom, who shrugged. "I was a fool for not listening to you. I should've left this place." She patted Diane's hand. "Please come with us. I worry about you."

"I promise to protect myself," she said, rubbing Mom's back.

A few minutes later, Diane watched her family begin their escape to Atlanta, and then she returned to the foul Gulf Coast. The best way to protect them—possibly the only way—was to complete the experiment.

• • •

A white truck with an OSCF emblem was parked in the driveway when Diane returned to her family's home. In the shed, she found Brandon and Todd listening to Nicole explain the setup. Todd laughed under his face shield. "A mad scientist's shed."

Brandon lifted his mask to reveal a sweet grin. "Have you found anything?"

Nicole pointed to the small container of River 10 contents, now a thick mixture of salt and fertilizer. "Maybe here?"

Diane shrugged. “I thought there was a resting cyst with physical properties of the red dino. I haven’t seen it again.”

Nicole told them about Jenson’s visit to the shed. Todd raised one eyebrow. “You tell him off in the lab; you don’t get fired. He approves an experiment with freshwater plankton in a shed. Do you have secret powers?”

Brandon beamed at Diane. “She’s got me under her spell.”

Diane knew he was joking, but the way he looked at her was enchanting. She also knew that Jenson was too smart to rule out unconventional methods.

“What are the bots reading?” Nicole asked. “Gulf now a thick floating red blob?”

The smile on Brandon’s face disappeared. “Bots in the Gulf are malfunctioning. The red algae are affecting the instruments. Thankfully, the Atlantic bots are working for now. But, they’ll need maintenance soon. When Dr. Bennett comes back from the cruise, I’ll be heading out.”

Diane thought about the grasshoppers floating in the Gulf and the map of red dots showing large numbers of red dinos. “Can we get satellite images of the influx of the Mississippi River into the Gulf of Mexico during the floods? Maybe get an aerial view showing how far the river pushed sediments and nutrients into the Gulf.”

“I’ll contact the center and place a request,” Brandon said, typing on his phone.

Diane helped them take their belongings to her mom’s and uncle’s rooms.

“Where do you sleep?” Brandon asked. She pointed to the couch, and he shuffled back a step. “No, no. I’ll take the sofa. You take the bed.”

Raised in the South, she needed to be hospitable. “The couch is comfortable.” *Though having my own room would be great.*

Brandon insisted and put his things on the sofa. He spotted a child’s drawing mounted on the wall. Leaning near the picture, he read the large printed letters: “*Daisies* by Diane.”

She looked down, pushing a strand of hair behind her ear. "I was six years old when I drew it. Don't know why Mom framed it."

He moved closer to her, revealing the smile that she adored. "Well, I could tell they were daisies. It must be a mom thing. I was terrible at sports, but mine kept all those silly participation medals."

She loved the way he wanted to relate to her. He had a genuine sweetness about him. She remembered when he'd found her gaming. "Someone built a castle using my Minecraft profile. None of my friends made it. I wonder where it came from."

He grinned sheepishly as his cheeks turned red. "Guilty."

"How'd you do that?"

"Ah, that's a million-dollar secret." His smile broadened. "Let's just say I know people. Did you like it?"

"Yeah. Except the mob blew it up."

His mouth dropped open. "What?"

After Brandon and Todd got settled, they headed back to the shed. Brandon and Todd worked with Nicole, treating the experimental containers with salt and fertilizer. Though the shed was twenty feet long, it was cramped with containers and four people. Diane stayed at the microscope. Nothing but the usual plankton. She sat back in her chair and rested her eyes. *Is this a waste of time?*

Between missing her family and working late nights in the shed, she felt drained. She rested her face between her hands.

A chair scooted across the floor, and she looked up. Brandon sat close to her. He pulled down his mask. "I know why we're not finding the red dino in these containers."

Everyone stilled and stared at him.

"They heard Dr. Dino was here and said, 'Let's split!'" A smile spread across his face. "Get it? Cell division? Let's split?"

It could have been the long nights with fatigue bordering on delirium, but Brandon's broad smile, nodding head with arched brows over shiny eyes, and amusement at his play on words caused Diane to laugh uncontrollably. Nicole laughed at her.

Todd groaned. "Dude, it's a bad joke when you have to explain it."

Brandon pointed to Diane. "All that matters is I made her laugh."

• • •

On day six of the experiment, Diane used a microscope to examine water in the experimental containers that had reached the salinity of the Gulf. No red dino.

At the end of the day, everyone except Diane returned to the house. Her thoughts returned to the cyst resembling the red dino in the River 10 sample collected upstream from New Orleans. She pipetted out more of the silty water that had been collected from the segment of the river nestled between an industrial lot and low-income housing units. After placing the contents under the scope, she searched for over an hour. Nothing.

Her eyes were tired; her body felt stiff. She stood up from her chair and stretched her arms. After moving her sore neck from side to side, she turned toward the small container with the leftover contents from the petri dish. Though it had remained on track with the experiment and had received daily amounts of nutrients, Diane had paid little attention to it because it had stayed out for too long and wasn't reliable.

With nothing to lose, she retrieved a sample from the small container and placed it under the microscope. The lens was set to a power for viewing resting cysts. At first, all she saw was empty space. But when she decreased the lens' power, a whip of flagella moved out of the light. A red dino with an orange spot. She held her breath as four more dinos swam under the lens. They looked like the ones they'd collected from the Gulf but with a thin, almost nonexistent exterior.

Diane placed some of the crimson-colored cells into dishes containing tap water. They died instantly.

Same organism but without the thick cell wall. Was the Gulf dino a mutation?

Her heart raced as she prepared a sample for DNA analysis. If OSCF molecular biologists determined this was the same organism plaguing the seas, then everyone would know that the parasite originated from the river. The next step would be to figure out what triggered its transformation.

Brandon stepped into the shed. Her voice was jittery with excitement when she said, "You're not going to believe what I found."

She set the scope lens focused on the red dinos for him to view. "You see the spiky red thing moving with stringy protrusions? I believe that's our parasite."

His eyes got big. "No way." He sat for a moment in front of the microscope, then inched away.

"Salinity matches the Gulf, but the levels of nutrients are off the charts," Diane said while frantically writing down measurements of the water from the small container.

"Um, maybe, it, um"—he moved toward her—"maybe it likes a little salt with its fertilizer."

"I ignored this sample because it sat out for so long. Looks like Nicole didn't adjust the fertilizer concentration from the large to a small container."

"Serendipity," he said, leaning closer to her.

Diane spun around, reached for her laptop, and ran right into Brandon. Instead of backing away, he held her close. Looking into his eyes and feeling his arms pulling her nearer, she forgot what she had been doing.

After a few seconds, she caught her breath. "Sorry about that," she said, her voice cracking.

"I'll try to stay out of your way," he said, his voice low, soft. Sultry.

Behind them, someone cleared their throat, and Diane quickly backed away from Brandon. Nicole and Todd had walked in, and Diane wondered what they'd seen. She pointed at the microscope, trying to quell a smile.

They both rushed over, and first Todd, then Nicole looked through the scope. Realizing she'd made a mistake in the addition of fertilizer,

Nicole helped Diane in recording concentrations. Brandon stood back, out of their way.

"Let's set up a culture of them. That way we have a constant supply to test," Diane said to Nicole.

"It looks just like the red dino except it appears thinner," said Todd, who kept looking through the microscope. "I'll make sure we have instruments available to measure the water and soils from River 10."

"Where's River 10?" Brandon asked.

The rapid clicking of laptop keys matched Diane's hurried answer to Brandon. "Forty miles upstream from New Orleans. Near an industrial lot and low-income housing." In a burst of adrenaline, she completed and emailed the report to Jenson.

No one slept that night. They sprawled out on the shed floor and took turns feeding the red dinos large amounts of plankton. The single-celled organisms divided until the water inside the petri dish turned bloodred.

When everyone got quiet, Nicole whispered to Diane, "It's day seven of the experiment. Do we get to rest?"

Diane looked at Nicole with a tired smile but said nothing. She wouldn't stop until she figured out what had turned this river dino into an unrelenting sea monster.

CHAPTER 19

The next day, Diane packed the sealed vial of river dinos into an impermeable case, which fit inside a watertight container. After placing the contained sample into a sturdy box lined with a thick orange bag and a biohazard sticker, she shipped it using FedEx Overnight. The others deep-cleaned the containers and prepared to take the equipment back to Fort Lauderdale.

Diane called her mom and uncle and told them about the discovery.

"Does that mean we can come home?" Bo asked. He was joking, but there was hope in his voice.

She told him about the high concentrations of nutrients in the container that allowed the resting cyst from River 10 to become a red dino.

"I remember the low-income housing," he said. "Not much there but concrete. How could that much runoff of something like fertilizer come from there?"

"I know, but I retested the sample many times. Even though the Mississippi basin runs through most of the central states, the nutrient concentrations would disperse and become diluted traveling downstream. Has to be near River 10."

She heard a commotion in the background.

"I'm sorry to cut this short," Bo said, sounding distracted. "Cousin Marnie's waving at me like a damn flag in a storm. Stay safe and call when you can."

The background chatter got louder, and her uncle hung up before she could respond.

Diane was still looking at her phone when her labmates came into the shed. Brandon opened his laptop and motioned Diane over. "I superimposed the satellite image of the river discharge onto the initial bot measurements of the red dinos in the Gulf. The murky brown stuff is fresh water and sediment coming out of the river during the spring floods. Normally, it's smaller and fans out toward Louisiana and Texas. With the continuous rains and flooding in the spring, the force of the river moved the freshwater and sediment out to deeper waters."

She studied the map. "Influx from the river lines up perfectly with your red dots showing highest concentrations of dinos."

Nicole walked over to Brandon's computer. "Most of the brown stuff is right off the Panhandle," she said in a muffled voice just before sneezing under her mask.

Todd backed away from Nicole. "Whoa, sounds like you need a doctor."

Nicole suppressed a cough. "It's just a cold."

Diane watched Nicole warily. The pungent smell from the shores was getting worse. Even when wearing a mask, Diane's nostrils burned. They all needed to be more mindful of symptoms as the onset of contamination could be mistaken for a common illness.

Her phone rang, and she looked at the screen. "It's OSCF," she said to the group and answered the call.

Jenson's voice came down the line. "Diane, congrats on the results from your experiment. I expect to receive your specimen by tomorrow. We'll get the DNA analysis done ASAP. I have to admit your fresh-water-to-salt-water theory took me by surprise. Great work."

His praise lifted her spirit. "Thank you. I think it's the same species, but the Gulf dinoflagellate has a point mutation."

"We'll know more soon. We're making progress, which leads to change. Now I have another issue I'd like to discuss with the group. Is everyone there?"

Diane motioned her labmates over to the phone and put Jenson on speaker.

"One of our research vessels sent out a distress signal yesterday," Jenson said. "The ship experienced a mechanical failure and is stuck in the Atlantic, a few miles off the South Carolina coast. The crew, including Dr. Bennett, are sick." Jenson paused and coughed before continuing. "In fact, I can't reach anyone by phone, email, radio . . . nothing. I've tried to find a medevac team that can evacuate them. They're refusing to go out because many of them have fallen ill. Some have died during recent rescues."

Diane and the others glanced at each other worriedly.

Jenson continued, "Just yesterday, the Coast Guard temporarily halted their operations in the Atlantic. Several of their ships were forced to return to shore due to crew members experiencing severe reactions and respiratory issues. They lost seven people, and many of their ships are having mechanical problems."

"We've lost the Coast Guard?" Todd asked in an incredulous tone.

"They're no longer monitoring the seas, only the coastline," Jenson answered. "It's all over the news."

Diane realized she hadn't kept up to date on the goings-on outside the shed.

"How about the navy?" Brandon asked, moving closer to Diane.

Jenson exhaled. "I don't know what the hell is going on with the navy. I certainly don't see their ships out there."

Todd shook his head. "Wow. We really are on our own."

"There are government ships at sea working with us, but their vessels are running into trouble as well," Jenson said, his voice weary. "I contacted a physician in South Carolina whom I'm friends with. He's willing to go out to the ship, assess the crew, and help get them to shore. I need someone who can get him out there. Right now you guys are my only available marine scientists who can handle a boat."

They all looked at each other and waited for someone to speak up. Like the ship with blubber in the propeller, the ship in the Atlantic wasn't moving. Like Brandon's bots, systems were failing.

Brandon crossed his arms. "I was supposed to go on that ship when it returned. I can go."

"No," Jenson retorted. "I want you on a different ship leaving out of Delaware. It's important for you to keep the Atlantic bots functional."

Nicole coughed again. She didn't look well. Todd and Diane glanced at each other.

Todd mumbled, "Guess we're it."

Diane nodded. "Todd and I can go. We'll get full-face masks with respirators for this?"

"Yes," Jenson said. "Should be okay for a day. Any longer than twelve hours and you'd have to change the filter. Assist the doctor, get them off the ship, and get back."

"What about the ship?" Todd asked.

"Leave it. I'll deal with it later. And whatever you do, do not go in the water. I don't care if you see a cute dolphin waving a sign that says 'Help!' Keep your asses on the boat."

They exchanged glances of wide-eyed disbelief.

Jenson feeling guilty about losing divers in the Gulf?

Jenson coughed. "I'm emailing your airline and rental car information with directions to the Charleston Harbor." He stopped for a moment, cleared his throat. "We've incorporated a new cleaning procedure on all vessels to eliminate algae on the surface. That should reduce the possibility of mechanical failure. Your boat will be cleaned and ready to go when you arrive."

Engineers had worked on reasons why the algae interrupted machinery. Diane hadn't read about those details. Her concern was the disruption of organic life.

Jenson ended the call, and just then, Nicole started another round of coughing. Diane turned to her. "Please go to a doctor about that cough, Nicole." She rubbed her temples and thought the hacking cough from both Nicole and Jenson sounded similar. Maybe they should convince Jenson's doctor friend to check on him.

Nicole agreed to seek medical attention while pointing at the small jar containing the River 10 sample. "We haven't touched it. The jar belongs to your uncle."

Diane examined the contents. "I don't think he wants it back. I'll dispose of it as hazardous waste. You packed and secured a sample for culturing?"

"You betcha." Nicole pointed at a small white cooler marked, with large black letters, "BIOHAZARD."

Wearing masks covered by bandanas, they packed the equipment into the truck. The other OSCF vehicle that Nicole had driven would remain for Todd and Diane.

Brandon approached Diane, and they both lowered their masks. "Be careful out in the Atlantic. Its shores are drenched in toxins." He fidgeted a little and stammered, "When we're not swimming in toxins . . . maybe we could go out one evening?"

"I'd really like that," she said, hoping her smile displayed interest without appearing too eager. She was thrilled about going out with Brandon. Everything she'd seen up to this point gave her hope he'd be different from her last cheating boyfriend. It was a strange time to be asked out, but a sense of normalcy was something they all needed right now.

Brandon grinned and then climbed into the truck with Nicole. The small white icebox labeled "BIOHAZARD" was in the truck's cargo bed, securely fastened and nestled between other boxes. Unearthing the river dinos was like finding diamonds in her Minecraft game. She recalled the online mob blowing up her gems and destroying her work. She also remembered her tremendous joy when Jenson praised her discovery. Charged with saving the oceans, OSCF had to protect this rare blackwater gift holding the mystery behind the red scourge. They could fail without it.

CHAPTER 20

Diane and Todd met the physician at the South Carolina harbor. After exchanging greetings, Diane said, "Dr. Jenson called us yesterday. He didn't sound well. After we're done here, could you call and check on him?"

Dr. Harris, the physician, didn't reply. Diane wondered if he'd heard her through the thick face cover she was wearing. Before she could repeat herself, Dr. Harris wrung his hands and yelled, "Let's get this over with!"

Diane and Todd exchanged glances and then followed the doctor toward the boat. Decomposing marine creatures covered in slime filled the harbor. Red algae on the docks competed with barnacles. Seawater caked in bloodlike goo lay a hundred yards away from the docks.

Her phone beeped with a text from Nicole. *Feeling much better after doctor's visit.*

A wave of relief washed over Diane, and she replied, *Thank goodness. I was so worried.*

Her thoughts drifted to Brandon retrieving and resetting bots off Delaware. Thinking of him was a nice diversion as she watched the ocean waves crash into pink foam. She thought about sending him a text but didn't want to look overeager.

He's busy on the ship. I should wait.

The beachcombers, anglers, birds, and boats that once crowded the shores were missing, and an eerie silence surrounded them.

They spotted the research vessel a half hour later. The immobile ship made no sound.

Todd blasted a horn. Dr. Harris covered his ears. "Damn thing's loud enough to wake the dead." No movement on the ship.

In the hot, muggy air, Diane felt a chill run down her spine. She glanced at Todd, who dropped the anchor about ten feet from the ship. They lowered the raft and floated toward the vessel. Todd fidgeted with his gloves. Dr. Harris didn't move. No one spoke. Their faces were hidden behind the respirators, but Diane sensed their dread.

Once on board the ship, Todd ran straight to the captain's quarters while Diane and Dr. Harris made their way down a narrow hallway to the passenger cabins. "Hello?" she called out, her voice shaking with fear.

Foul whiffs of decay mixed with smells of urine and feces flowed through the respirator, causing Diane to gag. Suddenly, she heard a shrill, small voice. A young woman was lying in a bunk, a stained sheet covering her sallow body. Her face was covered in hives and traces of saliva and vomit. Her eyes were bloodshot. A bowl of vomit on a makeshift stand was at the head of her bunk.

The woman tried to catch her breath between coughs. "A . . . shark," she managed, her voice hoarse and feeble.

Diane bent closer to her, feeling the respirator slip a little. An overwhelming stench of sulfur caused a burning sensation in her sinuses. The woman's pallid skin appeared to sag. She lost consciousness.

Diane ran toward the galley to look for bottled water.

Dr. Harris was in the next cabin, attending to another person who looked as ghastly as the young woman.

This is much worse than we expected.

No bottled water, juice, or soda in the galley. The refrigerator had lost power. Everything was spoiled. She turned on the tap. The water was brownish red.

Did the algae infiltrate the ship's water supply?

Todd found her and huffed, "Captain's dead."

A loud thrashing came from the starboard side of the boat. Diane and Todd ran toward the sound. A ten-foot bull shark, covered in red slime, writhed in the water. It was entangled in a line from a buoy that kept the massive fish afloat.

The sound of shuffling feet came from behind her, and Diane spun on her heels. A gaunt, ghostlike version of Bennett stood before her, saliva on her cheeks and chin. Diane and Todd ran to her and held her between them.

Bennett gasped for breath then whispered, "I come out when it moves. If it survives, maybe I will." She gazed into Diane's eyes behind the mask shield and asked in a childlike voice, "Won't you help it?"

Diane and Todd exchanged worried glances. Todd murmured, "Dr. Bennett's delirious."

"Let's get her to the boat."

They held onto Bennett and guided her toward the anchored raft where Dr. Harris stood holding up a man with grayish-green skin. If Diane hadn't known better, she'd have thought he was suffering from horrible seasickness.

"Six alive. All in critical condition," Dr. Harris said, gasping for air. "Rest of the crew's dead. We need to get the sick back to shore. I've called 9-1-1."

Diane helped Bennett onto the raft and then joined Todd to guide the others out of their rooms. One man asked, "What day is it? Where am I?" He trembled so much, she wasn't sure if he was feverish or convulsing.

Sweating under her mask, she took rapid breaths and helped Todd carry an older woman who could not open her eyes.

The shark pounded its gigantic body against the water as they drifted on the raft toward their boat. Bennett closed her eyes and covered her ears.

Todd steered the ship while Dr. Harris and Diane attended to the sick. A blazing sun kept Diane's face clammy under her mask. She sat next to the young woman lying flat on her back, staring up at the sky.

The whites of the woman's wide eyes were a fiery red, her lips cracked with dried blood. Diane held her hand. "We're getting you help."

The woman's body heaved as if she were going to vomit. Nothing came out. Meekly, the woman said to Diane, "I want to see my mom."

She squeezed the woman's hand. "You will." Diane took off her mask and forced a smile, despite the air stinging her face.

Paramedics in protective suits stood on the dock. She held the young woman and cried, "She needs help! Now!"

The young woman, clinging to Diane's hand, pleaded. "Don't leave me!"

Two paramedics rushed to the woman and placed her on a stretcher. One of them nudged Diane and shouted, "Stand back!"

She followed them to the ambulance. The woman's head rolled to the side, her eyes finding Diane. A red-stained teardrop crept down her cheek. She cried out, "Don't leave me!" The paramedic forced Diane backward. She stood outside the emergency vehicle and watched the double doors close, the woman's last words haunting her.

Bennett and the others were taken away into different ambulances.

She found Todd standing with Dr. Harris, who climbed into the last ambulance. "I'll call Dr. Jenson," he said, fumbling with his phone. "Let him know the status of survivors and his cursed ship with *twenty-six dead*."

"What about the bodies on the ship?" Todd asked.

"I'm not going back out there."

Diane thought of the families who would learn their loved ones were left on a ship to rot. She crumbled onto the dock and put on her mask. Her limbs were weak; her stomach was in knots. It felt as if someone had thrown hot coals into her eyes. Todd sat beside her.

After taking in a ragged breath, she glanced back at the crimson-stained waters. "Another soul needs help."

"I know."

They sailed back to the death ship and found the shark floating.

Todd maneuvered the boat to the other side of the buoy away from the large fish in case it began thrashing. She put on gloves, reached out with bolt cutters, and snipped the chain.

Released from the rust-colored shackles, the massive shark sank, disappearing into the depths.

Diane and Todd returned to the dock in silence.

• • •

The national news reported thousands experiencing symptoms of contamination and at least a hundred dead. Most hotels were closed along the Eastern Seaboard. Many coastal cities were occupied by the military.

Jenson arranged for Diane and Todd to stay at a Charleston hotel used by the National Guard. It had rooms with filtered water in jugs supplied by government tankers. Frazzled after the death ship, she barely remembered the drive to the hotel or getting to her room. There, she sat on the edge of the bed and wept. Soon the cries turned into full-body heaves.

I was supposed to be on that ship.

Jenson had sent Bennett in her place. The young woman covered in filth, gagging on her breath, and wanting to see her mom could have been Diane.

She took a deep breath, wiped off her face, and called her mom, who answered on the first ring. "I was thinking about you."

Diane forced a breezy tone. "You sound better. How's Atlanta?"

"What's wrong? You okay?"

Her mental image of the abandoned ship with its cargo of dead bodies caused Diane to shudder. She wanted to scream the truth in a desperate attempt to conjure words of encouragement, needing to hear that everything would be okay. Knowing that reality would cause her mom to worry, she forced a normal tone. "I'm just tired."

Mom was silent for a few seconds. Diane expected to be bombarded with questions. Instead, her mom told her about a cousin who had visited with a newborn baby. All Diane could think of was that the unlucky kid had entered a dying world.

After the call ended, she wondered if the young woman would survive and reunite with her mother. She poured water from a small jug sitting in the bathroom. The tank water was clear but had a musty smell and a stale taste. While she brushed her teeth, her mind scrambled to make sense of the death ship and its crew. She splashed her face with tepid water and fantasized about a long, warm shower. Maybe people in the West were taking hot baths and breathing clean air.

She went to bed wearing her respirator and imagined what would happen if the bloom continued to spread. Bleeding seas would bathe Earth with lethal rainwater, turning the blue planet with white clouds into a crimson sphere with toxic vapor.

CHAPTER 21

The next morning, Jenson, who was in Washington, DC, called Todd and Diane at the Charleston airport, which was occupied by commercial and even more military planes. "Dr. Bennett is in stable condition," he said matter-of-factly. His voice sounded firm, not strained like in their last phone call. "Dr. Landry and I appreciate your help."

"What about the other survivors?" Diane asked into the speakerphone.

"One person died," Jenson answered.

She was quiet for a second. "Was it a woman around my age?"

"Yes."

Remembering the dead woman's request, she asked, "Did she get to see her mom?"

"What?" Jenson asked.

Diane covered her face with both hands, remembering the young woman with red-streaked eyes fixated on a sunny sky.

Todd squeezed her shoulder and asked Jenson, "What about the twenty-six bodies on the ship?"

Jenson muttered something under his breath before responding. "I've reported it to the navy and Coast Guard. The families will have to wait until it's safe to retrieve the bodies."

Diane gasped. "That's awful."

Jenson let out a heavy sigh. "Yes, but I have good news. Your specimen came back as a match to the Gulf dino. We've confirmed the mutation: a thick cell wall that maximizes nutrient intake while minimizing environmental influences. Remarkable and devastating."

Normally, she would be jumping at the news. Instead, she kept hearing the woman's frightened voice begging, "Don't leave me." A cold tremor shot through her body, numbing her senses. *She died alone.*

Todd smiled, and she looked at him blankly. He whispered, "That's great news."

"Brandon's coming back from Delaware," Jenson said. "Their ship reported mechanical problems, and I won't have another stranded ship."

"Yesterday was a nightmare," Todd said, rubbing his forehead. "Ships going out have to be more careful."

"OSCF's running out of staff and ships." Jenson sounded more anxious talking about the logistical problems of his foundation than he did talking about lives lost at sea. "We're going to support crews of government-owned ships. Everyone in full-face respirators, and if they don't have bottled water, the onboard filtered water should be tested regularly." He was quiet for a few seconds. "Todd, I need you on the NOAA vessel leaving Miami tomorrow."

Todd nodded. "That makes sense. I have the most experience. If the ship's using filtered water, I'll work with the crew to make sure it gets closely monitored for contaminants."

"Diane, I've asked Brandon to help you with river measurements. He'll bring a new soil tester to measure nutrients."

Todd cleared his throat. "Um, you know I minored in geology and have experience in testing soils. I should help Diane."

"As you said, you're my experienced oceanographer. I need you on the ship. We can't afford another disaster."

When they got off the call, Todd gave her an uneasy look. "Brandon has no experience in sampling sediment. Do you?"

"I had field labs in geology. Not an expert but pretty sure I can measure nitrogen and phosphorus in the soil."

"You may be on your own testing river mud and figuring out how a dormant cell grew into a red plague of the sea."

She gazed at a military transport helicopter landing on the runway and murmured, "I have to figure it out. It's killing us."

CHAPTER 22

The stench was thick and rancid when Diane returned to her home on the Panhandle, a home that felt strange and lonely without Mom and Uncle Bo. The full-face filtered mask she'd ordered for her mom sat in a box at the front door. She put it on and went to the shed.

The only thing left from the experiment was a small jar containing the River 10 sample. She opened its lid and found a thick reddish-brown goo. It reminded her of the primordial-like ooze that covered the Dead Zone. She had emailed the OSCF staff about the protocol to destroy a biohazard, but no one had responded. Losing people and ships took precedence over responding to an inquiry about hazardous waste disposal. She secured the lid to the jar and placed it back on the shelf. The innocent-looking container with its lethal contents was like a monster on a leash.

Wily, the wandering cat, was missing. News footage showed some animals with access to clean water could survive. Her home was no longer a haven for the streetwise cat.

She entered the quiet house and turned on the TV. The president was speaking to reporters in the White House briefing room. "We have the best scientists from all over the world investigating the bloom," he said, glancing back at Jenson, Landry, and a team of other scientists. "The Coast Guard is no longer at sea due to mechanical failures and health-related dangers. They are using land-based stations to patrol the Gulf of Mexico and the Eastern coastline. Waterways are open only to research vessels. We're working to send more large tankers with filtered water and masks with filters to coastal states. We encourage every citizen to protect themselves and not to panic. All branches of the government alongside OSCF and some public and private companies are working nonstop toward a solution."

The president motioned to Jenson. "Dr. Shaun Jenson will answer questions you have about the bloom."

The camera panned over the press room crammed with reporters sitting on the edge of their seats. Diane recalled Isabelle, the *Miami Herald* reporter, but didn't see her.

A reporter, with a baritone voice, asked, "Can you explain why people who live away from the coast are showing signs of contamination?"

Jenson nodded as if expecting the question. "According to our models, the toxin can be carried inland through air and precipitation. Increased precipitation can cause exposure to toxins in areas up to five hundred miles away from the coast."

Diane's mouth gaped open. *Mom and Uncle Bo could be affected.*

Another reporter turned her laptop for the camera to see a picture of water the color of pink bubble gum. She asked, "Why is Lake Ontario turning into Pepto-Bismol?"

"We can only speculate that the red algae have infiltrated the St. Lawrence Seaway, which connects the Great Lakes to the Atlantic. The algae may react with freshwater microbes, causing the pink color."

The camera zoomed in on Jenson, who continued, "Our focus is on the Gulf and the Atlantic. If we can get a handle on the problem in our oceans, other related issues should resolve."

Diane clicked on an online video that showed people punching each other over a six-pack of bottled water, which ended up crushed on the floor. Pictures of empty store shelves and highways packed with cars full of people leaving the Eastern Seaboard. Long lines at gas stations with people filling multiple gas cans. Cars had signs that read, "Go West!"

The president ended the press conference with a final statement. "Our government has approved an increase in federal dollars to mitigate this disaster and provide additional resources to help clean our oceans and waterways. We'll have more ships, technicians, and equipment devoted to the mission of restoring our environment."

Diane turned off the TV. Her throat felt sore. A jug of filtered water from the government sat next to a case of bottled water in the bathroom. She thought the filtered water had a peculiar taste. Using the bottled water, she washed off, brushed her teeth, then swallowed ibuprofen and went to bed.

What would happen if they discovered how the red dino got what it needed to become an impermeable parasite? Someone would ask, "Now what?" Any answer would have to acknowledge the bloom already had a death grip on their waters.

CHAPTER 23

Diane awoke to someone knocking on the door. Her head felt heavy, as if someone was sitting on it; her throat burned. She crawled out of bed and rushed to the bathroom. "Just a minute," she croaked.

"I have a package for Dino Diva!" Brandon shouted.

His voice made her grin. The smile disappeared after she saw her stringy hair and puffy eyes in the mirror. She tried brushing her tangled strands, but a pain shot through her right temple, causing her to double over. After a few seconds, the throbbing subsided, and she made her way to the front door and opened it.

Brandon held a box in one hand and handpicked daisies in the other. "For you."

She took them and smiled, recalling his interest in the flowers she drew as a child. "Thank y—" A coughing fit came out of nowhere.

Brandon stepped back. "Whoa. That sounds bad."

"The beginning of a bad cold." *Or toxins in my body.*

His eyes narrowed, brow creased. "This is serious. I'm taking you to the doctor."

She didn't want to waste time sitting in the ER. "Too much to do. If I get worse, then I'll go."

"People who had less exposure to contaminants are dead." He dropped the box on the kitchen table and stared at her.

She walked around him and opened the box. "Only one soil tester?"

"I'll be your mule. Carry and fetch things for you."

Todd warned me.

Brandon inched closer and lowered his voice. "I should take you to a doctor. You don't look well. I mean . . . normally you look nice, but—"

She shook her head and held up her hand for him to stop. A sharp ache that felt as if it were ripping her scalp open caused her to drop onto a nearby chair.

"Unbelievable," he said, sitting next to her. "Let's go to the hospital."

"No," she insisted. "We don't have time for that."

He stood up and took a couple of steps back. "I wonder how many people taking their last breath say, 'I don't have time to die'?"

"A helluva lot more if we don't do our job," she snapped. Diane stood, her legs wobbly.

Brandon rushed to her side, his hands out. "You're going to topple over. Please sit down."

"I'm sorry," she said, steadying herself against the table. "I'm remembering a woman around my age who worked on OSCF's ship. She wasn't ready to die."

"Todd told me what happened. You're traumatized and not feeling well, so—"

"I just want to get to the river."

Brandon slumped and was quiet for a minute. Slowly, he started searching through the cupboards. "I don't want to argue. How about some soup? "

"No thanks," she croaked, then found a soda and sipped it. Her throat burned as the bubbly liquid went down.

She walked out of the kitchen, intending to head to the bathroom, but she ended up on the couch and closed her eyes.

Need to rest for a minute.

It was dark outside when she opened her eyes hours later. Brandon sat across from her, studying his phone. When she sat up on the couch, he moved close to her. "How are you feeling?"

The back of her neck was sore, and her throat felt as if she had swallowed glass. Her voice was hoarse when she said, "Not so good. Sorry we lost a workday."

"I'm more concerned about you." He offered ibuprofen and bottled water, then placed his arm around her. She took the pills and laid her head on his shoulder. His warm skin had a light vanilla scent.

He whispered in her ear, "I'm taking you to the doctor if you're not better in the morning—by force if necessary."

In the middle of the night, she awoke in his arms, scooted off the couch, then went to the medicine cabinet. If she had to keep popping pills to get herself moving, then so be it. No time to waste with busy waiting rooms and doctors with their medical tests. The bloom was getting worse, and its secret was buried in the Mississippi, waiting for her.

CHAPTER 24

The next morning, Diane's throat still felt a little scratchy, but her headache was gone. She slid out of bed, took more pills, then gathered her things for the trip to New Orleans.

Brandon stood at her bedroom door. "Are we going to the doctor?"

She grabbed her bag and answered in a raspy voice, "I'm better."

His eyes narrowed. "Really?"

"Yep."

A white Dodge Ram truck was parked in the driveway. "I'm surprised OSCF owns that gas guzzler," she said. "The news showed long lines at the pumps yesterday."

"OSCF has plenty of fuel. We've got full gas containers in the back of the truck." He studied her. "Glad I have the Ram. Plenty of horsepower to rush you to the hospital."

Wanting to avoid another confrontation, she pointed at her GPS. "This is the location of River 10."

Brandon opened the truck door for her while glancing at the map. "I'm familiar with the area."

After he got in the truck and started pulling out of the driveway, she asked, "How so?"

He didn't answer at first, following the truck's GPS to alternate roads, avoiding traffic jams. Finally he said, "I'm from a town not too far from New Orleans."

"Isn't Landry from a town near New Orleans?"

"She and her husband own a house in my family's neighborhood. They're popular among the locals. Her husband's a state senator."

Brandon and Landry from the same place shouldn't mean anything, but it was peculiar.

She leaned her head against the passenger window and slowly nodded off. After almost an hour, she opened her eyes to find Brandon watching her. "Feeling better?" he asked.

"A little woozy, but I feel a lot better." *Thank you, ibuprofen.*

"Music has healing powers," he said and turned on the radio. At the end of a Nirvana song, a reporter speculated that the number of deaths along the Gulf Coast and the East Coast was in the thousands.

Brandon turned down the radio. "I can't believe we're getting our asses handed to us by algae. I imagined doomsday would come from a nuclear war, a meteorite, or a deadly virus."

"What's that saying? Whence we came, we shall return."

He raised his eyebrows. "Sounds like scary Old Testament scripture."

She gave him a playful grin. "Don't worry. I'll protect you."

A smile lit up his face. He stared at the road in silence for a moment. "I know of some slimy people, but I don't get how humans came from seaweed. Plant reproduction is different. You're a biologist. Tell me, why don't algae have sex?"

She had heard this joke and beat him to the punch line. "Because they have a planktonic relationship. Platonic, like you and me." After hearing her last words, she stopped and looked out the window. *Why did I say that?*

Brandon laughed out loud. "She's got jokes!" He leaned close to her. "I think you took too many pills because you've already agreed to go out on a date with me." He glanced down at the dashboard. "Shit. Tank's almost empty."

They pulled off to the roadside. While he filled the tank, she found a Dolphin Bar & Grill matchbook on his seat and guessed it had fallen out of his pocket.

When he got back in the truck, she held it up. “Does this place have good drinks?”

“You plan on chasing ibuprofen with rum?” he asked with a chuckle. “It’s not mine. Whoever last used the truck must’ve left it.”

She dropped the matches in her backpack. “May come in useful if we get lost at sea and end up on an unknown island.”

“I can see us marooned together,” he said with a playful smile before placing his hand over hers. “Glad Jenson asked me to come. I enjoy spending time with you.”

She gazed into his eyes. “Me too.”

He leaned toward her, moving closer until their lips touched. Her body tingled all over in his warm embrace. They held each other after the kiss.

“I hope you don’t get whatever I have,” she whispered.

“I’ll take my chances.” He caressed her face. “For our first date, I’m thinking of a plane ticket to anywhere but here.”

“Sounds nice. But, if we don’t solve this problem, eventually there’ll be no place to go.”

Brandon located a major road with moving traffic while Diane found a news station, “Let’s find out if there’s one piece of good news.”

He mimicked the tone of a news reporter, “Just in! NASA has revealed spaceships leaving for Mars with biospheres ready for humans. Tickets are free.”

She squinted. “I wouldn’t want that ticket.”

With a wild, bewildered expression, he asked, “If this thing takes over the Earth and there was another place to live, you wouldn’t go?”

She thought for a few seconds. “It’s like a terminally ill person who knows death is around the corner. They choose to die in their own bed instead of going to a cold hospital. This is my home.”

Brandon’s mouth dropped. The truck was quiet except for the radio. Finally he said, “Anybody else saying that, I’d say they’re full of shit. But you mean it.” He pushed a few strands of hair away from her face. “You’re one of a kind.”

The radio reporter announced, "Thousands of people fleeing the Eastern Seaboard have jammed major roadways. We found one man returning to his home in South Carolina."

"Can't find a job or a place to live," the man said in a thick southern accent.

A different reporter cut in and said, "There's been a major accident off Interstate 64 in eastern Kentucky involving FedEx double trailers. All westbound lanes are closed."

She thought of Matt's family in Kentucky and asked, "Do you know if the police completed their investigation into the attack on OSCF?"

"They closed it a week ago. They said Matt lost it after he was fired. In a struggle with Jenson for the gun, he killed himself." Brandon showed no emotion.

"You didn't like Matt, did you?"

His eyebrows furrowed. "Oh, I have great respect for someone who brings in weapons to terrorize a building full of people." He took a deep breath, and his muscles relaxed. "Sorry. It just bothers me. He could've killed you."

The police would have sent Matt's belongings to his family in Kentucky. If she learned nothing from the river, asking Matt's family for help could be the only alternative.

CHAPTER 25

Diane and Brandon parked close to a cluster of low-income housing units located near the River 10 site of the Mississippi. They put on waders, boots, and gloves. The hot, humid midsummer air caused her clammy skin to stick to her clothing, and breathing was a chore.

She held up a mask. “What do you think?”

“EPA reported low levels of airborne toxins here. I’m already sweating bullets.”

They left their respirators behind, gathered supplies, and walked through a paved lot between two-story brick buildings. The lower part of the structures was darker, revealing how high the waters had reached during the flood. The watermark stretched from the ground to the second floor. A few units closest to the river appeared abandoned with broken glass panes while others had newer-looking windows.

Brandon nodded at some residents outside watching them. “Nice to have an audience.”

Walking off the cement into mud, Diane took a deep breath. “At least the air doesn’t reek of death.”

The soil tester was a handheld instrument attached to two metallic probes for measuring nitrogen and phosphorus. Every few feet up to the river, Diane pushed the probes into the ground and recorded the results. Brandon marked each location on a GPS.

“Any weird spikes in nutrients?” he asked.

“Not enough to wake up our sleeping red dino.”

They'd been at it for a while when they heard rustling behind them and noticed a couple of kids in the bushes. Diane smiled and waved at the pair of wide eyes spying on them between the branches.

Brandon followed her gaze and threw up his hand in a friendly gesture. Two young boys jumped from the shrubs and ran toward the housing units.

"Wow," Brandon said, "they leaped out of the woods like a couple of deer."

She giggled and pointed at their outfits and instruments. "I'm sure we look like crazy people to a couple of kindergartners."

They collected data until dark, covering over a mile downstream. Brandon wiped the sweat from his brow. "Don't forget we have to walk back."

She swatted at the buzzing gnats. "Maybe the resting cyst was dislodged by the flood and carried by currents to nutrients farther downstream."

Brandon bent over and rested his hands on his knees. "We'll need a four-wheeler if you want to sample the banks from here to the Gulf."

The warm dampness on her face attracted more no-see-ums. *I should've worn the mask.* They stopped sampling and headed back.

When they reached the truck, their phones rang almost simultaneously. She took her call from Uncle Bo but was distracted by Brandon's pacing. *Who is he talking to?*

Diane said to Bo, "I'm covered in river muck. I'll call you back when we get to the hotel." When she hung up, Brandon ended his call. Beads of moisture covered his forehead. "What's wrong?" she asked.

He shook his head, perspiration dripping from it. "Nothing important."

Tired from traveling and trudging through mud, she dropped the subject and focused on locating their hotel.

After checking into the two rooms they'd reserved, she made a beeline to her room and discovered traces of mud caked on her nose, cheeks, and forehead. She scraped some off and noticed that the earthy smell mixed with the salt on her skin was reminiscent of the rotten odor that had permeated the dying young woman on the ship. Grabbing a wet cloth and soap, she scrubbed her face until the mud was gone and her skin was red. While staring at her reflection in the mirror, the woman's words "Don't leave me" echoed in her mind.

To distract herself, she returned Uncle Bo's call.

"Your mom's feelin' heaps better," he said. "What're you up to?"

"I'm with a coworker, Brandon. We're sampling the banks where you and I collected the River 10 sample."

"Who's this Brandon fella?"

She smiled. "A colleague."

"Your voice got a little chipper when you said his name."

"He's nice."

Diane didn't want to tell him about the death ship or waking up with an odd illness. Besides, she was feeling better. "How's the concrete jungle?" she asked.

"A family visit is okay for a few days. But I'm ready for you to clean up the Gulf so I can get the hell outta here."

When their call ended, she received a text from Nicole. *Heard about the DNA match. Exciting stuff!*

We did soil measures in River 10. Found nothing. Try again tomorrow.

Diane found the contact information for Matt's family. People in the lab had written Matt off as a nutjob. The only way OSCF would learn about her reaching out to Matt's family would be if Matt's family told them. For some reason, she didn't think they would tell. After typing in their email address, she wrote:

My name is Diane Nelson. I work for OSCF. I wanted to reach out and express my sympathies. I saw Matt only once but heard he was a brilliant chemist. I have an interest in his research. Would it be okay if I called you or came by to visit? Maybe you could share what Matt left of his work?

Thanks so much,

Diane

She reread the message four times before pressing send. It felt awkward, and she wondered if they'd respond.

A few minutes later, an email appeared in her inbox. *Come by anytime. 808 String Road, Akers, KY. Carla*

The quick, simple response was a surprise. Perhaps Matt's family had something they wanted to share.

Diane brushed her teeth with the musty-smelling government water while watching news footage of Pensacola, where body bags on stretchers were being removed from a house.

A reporter wearing a full-face respirator said, "A family of four found dead from contamination." He turned to a woman holding a crying newborn. "You live next door to this family. Do you have concerns for yourself and your baby?"

The woman had on a particle mask covered by a kerchief. The whites of her eyes were pale pink, her skin a chalky white. "Of course I do," she huffed. "We tried to leave, but I went into labor. Then my husband got sick. He's in the hospital." She paused, then in a shaky voice said, "All we have is each other. We have nowhere to go."

The reporter faced the camera. "Ongoing discussions between state governors and the president concerning mandatory evacuations and the creation of temporary shelters continue to be unsuccessful. Our sources tell us that no one could come to an agreement, as more states and people are being affected. A mandatory evacuation would cause more displaced people."

Other news coverage showed people weeping and walking the streets in the Midwest, looking for a place to live. Reporters showed pictures of overcrowded airports and police removing people who refused to leave the terminals.

TV pundits gave opinions on how the bloom would end, but no one postulated its origins. There were fervent discussions on theoretical ways to eradicate the new algal species. One radical talking head believed the bloom was a hoax perpetrated by "those Greenpeace people who just want to scare us."

Hearing a knock at her door, she opened it to find Brandon holding a pink daisy.

"You're sweet," she said, smiling. "You don't always have to pick me flowers."

"It was growing in the middle of a bunch of weeds next to the hotel."

"Thanks. You're in better spirits."

"Sorry about earlier. My mom called. She can be . . . let's say, overbearing. She's invited us for dinner tomorrow. Their house isn't far from here. Interested?"

Diane wanted to take measurements near the industrial park, and she had a habit of working late into the evening.

Brandon must have sensed her hesitation because he quickly added, "My family has an amazing cook. Delilah is making her homemade chicken and dumplings with sweet apples. It'll melt in your mouth."

He has a cook?

"Count me in." The riverbank wasn't going anywhere, and a scrumptious southern meal was food for the soul.

They sat next to each other on the bed, and she told him about the dead family found in Pensacola and their young neighbor. "The mother didn't look well, and her newborn's cries were high-pitched squeals. I don't know if the baby's hungry or in pain."

He scooted closer. "Either is awful. I'm sure that poor mother is frightened and confused."

Diane looked into Brandon's eyes. "Are you afraid?"

"Work keeps me focused. I'm too busy to concentrate on the what-ifs." He put his arm around her. "I'm surrounded by strong people . . . like you. You're like that daisy demanding its place among the weeds."

The flower's pink shade reminded her of people's eyes, ocean foam, and luminescent waves. "I'm not so strong. I'm scared too."

"You need a little break." Brandon opened his laptop.

"Wow," she said and widened her eyes. "I didn't even notice you carrying it."

With a whimsical tone, he said, "I made it appear, " and wiggled his fingers like a magician. "Let's do some Minecraft tricks."

She logged in to the game. Brandon navigated her to secret treasures and hidden rivers of blue-colored diamonds and dark soils containing brown netherite.

"You are a computer wizard. How do you know this?" she asked in awe.

"Sorcerers don't reveal their secrets."

Diane laughed as they stretched on the bed with the laptop between them, and then Brandon helped Dino Diva lay the foundation of a diamond fortress.

She looked at her treasure trove and then gazed into Brandon's eyes. "Thank you. Not just for this but for helping me . . . and saving me."

Brandon watched her under hooded eyes as he placed the laptop on the nightstand and then pulled her close to him. His wet, warm lips felt familiar, as if she had kissed him many times in another life. A rush of excitement flooded her body as they undressed each other. As he lowered her to the bed, Diane unfurled, releasing the tension she'd been holding in her body for longer than she cared to remember. Being with Brandon was the escape she desperately needed from a world on the brink of extinction.

CHAPTER 26

The next morning, Diane and Brandon held hands as they drove to an industrial lot across the river from the low-income units. He kissed her cheek before getting out of the truck to gather their gear.

Air toxin levels were still low, and the summer sun was fierce, but Diane put on a respirator to avoid another gnat attack. She tested the soil along the riverbanks. Brandon followed with the GPS. They trudged two miles south along the muddy shores. None of the readings showed abnormal amounts of nitrogen or phosphorus.

Beads of sweat ran down her face, irritating the little red bumps that had formed from yesterday's bug bites. She slid off the mask and inhaled the thick, muggy air. Brandon plopped down on a spot that had more pebbles than muck.

"Can't find one spike to wake up the dino," she muttered.

"Could be like you said." Brandon gasped for breath. "Nutrients farther downstream. Maybe we could rent a boat with a cabin for two," he said with a mischievous glint in his eyes.

"Do you think we'd get any work done?"

Brandon grinned and got to his feet. "I hope not."

She returned his smile, then looked across the river. "We have some time before we need to leave for your parents' house. Let's retest the banks near the housing units. I feel like we've missed something."

Twenty minutes later, they parked in a space near the units and followed the cement path between the two-story brick buildings to the river. Diane heard kids giggling. It was the two little boys who had followed them yesterday. "Hello," she said, taking off her mask to reveal a friendly smile. "It's okay."

They froze with gaping mouths and wide eyes.

A tall, skinny teenage boy wearing high-tops and a short, plump older woman in a short-sleeved floral housedress approached. The woman yelled in a Cajun accent at the children. "How many times do I have to tell ya to stay away from folks ya don't know?" She squinted at Diane and Brandon. "They botherin' you?"

"They're fine," Diane said. "We're taking measurements off the bank."

The teenager looked at the woman. "What she say?"

The woman shrugged and whispered, "Couyon."

Diane had heard of that Cajun expression meaning "idiot." She suppressed a giggle. "We're trying to figure out if anything unusual occurred during the spring floods."

The teenager snickered. "Ya kiddin'? Everywhere covered in water. Lost most of our stuff. What little we got back smelt like crap."

The woman nodded. "Yep, it was real bad. Dirty water."

One of the kids shouted, "Daddy says it's *turdy* water! He saw floatin' *shit*!"

"Watcha mouth," the woman said to the boy with a narrow-eyed look that warned *if you know what's good for you.*

"Raw sewage?" Diane asked, hoping for more information and for the woman to release her death glare at the boy.

"Yep," the woman answered and faced Diane. "Floatin' everywhere. Lawdy, the things I saw."

Diane gestured toward the surrounding area. "Is there a wastewater treatment plant near here?"

Brandon leaned close to Diane. "We should start sampling. We're losing time."

The woman nodded and pointed northward. "Not sure how far up, but it's there."

"Where do you live?" Diane asked.

The woman pointed to the third building from the river. "Over there."

"Besides me, has anyone come here to test? Like people from the state health department or from the Environmental Protection Agency?"

"After the hard rains, me and Luke—that's their daddy—got a boat. Got what we could out of our place. We saw boats headin' downstream with huge silver shiny barrels of thick liquid. They's pourin' it into the river. Looked like clear molasses. People from the state department came out. Waters cleared up."

The woman clapped her hands at the kids, who had started to play fight. She continued, "I'd say 'bout two weeks later, Senator Landry came by. He hired contractors and a cleanup crew. Our place is better than when we first got here. Cleaned it up like new."

Diane nudged Brandon, who was staring at the ground. She said, "I want to go to the wastewater plant."

Brandon smacked at a fly on his neck and grimaced. "Sure."

Diane got close to him and whispered, "C'mon. You don't think wastewater is sexy?"

He frowned. "I voted for floating down the river on a boat with a cozy cabin."

"Thank you," she said to the woman. She waved at the little boys, who halfway raised a hand and frowned while dragging their feet behind the woman and the teenager returning to the units.

• • •

The wastewater treatment plant was ten miles north of the low-income housing units.

During the drive, Diane asked Brandon, "Why do you think Senator Landry was there?"

"I'm sure to help people get back on their feet. He's working on rebuilding communities most affected by the flood."

"Sewage everywhere. What else could it be except a spill from a wastewater treatment plant?"

Brandon let out a heavy breath. "A raging river can do a lot of damage and remove tons of soil. Maybe the waste was from residential pipes that ruptured during the floods."

"Talk about an overload of nitrogen and phosphorus. I'd guess the currents pushed most of it into the Gulf. Anything left over eroded or dissipated." Brandon shook his head as she continued. "What do you think was in the barrels?"

He gazed at the road but said nothing. They drove up to a gated entrance to the plant. The guard recognized the OSCF tag on the truck and waved them through.

Brandon parked the truck and turned to face her. "Wastewater from nearby cities and towns flows to this facility, treating at least four hundred million gallons of water daily. It's a pilot plant used to test an experimental method to eliminate waste from water with zero gas emissions, a part of OSCF's research that's been operating for about nine months."

Diane wasn't surprised because Jenson was known for spearheading and supporting innovative research. "Didn't Matt work on a chemical process for reducing greenhouse gases?"

"He, Jenson, and Landry worked on getting this place operational and tested. Dr. Landry did a presentation on it. She showed significant reductions in nitrous oxide and methane by using this new mechanism to treat wastewater. It's a big deal for OSCF, costing millions of dollars."

"You know a lot about it."

"Most of our colleagues know about it. Also, my family and their neighbors helped support its development. They believed it was a good investment for the community and the environment."

Diane decided not to elaborate on her concerns. His family was committed to this venture. She relaxed and said, "I'd like to learn more about it. Do you know what type of chemicals they're using to clean the wastewater?"

"I'm a computer engineer, not a chemist. I know you're suspicious." He pointed to a location near the river. "You can start doing your measurements. I'll let the operators know what we're up to."

After spending twenty minutes of collecting data, her readings showed nothing out of the ordinary.

A few minutes later, Brandon joined her beside the river. "I would think high levels of nutrients would be normal here."

She believed the woman and her children. Their description had fit a wastewater plant spill, not a broken pipe.

Brandon watched her for a few seconds. "Do you want to take more measurements?"

They spent an hour sampling downstream. Again nothing.

Both exhausted and wet with perspiration, they sat down among tall blades of grass a few feet from the river. Grasshoppers on the ground next to her looked like the ones fished out of the Gulf. The chirping insects provided a soft cadence to the soothing beat of the Mississippi's small waves rolling onto the bank. The dark, rippling surface concealed a powerful current that unleashed hell in the spring storms. After catching a scent of odors reminiscent of an overused porta potty at a county fair, her thoughts returned to the wastewater treatment plant.

Jenson and Landry had funded the research and initiated the pilot facility, but Matt had been the chemist and engineer. His family had said she could visit anytime, but she wanted to get more information before traveling to Kentucky.

She turned to Brandon. "It's not impossible that a plant testing a new process accidentally released gallons of raw sewage into the Mississippi during a record flood event. What's odd is that it never made the news."

"Exactly. We live in a world where people walk around with their phones. I doubt a massive wastewater spill would go unnoticed."

What if it was noticed and then covered up?

She lifted herself off the ground and headed toward the truck.

Brandon called after her. "I don't think you'll find what you're looking for here."

It's the only thing that makes sense.

He hustled to catch up with her. "Let's go back to the hotel to clean up. Pack an overnight bag. My parents' house has plenty of room. We can relax after the meal . . . that is, if you're in the mood for homemade dumplings."

She gave him a small grin. "I can eat and disagree with you at the same time."

Diane hoped OSCF's pilot plant technology didn't have the power to destroy life on Earth. A wastewater plant employing a pilot technique ten miles upstream from River 10 was suspicious.

CHAPTER 27

Brandon's family home was a two-story plantation-style house with white columns and a wraparound porch flanked by weeping willows. Diane glanced down at her jeans and hoped this was not a formal dinner. "I packed only field clothes."

Brandon, who looked handsome in khakis and a navy button-down shirt, noticed her touching the red bug bites on her face and tugging at her shirt. "You look great," he said and pecked her on the cheek.

"Not even a remote possibility. I have enough bumps on my face to play connect the dots."

"Hey, let's tell my mom they're hickeys. I'll give you some now to make it more believable." He lunged at her neck with a mischievous grin. She half-heartedly fought him off. Still smiling at each other, they stepped out of the truck. Brandon put his hand on her back, and they walked up to an archway with a crawling jasmine-scented vine. He punched numbers into the door keypad and motioned for her to enter a foyer with a large staircase.

"Your home's beautiful," Diane said.

A woman with brown doe-like eyes and a contagious smile beamed when she saw Brandon. She hugged him, then turned to Diane. "I'm Rose, Brandon's mom." She reminded Diane of an exchange student from Italy who had stayed with her high school classmate from the north side of town, where people with better-paying jobs lived in nicer houses.

A large, tall man entered with an animated laugh and a big welcoming smile. He embraced Brandon. "Glad you could join us, Diane. I'm Glen." He pointed at Brandon. "This boy's dad."

Their living room had floor-to-ceiling windows, furniture that appeared antique but well kept, and a baby grand piano. Near the instrument was a picture of a younger Brandon with his fingers on the keyboard and a small boy behind him.

"That's our youngest, William," said Rose, pointing at the younger boy in the photo. "He's a student at Vanderbilt. I don't know why he's still in Nashville. Courses went online because the campus is being used as a shelter for people who've been displaced by the bloom."

"He's joined the Clean Water, Clean Air movement," said Glen while finding a comfortable position in an oversized recliner.

Rose wrinkled her brow like Diane's mom did whenever she was frustrated. "We found a picture of him on the internet carrying a banner that read, 'Stop Killing Us.' I support him, but he could protest closer to home. "

Diane spotted a photo, nestled among other pictures on a shelf, of a small group of people. She moved closer to it. "Is that you and . . . Dr. Jenson?"

"An old college picture," Rose said with a giggle as she picked up the frame. "I met Shaun in freshman biology. This was our Bio-Boss Club." She placed the photograph back on the shelf. Her smile disappeared. "Then he met Susan, who majored in meteorology, same as me. He didn't come around our group as much after that."

"Susan?" Diane asked.

Rose put a hand to her face. "Sorry, that's Dr. Susan Landry."

Brandon cleared his throat. "Dinner almost ready? We're pretty hungry."

"Shortly," Rose answered, giving her son a stern look before turning back to Diane. "I do a lot of outreach projects on global warming. I was once a meteorologist on the news. Gave it up and became a stay-at-home mom."

Brandon sat on the couch. He spread his arms apart in a grand gesture toward Rose. "My mom is a philanthropist of all things related to climate change."

"That's right," Rose said and sat next to Brandon. "OSCF's done a lot for the environment. I'm relieved it's investigating the bloom. So many dead animals. People dying and fleeing the coast. I heard someone say it'll eventually spread into the Pacific." Rose paused to look at Glen, then continued. "One of our close friends works as an ER physician in Galveston, Texas. He described both the young and old walking into the hospital. Many never leave."

Glen rummaged through his pockets and found a tissue to wipe his nose. "NASA took pictures of the bloom from space. Miles off into the Atlantic is bloodred. The Gulf of Mexico looks like it's on fire. At night, it's all lit up."

Brandon motioned to Diane. "Our brilliant postdoc specializes in plankton causing toxic blooms. I bet she'll put out the fire."

Glen scooted to the edge of his chair and studied Diane. "On the morning news, a botanist from Sudan claimed fossil evidence showed the same type of algae existed in the Nile River thousands of years ago."

"Really?" Diane asked and sat on a small chair next to Glen. This was the first time she'd heard anyone connect the parasite to fresh water.

Glen nodded. "He said the fossil history showed it had been short-lived. Every scientist on the panel said his claims were bogus. What do you think?"

Brandon raised his eyebrows at Diane, who answered, "They should reconsider his observations. That said, short-lived means something in the environment killed the ancient organism. Nothing is destroying our pestilence."

Glen watched her as if waiting for her to say more. Maybe he needed to hear something optimistic.

"Hopefully, something will stop it," she said.

They headed to the dining room table where she met their cook, Delilah, who didn't say much. Rose smiled as Diane reached for a second helping of chicken and dumplings. She restrained herself and didn't go for a third.

Brandon's parents elicited the usual information from Diane: where she was from, where she went to college, and details about her family.

Rose leaned forward in her chair. "You live with your mom and uncle . . . and your dad?"

Diane fidgeted a little. "My mom and uncle raised me. I've never met my father."

"Your uncle sounds like he's a wonderful father figure," Glen said and nodded at Rose.

Glen was a businessman and a volunteer minister for a local protestant church. He talked about his oldest parishioner. "She never misses a sermon. Told me about having nightmares and quoted a verse from Psalm 105: 'He turned their waters into blood, causing their fish to die.' I told her to pray and have faith."

Reflecting on Glen's account of the Sudanese botanist, Diane wondered if the bloom was a revival of a Biblical curse.

Glen observed Brandon gazing at Diane, then shifted his attention to Diane and declared, "I firmly believe that those who follow their heart and do what's right can perform miracles."

Just then, Delilah entered with a round tray. "Dessert time!"

Brandon smiled. "Speaking of miracles, wait till you get a taste of Delilah's pecan pie."

Diane took big bites of the scrumptious dessert. If her stomach exploded, it would have been a happy death. Recalling Brandon mentioning his parents' support and knowledge of the pilot facility, she asked, "What do you know about the wastewater treatment plant near here, using a new method that doesn't emit greenhouse gases?"

Rose's eyes lit up. "Of course, OSCF's breakthrough technology. The plant employs around fifty people from the community. We're very proud of it."

"I'm interested in learning more about it. Is there a way I could get a tour?" she asked.

Rose responded in rushed excitement. "We know the people who lead operations. I'll contact them in the morning."

Brandon, sitting across from Diane, nodded and grinned.

Diane, exhausted from a long day, excused herself after dinner. Brandon showed her to the guest room. They lingered in the doorway. "Nice work back there," he said.

"Your mom was excited to help."

"Sorry she asked about your dad."

"You don't have to apologize." She held her hands up in a what-are-you-going-to-do gesture. "So your mom went to college with Jenson and Landry?"

Brandon shrugged. "A long time ago." He leaned in, pulling her toward him. "I'm interested in the present." They moved out of the doorway and into the room.

Diane hugged him, circling her arms around his neck and resting her face against his. She closed her eyes, enjoying the heat from his moist, vanilla-scented skin. His strong arms that had pulled her out of the red water tightened around her waist.

Rose yelled from downstairs, "Show her where the towels are."

Diane tilted her head and smiled. "You gonna show me?"

He smirked and ran his fingers through her hair. "Not exactly what I had in mind."

His cell phone beeped, and he let Diane go. He read the text. "Shit. Urgent request to get the bots out of the Gulf and repair them for a new expedition. Something's happening in the North Atlantic. I have to leave tonight." He texted while he spoke. "A taxi's being sent to take me to the airport. I'll leave the truck here for you. Could you drive it back to OSCF?"

"Of course."

He put down his phone, touched her arm, and lightly kissed her. "I'd really like you to come with me. I can get the truck later."

It would be easy for Diane to forget about the river muck and fly off with him. However, the sewage that had inundated the woman's home must have come from a wastewater plant; that would explain the large amounts of nutrients needed for the red dino. The bigger question was the dino's mutation. A new chemical process was suspect. She lowered her eyes. "I'll stay and learn what I can. If I find nothing interesting, I'll return to OSCF."

Brandon said goodbye to his parents, then grabbed Diane's hand and walked to the taxi. Before getting into the cab, he pulled her close to him. "You really prefer wastewater to me?"

She shook her head and hugged him, inhaling the warm vanilla scent that almost lured her into the yellow-checked car. Instead, she watched him climb into the vehicle that disappeared into the darkness, leading him back to the deadly red waters. OSCF must have had a compelling reason to order people back to the Gulf. Ghastly images of the Gulf Stream stained with crimson parasites aiming for European shores raced through her mind.

• • •

Rose, dressed in a pleated white skirt and a light blue polo shirt that matched her earrings, came to Diane's room the next morning. "I managed to get a tour of the plant this morning," she said in hurried excitement.

Diane, in a T-shirt and jeans, was amused by her enthusiasm. She thought Rose should be heading to a golf course instead of a wastewater plant as they got into a teal-colored Mercedes. Curious about what had happened between Jenson and Rose, she asked, "What was Dr. Jenson like in college?"

"Oh my." Rose smiled. "In class, he came up with incredible ideas to predict weather patterns. Guys circled him because he was a popular football player. Girls buzzed around him because he was a hunk. I thought he was brilliant."

Diane had been a freshman in college when she had first seen a picture of a younger Shaun Jenson surrounded by instruments on tripods in her online textbook describing the effects of global warming on marine life. Mesmerized by his work and dazzled by his determined gaze, she had ordered a hard copy of the book, now dog-eared and displayed on her apartment shelf. “My uncle said he could’ve played in the NFL.”

“He told me that he grew up poor in Tennessee. His ticket out of there was an athletic scholarship. Protecting the planet meant more to him than putting points on a scoreboard.” Rose spoke cheerfully about the young man who had grown into an industry hero adored by many, including Diane.

Rose was silent for a second. “Shaun’s done incredible work with all the OSCF divisions, but I’m especially glad Brandon is working in Jane Bennett’s lab. I trust her the most.” Rose glanced at her. “She’s good people.”

Diane agreed but was eager to learn about OSCF’s cofounders. “You mentioned at dinner that Dr. Jenson no longer hung out with you and your friends after he met Dr. Landry. What happened?”

“Susan was smart and also the pretty, fun rich girl in a popular sorority. After Shaun met her, I didn’t see him as often. I found out from a mutual friend that he wrote her a letter with a picture of himself in his football uniform.” Rose paused with a faraway, sad gaze. “She never wrote him back but continued to flirt with him. Maybe I don’t like her, but she seems to get her way with men.”

“Are Jenson and Landry still . . . ?”

“Shaun knows what she is.” Rose snickered. “Between you and me, I think he exploits her access to money and political connections.”

Diane watched Rose grip the steering wheel tightly, practically molding it with her hands. Perhaps Landry had quashed a budding relationship between Rose and Jenson. She’d seen interviews with Landry. Despite her alluring smile and hypnotic gaze, there was something cold about her.

Rose nodded at the guard waving them through the metal gate to the plant. "Our community is proud of this new technology to protect the planet."

OSCF had a history of outstanding endeavors. Though suspicious, Diane wanted the facility to be successful, elevating Jenson to legendary status for his efforts in tackling global warming.

CHAPTER 28

The wastewater treatment plant consisted of several light green and brown multistory buildings arranged around circular ponds. Diane recalled a pungent smell the last time she had been downwind of the plant while measuring soil nutrients with Brandon. Expecting the facility to reek of sulfur, she was surprised it had a hint of something like garlic mixed with ammonia.

A man sporting a thick red beard and wearing a bright yellow vest approached Rose and Diane. He nodded at Rose. "I know you're familiar with the plant." He gave a soft laugh and glanced at Diane. "You must be the OSCF employee wanting a tour. Are you familiar with wastewater plant systems?"

Diane rubbed her chin. "Kind of."

"Our plant is laid out like most others. Major difference occurs when the wastewater first enters the facility in underground pipes. Other facilities have bar screens that capture large solids. Trucks take those to landfills. The water then goes through a series of purification steps, releasing large quantities of nitrous oxide and other greenhouse gases."

The operator, who walked with a noticeable limp, motioned for them to follow. They walked to the other side of the facility and stopped next to a line of trees. He pointed to the ground. "Wastewater goes directly into a buried chamber surrounded by compartments that contain what is called reduction fluid, which goes through a timed series of cooling and heating procedures. It's added to the wastewater containing raw sewage. It destroys all solids and cleanses the water with no emissions of greenhouse gases. Treated water is discharged into the river."

Diane's eyes widened. "If everything is underground, then why does the plant have holding ponds and extra machinery?"

He chuckled. "We're required for at least a year to have the plant capable of using traditional procedures in the event something goes wrong."

Rose waved at a group of women dressed in business suits who were heading into the main building. "I'm going over to say hi," she said. "I'll meet up with you soon."

Diane knelt and examined the soil. "Since everything is buried, how do you know if something goes wrong in the compartments?"

He scooted his mud-covered boot across a small brown patch of grass. "All kinds of sensors. Some monitor the temperature and amount of reduction fluid going into wastewater. Others check for unclean water leaving the chamber. If any alarm is triggered, the water is diverted toward a set of bar screens, and the traditional process of wastewater cleaning is initiated." He exhaled, putting his hands on his hips. "We can also manually divert to the traditional method in case of other issues like running out of reduction fluid."

"You've never had to use the traditional method?"

He pulled out his phone, glanced at the screen, and returned it to his pocket. "There was a problem during the spring floods. Someone sneaked into the plant and turned off the controller to the reduction fluid, preventing it from going into the chamber. Normally, the system would divert the wastewater toward the bar screen, but there was a glitch in the system. Eventually, the plant got the fluid back into the chamber and resumed normal function."

"Did any of the raw sewage make it to the river?"

He shrugged. "I was out that week. When I returned, everything looked normal."

"Is there anyone here who was working when the incident occurred?"

"No. Everyone working during that time belonged to a different company that lost the contract rebid. I was the only one brought on by the new company, probably because I'm the lead operator."

Or because you weren't around during the accident.

"Did they catch who broke into the plant?"

He shook his head. "An engineer had been fired a week before the incident. There's no evidence it was him, but he's the only person with a motive. I mean, why would anyone want to break into a wastewater plant?"

Diane thought of Matt, who'd helped create the system. He had suffered a nervous breakdown, but why would he shut down the controller? She pointed to security cameras mounted on the main building. "No footage of the intruder?"

"Those are brand new." He pulled out his phone again and stared at the screen. "Installed after the break-in," he said, his words trailing off.

Diane worried he'd find an excuse to end her fact-finding journey. "I really appreciate your taking the time to explain everything. My uncle once said if he had a penny for every one of my questions, he would've retired a wealthy man years ago."

The operator stopped gazing at his phone and smiled at her. "Amen to that. My little girl always asks, 'Why?' every time I say something to her.

Diane grinned, hopeful he'd stick around for a few more inquiries. "Is there a material safety data sheet on the reduction fluid?"

He brought up the MSDS on his phone and handed it to her. "The fluid is comprised of different chemicals."

Diane reviewed the online document. The combined chemicals were designated as highly flammable and toxic. The ecological section described many effects as "unknown."

Within seconds, the operator took away his phone. "Sorry, I'm waiting on a text."

It was difficult to believe a chemical process could be applied to raw sewage with solids and make it clean to drink in one step.

How could something that powerful not leave a trace of itself?

The process was experimental, which meant someone had to measure the treated water to ensure standards were being met. "Who monitors the treated water?" she asked.

The operator pointed at a fenced-in area. Beyond it was the sound of water falling into the river. "The treated water is checked by the state watershed management organization. We've been passing with glowing reports."

He waved at ten people wearing thick white protective suits, long gloves, and hoods, walking toward the tree line. "Those guys are preparing to refill the reduction fluid compartments."

The group walked into a warehouse, somewhat hidden by the trees, and rolled up the large doors.

The operator pointed to the building complex. "We need to go inside now. No one without authorization and protective gear can be outside during fluid transport."

As Diane followed him toward the main building, she looked back at the workers moving large, glistening silver drums onto a truck. "Would it be okay to walk to the discharged pipes? I'd like to see the treated water returning to the river."

The operator shook his head and coughed. "There's a reason it's surrounded by a metal gate with the sign 'Authorized Personnel Only.' Too dangerous near the discharge. A lot of water coming out of those gigantic pipes."

"How does the state take readings of the treated water?"

"As I understand it, measurements are taken downstream using a boat."

The plant employees had on coveralls, vests, hard hats, and ID badges. She wanted to sample the treated water but didn't know how.

A few minutes later, they found Rose chatting with a group of people standing near the exit.

"Well, that's about it," said the operator. "I hope you enjoyed the tour."

Rose smiled at Diane. "Imagine if all wastewater treatment plants had this operation. We could reduce greenhouse gases by at least 3 percent worldwide."

Diane recalled the woman describing shiny barrels of clear, thick liquid being poured into the Mississippi inundated with raw sewage. So far, she'd learned that the effect of the reduction fluid on living organisms and the environment was undetermined. What caused a freshwater dino to morph into a sea-loving parasite was also a mystery. That was too many unknowns for Diane.

CHAPTER 29

Back at the house, Rose watched Diane pack her duffel bag. Rose's chattiness and cheery disposition from yesterday and earlier that morning had been replaced with a strangely quiet demeanor. This attractive, well-educated woman blessed with a beautiful family and gorgeous home seemed depressed, even lonely.

When Diane started for the door, Rose stopped her. She showed Diane a large box containing a case of bottled water, two full-face respirators with filters, and at least a hundred boxes of refillable cartridges. "I know there are government tankers with filtered water, and OSCF keeps you stocked on protective gear and bottled water," Rose said. "I still want you to have these. Glen has connections to get supplies through his company. You can give Brandon the other mask." Rose patted Diane's arm. "I'm a mother, so I want to make sure you both have what you need."

"That's so kind. Thank you, and I appreciate your letting me stay here."

After helping Diane carry the box to the truck, Rose smiled sadly. "I hope to see you again." Despite the strange melancholy, Rose's eyes had an inner light and warmth that reminded her of Brandon. Rose kept waving at Diane as she drove away. Perhaps Rose felt isolated in a big house with her sons gone and her husband at work.

Later that evening in her hotel room, Diane called Yan, a chemist and friend from college. "Long time no talk," Yan said.

“I’m sorry. I got a job at OSCF.”

“I heard. Congrats and sorry. Working in toxic waters. Dangerous job.”

“We’ll talk more on that later, but right now, I have a question for you.” Diane described the chemical process at the plant and the information she’d gleaned from the MSDS. She didn’t mention OSCF.

Yan gave a swift assessment. “It’s a pilot experiment. They would’ve submitted paperwork to the state and the feds for approval. The fluid sounds similar to piranha solution.”

“What’s that?”

“A cocktail of sulfuric acid and hydrogen peroxide that destroys organics, even dissolves bone. Highly toxic. It can be flammable under certain conditions. I think they’ve got a lot more going on underground in those compartments than they’re letting on.”

“I remember sulfuric acid and some type of peroxide listed among the chemicals. It was a long list.”

“Do you remember any of the other chemicals?”

“No, it was on the operator’s phone. I had only a few seconds to review.”

“I’d have to get a sample of it in order to tell you the exact composition. Don’t forget, they’re altering properties by fluctuating temperature. Risky.”

Diane recalled the workers moving shiny barrels. “The fluid is in drums stored in a locked warehouse.”

“Can’t be piranha solution. Airtight storage will cause it to explode.”

“They’ve got cameras on the main building, some pointed at the warehouse.”

“But you’re interested in the treated water returning to the river. If you can get a sample, I can identify a chemical residue and determine if it exceeds regulations.”

“Do you think the state watershed organization would share their records from monitoring the discharge? Save us a lot of trouble.”

Yan, a speedy talker with fast responses, was silent for a few seconds. "You called because you believe something's not right. Would the government hand over records that showed they're not doing their job?"

Yan always got to the point quickly. Diane took a deep breath, knowing her friend had great instincts. "Got me there. I'll collect samples for you and for my experiment. Appreciate your help."

When she ended the call, Diane opened Google Earth and identified the tributary next to the plant. Though many places were not leasing kayaks due to reports of toxins in fresh water, she called every outdoor store until she found one still renting equipment. "I'll be there first thing in the morning." While she was speaking with the store owner, her phone beeped.

She felt like a giddy schoolgirl receiving a love letter when she saw Brandon's text: *When am I going to see you? Pick up where we left off!*

I hope soon. Pilot plant was interesting. Your mom's nice. Thank her again for me.

Something big brewing in the Atlantic. You should be here!

Nicole texted as well. *How are things between you and Brandon? We'll be cruising to Greenland. Get your butt down here. Need help.*

Diane texted her back. *What's happening in the subarctic?*

Dunno.

Need to use culture of red dino without mutation. Want to see if cells exposed to water I'm collecting will develop a thick shell.

Nicole answered a few minutes later. *Plenty of cells for testing. Easy to grow red dinos.*

Diane searched the news for information about waters near Greenland. Instead, she found reports of increased toxins in groundwater from states bordering the Gulf and the Atlantic. Another report covered news of a truck driver who had carried large crates of donated bottled water and food from Utah. The anchorman stared expressionless into the camera and reported, "He was found shot in the head, slumped over the steering wheel. They'd taken everything. Many truckers are now hesitant to carry goods to the eastern states, making provisions more scarce."

While cramming supplies needed to sample the treated water into her backpack, she noticed two small items resting at the bottom of it. One was the Dolphin Bar & Grill matchbook. The other was Isabelle's contact information. She picked up her phone and considered texting the reporter who wanted to know what had caused the bloom. The thought disappeared when her phone beeped.

Jenson texted her: *Need you on North Atlantic cruise. Depart in two days. Bring passport.*

I'll be there, she texted back and placed the card in the side pocket of her backpack.

Seconds later, Jenson responded. *Proud of your hard work. Doing a great job.*

Staring at his text, Diane felt tremendous relief at his recognition. He was a brilliant pioneer in climatology who was eager to fix the world's environmental problems. If the treatment plant were emitting illegal substances, then Jenson would correct it. She had to get a sample of the treated water leaving the wastewater plant even if it meant swimming in poison or in something as dangerous as piranha solution.

CHAPTER 30

The next morning, Diane launched the kayak upstream from the wastewater plant. She marked her location on the GPS, put on a full-face respirator, and used a handheld meter to measure water quality.

After paddling about a quarter mile downstream, the plant's fence, forming a sizable perimeter around the treated waters, came into view. The metal barrier started in the woods above the bank and extended down to the water's edge. She stopped paddling and let the fast-moving current push her toward the sound of water flowing. Her T-shirt and shorts clung to her in the sweltering heat and humidity. Gnats bit her arms and legs. *Forgot the repellant!* Flinging her arms and swatting at the tiny bloodsuckers did little to discourage them. She lifted her mask slightly to feel the breeze and smelled an odd mixture of garlicky ammonia.

Within minutes, the low-pitched sounds of a distant waterfall changed to a roaring, frothy cascade hitting the tributary with tremendous force. The two discharge pipes were at least seven feet in diameter. The treated water from the plant rushed out of the round steel cylinders, creating foam and spray.

Diane rowed at a safe distance from the pipes and dropped probes into the water. Meter readings indicated pH and dissolved oxygen were normal and comparable to upstream waters. Her rapid test for *E. coli*, a type of bacterium associated with waste, showed zero concentration.

She floated the kayak to the bank. Spray from the discharge pounding the waters dampened her clothes, skin, and hair. Thick perspiration mixed with droplets of treated water conjured up images of her covered in thick, sticky yolk after losing the egg toss challenge on field day in seventh grade. *I'd rather be here than in middle school.*

Carrying bottles in a bag slung across her chest and shoulder, she climbed out of the kayak and sank ankle-deep into the mud. She grimaced as she lifted her mask to examine the goo on her boot that smelled like rotten cabbage.

Setting her sights on a small red maple growing on the banks near one of the enormous pipes, she began tramping through the muck. The sinking of each foot and pulling it back up made a sloppy, sucking sound. She stopped frequently to look over her shoulder and scan the trees leading to the plant. Her legs became more unsteady with each step accumulating more mud.

As she got closer to the tree covered in dark burgundy leaves, she heard a sudden snap. She hunkered to the ground, her heart pounding. Next to her muddy boot was a branch she'd stepped on and broken. She stood up halfway, resting her hands on her knees. *Pull yourself together.*

After positioning herself between the tree and the pipe, she pulled out a bottle with one hand and grabbed a limb growing near the pipe with the other. Stretching out toward the rushing water, she held the bottle under the waterfall. The gushing white water almost caused her to topple over. Diane tightened her grip on the branch, causing it to bend. With her feet planted in the mud, she heaved the filled container back and fell to the ground. Some of the water spilled, and she scrambled to put the bottle upright. *Yan and I can work with half a bottle.*

After securing the sample, she plodded back to the kayak in her boots that felt more like blocks of lead. Thankful to be on the water, she paddled upstream.

Suddenly, she heard movement in the trees. Voices were coming from the plant.

She froze. The current pushed her backward toward the pipes.

Footsteps were getting closer.

With all she had left in her, she rowed frantically, getting distance between herself and those approaching the tributary.

Her whole body ached when she finally reached the riverbank near the parked truck. She dragged the kayak out of the water and into the truck bed. Her muscles cramped, causing her to double over. She pulled out her cell phone and noticed a missed call from Nicole. After taking a ragged breath, she called her back.

"Please don't be upset," Nicole said, sounding hysterical. "It's the cultures I grew from River 10. The red dinos without the mutation."

Nicole hesitated long enough to bother Diane. "What is it?"

"They're dead."

Diane weaved a bit and slowly dropped to the ground on her knees, fatigued and gasping to catch her breath. "What happened?"

Nicole didn't answer, but Diane could hear her moving around. "Hold on," Nicole mumbled. A minute later, she said quietly, "I wanted to talk where no one could hear. The cultures were thick and growing yesterday. When I came in this morning, I noticed a discoloration in the containers and a chlorine smell. It's as if someone poured bleach into the cultures."

Diane couldn't believe someone would do that. "Who has access to them?"

"Dr. Bennett, but she's still recovering in New York. Todd and Brandon. Of course, Jenson and Landry. Some in the biochemistry division come in every so often to obtain samples for tests. Division directors can get into most areas."

"Who was in the lab yesterday?"

"A couple of biochemists got samples from cultures. Todd and I were packing and shipping equipment. Jenson and Landry were in a few times checking on our progress."

"Didn't OSCF install surveillance cameras after Matt's attack?"

"There's one in our lab, but it's facing the doorway, not the walk-in chamber where we grow cultures."

Diane knew the plankton cultures were easy to find. Whenever someone opened the chamber door, all the containers were clearly visible on the shelves. “What about your other cultures?”

“I was checking the diatoms when you called. So far, everything else looks okay.”

“Who do you think did this?”

“No idea. Why would they?”

“Did you tell anyone that I planned to use the River 10 dinos?”

“I told my goldfish. Does that count?”

Diane ignored Nicole’s attempt at humor and glanced at her half-full bottle of treated water. “Is there a safe place in the lab to store samples? Somewhere hidden?”

“Behind large yellow containers in the back left corner of the walk-in. No one ever checks it.”

Diane remembered the small container of the murky mixture from River 10 left in the shed. If there was one live red dino left, she could set up an experiment exposing the cells to the treated water. She wasn’t sure how long it would take for the mutation to occur. Someone had to continually supply large amounts of fertilizer to viable cells swimming in discharge from the pilot plant. The other half of the treated water she’d hide in a controlled lab environment until she could ship it to Yan.

“Don’t forget we have an early morning flight,” Nicole said. “Jenson emailed the tickets and itinerary. Our ship leaves the Nova Scotia port tomorrow.” After a few seconds of silence, Nicole’s voice broke. “I’m really sorry.”

Maybe Nicole had accidentally ruined the cultures and didn’t want to admit to it, fearing the repercussions. Diane kept telling herself it had to be an error, but a lingering thought kept her on edge. Someone wanted them to fail.

CHAPTER 31

After returning the kayak to the store and tossing her muddy boots into a trash can, Diane began the three-hour trek on mostly empty roads back to her Gulf home. She dialed the number of the greatest seaworthy soul who could handle just about anything that could swim, the person who truly knew her and had never let her down.

"Hey, it's Miss Know-Nothin'," Uncle Bo answered. "Keep it down." The background chatter stopped. "Your mom wants the phone."

"Wait, before you put her on, do you think she's well enough for you to return home for a few days? I'm scheduled to leave on a cruise tomorrow and need help with an experiment."

He chuckled. "Gonna have to start chargin' a fee for my services."

Diane told him about the wastewater plant. "It's a pilot facility for testing a process to clean wastewater. Due to some kind of fiasco, their operations went offline. Folks downstream described seeing what had to be sewage." She paused when Bo shushed someone. "I think the treated water coming out of the plant contains residuals from the chemical process. It may be responsible for the dino mutant causing the bloom."

"Why can't this wait until you return? I know nothin' about mutants and rituals."

"It's re-sid-uals."

"Shitfire, I can't even say it."

"I have enough time to get back to our house and check the container for viable cells. The longer it sits without food, the more dinos will die. I could be out at sea for weeks, depending on what we discover. I need to set up the experiment now." Bo was silent as she paused to mentally review the steps needed for accurate results. "You'll only add fertilizer to the container. After three days, you'll preserve a portion of the sample and return to Atlanta. When I get back, I'll see if the dinos exposed to the treated water developed a thick shell." She heard Mom whispering something in the background. "We'll go over it when you get home. I'll write down the directions."

"Gives me an excuse to get away from these gossipy hens. Your mom's as happy as a lark up here. She won't miss me."

A wave of relief rushed over Diane. "Thank you, Uncle Bo. Get Mom on the phone. Talk to you soon."

Mom sounded better, stronger. "I'm concerned about you."

"Please don't worry. I'm careful."

No sense in telling her I almost fell into a huge waterfall.

• • •

Diane bolted to the shed when she reached the small brick house. After setting up her old microscope, she removed the full-face respirator. The thick mask was too bulky against the scope, making it difficult to see through the lens. Inside the small container of what used to be dark red slime from River 10 was a brown liquid. Expecting a pungent odor, she squinted, covered her nose, and peered into the fluid.

A rich, musky aroma made its way through her fingers. *Odd. Smells like a forest after rain.* She sat it down gently, used a plastic dropper to place a sample of the contents under the scope, then searched for a red dino with an orange eyespot. For at least an hour, she repeated the process until a single red dino, barely moving, came into view. After siphoning out water containing the cell, she expelled the contents into half of the treated water and then loaded it with fertilizer. She saved the rest for Yan to analyze.

Diane's throat felt sore, and her chest tightened. Lightheadedness caused her to lose balance for a second. She put on her respirator, and her breathing returned to normal. The dizziness subsided. It would be too dangerous for Bo to stay here. She texted him. *Turn around! It's bad here! Choking on air.*

If the experiment failed, she'd go back to the river and start over. Compromising her uncle's health was not an option.

Twenty minutes later, Bo's truck pulled into the driveway. Her heart pounded like a wild animal trying to escape her chest as she darted to the truck and grabbed the mask Rose had given her. She shoved the respirator at him. "Put it on! Now!"

Uncle Bo slipped on the respirator. "Kinda pushy, aren't ya?"

"The air is toxic here. You should go back to Atlanta."

"I just got here." He lifted up the respirator. "And I have this thing on now."

Diane stared at him. "If you stay here, then you have to keep it on. Day and night. That means sleeping in it."

Bo took a couple of steps back and studied her. "I got a better idea. You stay here and I go on a cruise."

She sighed, realizing her uncle had already made up his mind. Sending him back to Atlanta with the container, supplies, and chemicals was not feasible. Even if her cousin Marnie's suburban home were equipped like the shed, it would be too dangerous to have those things inside someone's house. Feeling exhausted and defeated, she mumbled, "Wish I could stay."

Bo helped her lug Rose's box of supplies into the house. After setting it down, Diane pointed at a stash of bottled water. "There's plenty of clean water." She pointed at the boxes of refillable cartridges. "You must replace the mask filter at least every twelve hours. If you don't, you need to go back to Atlanta."

"What about your experiment?"

"If it fails, we'll go back to the river and dredge some more."

"Hell no! Besides, I want to stay and check on things around here. I'll grow the algae and leave in a few days."

"You're going to keep the mask on. You'll sleep in it."

"I'm changin' your name to Ms. Bossy."

Diane shouted, "Are you going to sleep in the mask?" Her bottom lip trembled, ashamed for yelling at Bo, who was there only because of her. They gawked at each other. Bo nodded and shrugged. "You promise?" she asked in a softer voice.

He threw up his hands and hung his head. "Don't you have to leave soon? You got a long drive to South Florida." After a few seconds, he looked at her. "I promise."

Bo drifted from room to room. "I'm glad we got your mom out. Hate havin' to get rid of this ol' place." He stifled a chuckle and jokingly asked, "Know any buyers interested in coastal property?"

Diane sadly shook her head and recalled running in and out of the rooms as a kid, playing hide-and-seek with Bo, who would send his yellow dog, Catie, to sniff out her hiding spot. The kitchen was where Mom helped her boil test tubes and whip up concoctions for science fair projects. Leaving their home would be heartbreaking.

They walked to the shed, where Diane showed him the container, fertilizer, and preservatives. "If you start feeling sick, please leave and go see a doctor."

Bo's gray eyes narrowed. "What're the odds that you'd find this critter in the Mississippi mud again?"

Out of the fifty-four places they had dredged in the river, only one resting cyst of the red dino had surfaced. "We know where to look: River 10."

"I'm gonna stay put, make sure this fireweed gets what it needs. Don't worry about me. I'm careful." A few hours earlier, she had used the same consoling words masked with good intentions.

Outside the shed, the humidity was thick, neurotoxins percolating in the soggy heat. It was getting late. Just thinking of the long haul to Fort Lauderdale was as tiresome as the drive itself. Thankfully, the traffic was practically nonexistent because of the absence of tourists and the large mass of people who'd already fled.

Diane climbed into the truck, started it, and watched Bo enter the shed, desperately wanting him to be okay. *I should stay.* Losing her job would be crushing, but if anything happened to her uncle, she'd be lost. An uncomfortable heaviness crept through her body. Her stomach ached. She cut off the engine, glanced at the house and then back at the shed. Bo walked out and waved his arms toward the road, encouraging her to go. Her uncle was smart. No one was more trustworthy. Reluctantly, she restarted the vehicle and backed out of the driveway. *He'll be careful.* She hoped she was right.

Diane returned the truck to OSCF's garage in the dark hours of early morning, then hid the sample of treated water behind yellow containers in the walk-in chamber. She needed more time to prepare it for shipping. She would do that after the cruise and airfreight it to Yan.

Her eyelids felt heavy as she shuffled down a dark corridor on her way out of the building. The parking lot was empty except for her Jeep. After sliding into the vehicle, she turned on the ignition, then crumpled into the seat. The clock on the dashboard flashed 3:05 a.m.

Need to pack. Early flight. Sleep on plane.

Some big event was happening in the North Atlantic, but her thoughts kept returning to Uncle Bo surrounded by thick, hot air oozing with neurotoxins.

CHAPTER 32

Ten hours later, Diane boarded the 230-foot-long *Atlantic Splendor*, with its bright red sides and white decks, anchored at the Nova Scotia port. It was equipped with icebreakers, laboratories, computer rooms, and a large recreational space, including a half-court basketball floor with a hoop at one end. Smaller ships with hoses sprayed the vessel with a fungicide to protect its machinery from the red algae.

Stored in the below-deck compartment were bright yellow hazmat suits with hoods and portable breathing machines, referred to as 'breathers.' Though everyone wore a full-face respirator, it was required for anyone on deck to wear the suit and breathers after the ship left the port. Rooms inside the ship were outfitted with an air filtration system to eliminate pollutants. Large crates holding OSCF's bots were on each side of the ship.

Diane couldn't find Brandon, Nicole, or Todd, who had flown on different airlines.

After a crew member provided directions to her cabin, she texted Uncle Bo. *Wearing mask? Feeling okay?*

This is your tenth text! I'm fine was his immediate response.

"Diane!"

She turned to find Nicole, mask half-off and waving at her.

"How did you recognize me?" asked Diane, lowering her respirator.

"I yelled your name to see who'd turn around." Nicole grinned.

Diane noticed Nicole's swollen eyes. "Guess I'm not the only one who hasn't slept."

"I can't stop thinking about the dead river dinos." Nicole put down her suitcase and lowered her voice. "I keep wondering who was in the lab. Nothing makes sense."

Diane closed her fatigued eyes, wanting to trust Nicole and needing someone besides Uncle Bo to help her. "I have a guess as to why."

Nicole's puffy eyes widened. "Brandon said you didn't find anything in the mud."

"His mom arranged a tour of OSCF's pilot plant while I was there. The operator said the treatment process was disrupted by someone breaking into the main building." Diane paused, waiting for a few of the crew to pass. "I met residents who live downstream from the pilot plant. They described what could only be sewage released from a wastewater facility. I think the floods forced a sleeping dino into the Gulf. Raw sewage and salty waters woke it up, giving us the red plague."

Nicole gaped and whispered, "OSCF's grand plan to reduce global warming started this?"

She nodded. "And that's not the worst of it." Nicole shook her head, waiting. "Under normal conditions, the red dino we grew in the shed would have died when met with changes in temperature or water quality."

Nicole froze, her mouth hanging open.

Diane glanced at crew members moving equipment and moved closer to Nicole. "The dino underwent a mutation, giving it an abnormally thick exterior. *Something* changed its DNA, its very blueprint so it could grow that protective shell and not be vulnerable to its old weaknesses anymore. But what could've triggered it? How did it get the thing it needed to go so completely out of control and do so much damage?"

Nicole rubbed her cheek, mulling over what, at least to Diane, was the million-dollar question.

Diane lowered her head and her voice and moved closer to Nicole. "Chemicals can alter DNA. The plant uses experimental agents to process solid waste. If we expose the River 10 dino to the plant's treated water, let the dino replicate itself in it, and then see if the new cells grow that fancy armor, we may finally know what made this parasite such a tough customer."

"Isn't treated water leaving the plant monitored?"

"I was told it's checked by the state watershed management organization."

Nicole wrinkled her brow. "Hmm. I know nothing about wastewater." She looked over Diane's shoulder. "Incoming . . . our famous leaders."

Oceanographers greeted Jenson and Landry as if they were rock stars. In the midst of it all, Jenson saw Diane and motioned her over. Landry, wearing a forced smile, watched Diane. She wasn't sure if Landry recognized her.

Jenson gestured toward Diane and spoke to the scientists. "This is Dr. Diane Nelson, our new postdoc who's already proven to be an outstanding marine biologist." His warm smile and gracious compliment gave her goose bumps. "Her dissertation topic was harmful algal blooms."

Scientists Diane had cited in her thesis introduced themselves. They were all discussing the unusual red dino when, out of nowhere, Landry interjected, "I wonder if this new species is related to cara brave."

Landry was a climatologist and was not as familiar with the scientific names of plankton as the others. Diane tried to think of a friendly way to respond to Landry.

Jenson lowered his head, suppressing a smile. A few others did the same.

A scientist cleared his throat and abruptly said, "I think you meant *Karenia brevis.*"

Landry's face reddened. She fidgeted, shifting her weight from side to side as the conversation continued.

Diane wanted to calm Landry and hoped to make some kind of connection with the cofounder. She said, "I think Dr. Landry made an interesting point about *Karenia brevis*. It's a well-known dinoflagellate in the Gulf that also produces toxins harmful to marine life and humans."

Landry glanced at her, then at Jenson. "Of course! That was my point," she said, then glared at Diane, making it clear she did not welcome the assist.

Diane wanted to enjoy the discussion with the scientists she revered, but she could feel Landry's eyes burning holes through her.

Looking past the group, she found her three labmates watching the exchange. Nicole stood expressionless while Brandon and Todd smiled and nudged each other. Diane knew Jenson was attempting to widen her professional network, but Landry's visible contempt made her uncomfortable.

Finally, Jenson gave her the big, dimpled smile. "I'm sure Dr. Nelson has preparations to make in the lab before we set sail."

Controlling the urge to run away, she met his kindhearted gaze with a thankful nod, then walked toward Brandon and Todd, who were chuckling and whispering. Nicole shook her head.

"I've never seen Landry give such dirty looks. What'd you do to her?" Todd asked.

Wide-eyed, Diane shrugged, put on her respirator, then glanced back at the cofounders. "Nothing."

Landry smiled and nodded at them. Diane believed the kind gesture was not meant for her.

Brandon waved at Landry. "She definitely knows who you are."

"Is that a good thing?" Diane asked.

The men looked at each other and didn't answer.

"Normally, she's really nice," Nicole said. "But I'd suggest walking in the opposite direction from her."

Perhaps sensing Diane's anxiety about the tension between herself and Landry, Todd moved closer. "I think she's upset that you told off Jenson in the lab, and he let you off the hook."

Nicole nodded. "He also approved your work in the Panhandle."

"What matters most is that Jenson likes you," Todd said with a half grin. "Landry could love you, but if Jenson doesn't care about you or your work, you're out." Todd's voice took on a serious tone. "I think she does what he says."

Brandon glanced at Todd and Nicole. "I would like a moment alone with our postdoc for further interrogation as to why Landry's giving her the stink eye."

Nicole and Todd smiled at each other and moved toward the galley.

Todd turned around, walking backward. "Don't forget, bots go out when the ship leaves port."

"Got it," Brandon said, leading Diane down a hallway, away from everyone. They took off their respirators and embraced in a kiss that made her forget all about the odd-acting Landry and a spreading bloom. When they finally let go of each other, he brushed her cheek with his hand. "I'll be working like crazy with bot deployment. Every break I get, I'll be looking for you."

His sultry eyes and the way his warm body pressed up against hers, made her tingle. For a moment, she felt a connection that made her heart beat faster. They kissed again, not letting go of each other until the ship moved, heading out to the icy waters of the North Atlantic, which held a secret of its own.

CHAPTER 33

Standing on the deck, Diane and Brandon held hands and watched the port recede. Thick scarlet-colored swells faded into crimson ripples as the massive hull sliced through the rotting remains of sea life. A crewman shouted, "Everyone who's on deck! Get on your hazmat suits and portable breathers!"

Diane went inside and helped Nicole calibrate instruments. They suited up on their breaks and watched Brandon, Todd, and a team of technicians move bots into position on mechanical arms located at starboard. The ship's engine slowed, and the robotic arms swiveled like a crane over the water, then deployed multiple bots so they were spread out every few feet.

After working in the lab until dinner, Diane and Nicole went to the galley. Brandon was at a table with Jenson, Landry, and other scientists, discussing artificial intelligence. Diane and Nicole joined Todd at a less-crowded table and planned their schedules.

Diane tried to get on Brandon's shift, but Todd disagreed. "No way! He'll be looking at you and not working."

Nicole and Brandon would take the first twelve-hour shift. Todd and Diane would take the second. They were approaching Greenland, and the days were getting longer. This far north at this time of year, Diane would get to see the midnight sun.

Brandon joined them after they had finalized their work plans. Todd asked him, "How did the last batch of bot deployments go?"

"We started out with good measurements, but I just got word the readings are all over the place." Brandon's voice sounded hoarse. "I'm getting ready to work with the crew on testing a fungicide application on the remaining bots."

Todd clapped him on the back. "Hang in there, man. Gonna grab some shut-eye before my shift."

Nicole stood. "I'm sure you'll get the bots working again. I'm heading to the lab."

Brandon smiled, gazing at Diane. "I forgot to ask about the pilot plant."

Diane answered nonchalantly. "I didn't realize a chemical process existed that made raw sewage clean enough to drink in one step, nothing left behind. Incredible."

He leaned back in his chair, studying her. "I thought you suspected the plant. Maybe it started the bloom."

"Yeesss." She drew out the word, nodding. "That's why I went on the tour. They answered my questions."

He put his hand over hers. "Wish I could take you somewhere, just you and me."

She rolled her eyes. "What did you say about looking for me when you weren't working? An hour passed before you noticed I was here."

"Have to play nice with the researchers." He leaned in close, lightly pressed his lips against hers, then whispered, "And you're very noticeable."

The technicians found Brandon and whisked him away. He looked back, giving a little wave.

She touched her mouth, recalling his soft kiss and wishing he didn't have to go. Alone, she decided it was time to text Uncle Bo. *Be sure you're wearing a mask ALL THE TIME.*

Minutes later, he responded, *Your nagging will kill me before the toxins.*

She went to the cabin. It was cramped, like most accommodations on a research vessel. The room's porthole was a nice change, providing a round view of the choppy red sea. Nicole had placed her bag on the top bunk, so Diane took the bottom.

What did Brandon mean by "very noticeable"?

She was sure he meant it as a compliment. But it made her think about whether she'd been noticed by the people at the wastewater plant. Had someone seen her frantically rowing a kayak upstream to avoid detection?

CHAPTER 34

During their shift, Diane and Todd used a mass spectrometer to analyze samples other researchers had collected on the cruise. Only red algal cells were detected. After annotating the results, her thoughts returned to the wastewater plant. Todd had the most experience in the bio-lab. She asked, "Do you know much about OSCF's pilot treatment plant? Like how they monitor the treated water?"

"Everyone at the foundation knows about the plant. If you're interested in how it's monitored, your best resource would be Dr. Landry. Her husband used to be the director of Louisiana's state watershed management organization. I think he might have also worked for the EPA."

Diane remembered the story of how Senator Landry had visited the woman in the low-income housing unit. "Cleaned it up like new," the woman had said.

"What do you know about Dr. Landry's husband?" Diane asked.

"Like I said, he's worked in government for many years. I met him once. Kind of a wimpy guy. The complete opposite of Jenson."

Todd started organizing the glassware they'd just cleaned and pointed at a crate of plastic bottles. "We need to get the rosette ready for sampling."

"I'll do that."

She went downstairs, took off her respirator, and put on the hazmat suit. The portable breather fit like a backpack. After positioning the mask over her nose and mouth, she returned to the lab, picked up the containers, and headed outside. Though it was difficult to recognize people in hazmat suits and breathers, she guessed many on deck were technicians.

The ship had come far north. Even with all her bulky protective gear, she still could feel the strong, frigid gusts off the ocean. Ice from the freezing gales pelted her mask, forcing her to look down while leaning into the wind to reach the rosette.

After securing the crate of bottles next to the rosette, she fought to maintain her balance as the surging vessel made its way through churning seas. She made it back inside the ship just in time to receive a text from Jenson: *Everyone report to the muster station.*

The recreation area served as the muster station for the lifeboats. It was the only space below where everyone could gather at once. The technicians and scientists filed in, carrying their respirators. Some looked well rested such as Nicole, who was getting ready to start her shift. Others trudged along such as herself, ending a shift.

Brandon's respirator hung around his neck. He looked the most haggard, with shadowy circles around his dark eyes from working double shifts. Diane was making her way through the crew members toward Brandon when Nicole grabbed her arm and said, "This gives me some major bad vibes."

Before she could make another attempt to be near Brandon, Jenson began speaking. "The captain has informed me there's a huge storm shifting toward our trajectory. He's moving the ship quickly to stay ahead of it and get out of its path. We'll remain in contact with the weather bureau and keep tabs on the storm's movement. We may have to forgo regular stops for sampling."

The room filled with audible gasps. Some groaned and threw up their hands at the thought of a trip out to sea ending with no data. One scientist studied her phone and muttered, "Right now, it's a major hurricane. They expect it to become a strong tropical storm."

Nicole turned to Diane and Todd. "I thought hurricanes needed warm water."

"They form over warm waters and lose steam in the cold," Todd answered, rubbing his fatigued face.

Diane navigated to a weather app on her phone. "This storm is probably like the hurricane that made the news a few years ago that cut across the northern Atlantic and struck Iceland."

Nicole knelt down and stared at the floor. Diane glanced at Brandon, who was leaning against the bulkhead. His eyes were closed. Everyone was exhausted and worried.

Jenson gestured at those who were grumbling to quiet down. "A cargo ship reported a strange phenomenon involving the red algae: a visible barrier between the North Atlantic and the algae-infested waters. We want to get to that location and verify the observation." The room grew silent, amplifying the creaking noise the ship made as it was battered by strong winds and violent waters. The sound reminded Diane of walking on old floorboards in her Gulf home.

Jenson checked his phone and continued, "It's an area with a temperature variant located south of Greenland. Depending on the storm's path, we may have time to do some sampling and take measurements upon arrival." He snapped his fingers at Brandon, who jerked open his eyes. "We're going to be on station in eighteen hours. Bots need to be ready."

Diane looked at Brandon, hoping to make eye contact, but a couple of technicians had surrounded him, blocking her view. She overheard two scientists discussing the subarctic waters, and she joined them. One of them brought up Google Maps on her phone and said, "I think we're sailing into the cold blob."

Freshwater melt from the ice shelf, glaciers, and icebergs had caused a marked decrease in water temperature in that one spot in the North Atlantic. *The cold blob.*

The other woman agreed. "It's a place where the presence of fresh water continues to weaken the Atlantic Ocean current."

Diane guessed that fluctuating temperature and salinity alongside a weakened ocean current could mean the red dino would be forced to slow its drift toward new prey.

Todd walked up to Diane. "I'm going to work double shifts. Brandon needs help with the bots. Poor guy's exhausted."

She said goodbye to the scientists and watched as Todd joined Brandon, who was speaking with Jenson and Landry. Nicole nudged her. "Go to bed. Who knows what's going to happen when we reach our destination?"

Diane feared that if she closed her eyes she'd miss something important during the journey, but she needed rest. "Wake me if anything happens."

Nicole nodded and headed toward the lab. "See you in twelve hours."

Jenson and Landry left with Todd.

Brandon stood alone, watching her. She smiled and waved at him, but his blank expression didn't change. His fatigued eyes seemed darker and . . . cold.

She started to move toward him when someone yelled his name. Brandon looked down, rubbing his eyes, then joined the others suited up for deck work.

Had he found out about her kayaking near the discharge pipes? In his words, she was "very noticeable."

Back in her cabin, she sprawled out on her bunk and thought of Brandon, the hidden samples of treated water, and the cold blob. Her body ached for rest, but her mind raced with a grueling mix of worries and ideas running amok.

To calm herself, she recalled youthful memories of holding her breath while skin diving underneath the Gulf waters, and the surface above her breaking with the quick-moving paws of Catie paddling alongside Uncle Bo. Her uncle, wearing goggles, would look down at where Diane floated in the shallows and wave at her, a simple gesture that had filled her soul with joy. Nothing felt better than being underwater and knowing that Uncle Bo was with her. She wanted to text him but decided against it. Her constant checking in had become a nuisance to him. Her thoughts returned to what they would discover in the subarctic waters. Whatever it was, they were heading straight for it.

CHAPTER 35

Diane awoke to Nicole jumping onto the top bunk and letting out an exasperated sigh. "So boring. Nothing to do in the lab."

Through the porthole, Diane observed the calm seas. "Maybe we'll get the go-ahead for sampling when we reach our destination."

Nicole groaned. "You'll be sitting in the lab twiddling your thumbs. Maybe see if Brandon or Todd needs help."

Diane suited up and went to the deck crowded with people in bright yellow suits. Brandon motioned her over and held out the device used to control the bots. He pointed to the monitor with little blinking lights. "Those are the bots." He zoomed into the map and selected one of the lights. The bot's name, BID8087, popped up, displaying its water depth, signal strength, and other numbers she didn't recognize. He pressed a button that returned to the map of flashing lights.

"It's incredible," she said, gazing at the bright screen.

Brandon leaned into her. "You're a joy to watch, especially when you're fascinated."

She was excited to see his warm smile under the clear shield. Her bulky gear prevented her from acting on the urge to hug him. She was just about to ask him about his peculiar behavior the day before when technicians and scientists rushed toward the bow. Todd, following the excited group, yelled, "Something's ahead of us!"

She didn't want to leave Brandon, who continued to work. He got close to her, their masks touching. "Must be good if Todd's running. Go on."

"You don't need me to stay?"

He shook his head and kept working.

The front of the ship was crowded with people who had removed their breathers and were aiming their phone cameras at the sea. "Mask up!" some crewmen screamed at them.

Todd waved Diane over and gave up his position against the rail. He said in a loud, high-pitched voice, "This is crazy! I'll get Nicole."

Fifty yards in front of the vessel, the red bloom stopped and shimmering purple waters began. Were the dinos reacting to something in the water? Perhaps the North Atlantic contained something worse, gaining its strength from the algae.

Nicole showed up in gear, carrying a couple of binoculars. She handed one pair to Diane and yelped, "What the hell is that?"

"A nightmare or a miracle," Diane said, pressing the field glasses against her mask. Farther out, the waters were dark indigo. A shiny amethyst sea was breathtaking, but nothing could match the natural beauty of a blue ocean.

The ship sailed into grape-colored seawater. It seemed improbable that the red tide would disappear because of an anomaly in currents, salinity, or temperature. The purple waters reminded her of the pilot plant's reduction fluid. Red dinos entered it and—poof!—they were gone.

Congregated around Jenson and Landry were scientists excitedly shouting from behind their masks. Jenson held out his hands in a motion to calm them. "There's a tremendous storm not far from us. It's too dangerous to collect samples. We'll return when it's safe." Many tried to change his mind but were unsuccessful. Diane, chewing her bottom lip, walked up to him.

She avoided eye contact with Landry and spoke directly to Jenson. "I have a book with a picture of you holding equipment and standing next to a muddy truck. Behind you, in the distance, is an F4 tornado.

That day, you recorded data used to predict weather patterns. Imagine what we could learn from these waters."

Jenson's determined eyes softened behind the mask. "That was me and one other person on land. I wasn't at sea with hundreds of souls and a powerful squall. We have to leave within the hour to avoid it."

Landry tugged at Jenson's sleeve. Diane spoke before Landry could pull him away. "Something's destroying the red dinos. Beyond the purple water is a clear ocean. We can get the rosette in and out of the water in thirty minutes."

Landry whispered something in Jenson's ear. He didn't respond. Instead, he turned to Diane. "Just the rosette."

Landry stormed off the deck and into the recreation area.

Jenson kept talking as if nothing had happened. "Split the water samples to share with other researchers. I want the bots in the clear waters to confirm no trace of red algae. That gives you less than thirty minutes." He glanced down at his phone. "We need to be sailing on a trajectory toward Nuuk Port no later than 18:45."

Minutes later, Todd, Nicole, and a couple of technicians joined Diane. They secured the rosette to the winch and had it in the water collecting samples within minutes. Diane stopped every ten feet to collect samples to a depth of fifty feet. Going any deeper would have taken too much time.

The captain, without his mask, stomped down the ladder from the bridge and frowned at the winch holding the rosette. He screamed at Jenson, "We have to move! Why in the hell do we have equipment in the water?!"

Jenson remained calm. "It'll be out in a few minutes."

The captain huffed and trudged up the steps. "Damn eggheads."

It seemed unbelievable that a big storm loomed behind the southern sky filled with white, fluffy clouds.

When the rosette was brought up and hoisted onto the ship, Diane grabbed the crate of bottles and began emptying water from the rosette into separate containers labeled by the depth. Todd and Nicole distributed the violet-colored samples to the scientists.

The ship sailed out of the purple band of seawater and into a dark blue ocean. Technicians helped Brandon deploy bots into the clear water.

The large vessel listed slightly while making a sharp turn and headed toward Nuuk Port in Greenland, steering away from the storm's path. Diane looked at her phone. The sampling and the bots had taken twenty-nine minutes.

Diane, Nicole, and Todd carried their purple water samples into the lab. While prepping instruments to analyze the water, Diane's phone beeped.

Brandon texted, *Come look!*

Diane made her way up to the computer room, which was crowded with at least fifty scientists and technicians. She couldn't make it to Brandon, who was sitting in front.

Large screens mounted on the wall showed red dino concentrations represented by colored dots on top of a static map. Displayed on the screen was also a blue and black dashed line to show their vessel's path from south to north. At the end of the line was a red *X* to mark their current location.

An abundance of yellow and red dots showed high concentrations of dinos in the southern red waters, followed by a scatter of white dots in the purple waters, showing a very low number of dinos. Above the white dots was the last location of the bots deployed into the clear seas. No dots. Zero dinos.

The yellow and red dots on the lowest region of the map disappeared.

She texted Brandon. *Bots malfunctioning?*

The next row of dots vanished. Brandon was losing bots one after another from south to north. He replied, *More like destroyed.*

"The storm is tracking near those coordinates," someone said.

The powerful storm was almost on top of them. Stopping to sample might have been a mistake.

CHAPTER 36

In the ship's laboratory, Diane prepared the water samples the rosette had collected. The TV in the recreation area, located beside the lab, was showing pictures of dead wildlife. A scrolling ticker read, "Freshwater bodies near the contaminated coast continue to hurt wildlife and stray animals." While images of human corpses covered by black tarp were shown onscreen, an expert from the local environmental agency was being interviewed. "Measurements taken a week ago indicated trace amounts of toxins in the groundwater. We had a large rain event over the past few days, causing a significant spike in toxins." He fidgeted with his respirator. "Filtration has become inadequate. We urge everyone to use only bottled water."

"What about the filtered water brought in by the tankers?" the reporter asked while she glanced back at protesters waving signs that read, "Clean Air, Clean Water NOW!" and "Climate Change Kills!"

"We're calling back the tankers and plan to incorporate a new purification process. In the meantime, FEMA and the Red Cross will deliver bottled water and nonperishable foods to the coast." Gunshots rang out during the news report. People screamed. The broadcast signal was lost.

Diane turned away from the TV and focused on the small plastic container labeled "SAMPLE 10 FEET." She heard a loud rumble from outside the ship and paused for a second. Content that they were sailing away from the storm, she picked up the container and poured out water with swirls of violet into a petri dish. Under the scope, a tiny crustacean with long antennae and a round, transparent, blue-colored body fed on a red dino—the new copepod was twice the size of the dinoflagellate.

A single copepod consumed up to three-hundred thousand microorganisms a day. This tiny, fast-moving zooplankton fluoresced a bright blue under the light. It reminded Diane of a copepod that biologists had used as dye to visualize experiments. She watched a blue copepod snag a red dino, then noticed the crustacean shone purple as the crimson parasite entered its glassy body.

Ten short blasts of a horn caused her to jump away from the microscope—a warning signal. She stopped for a few seconds. Perhaps another ship was near and the captain was alerting them to their presence.

She returned to the scope and discovered a few dead copepods. Unsure if their demise was caused by the toxin, she monitored an individual copepod feeding, waiting to see if it would perish.

Her phone beeped, but she ignored it. Someone brushed her arm; she didn't look up.

I can't lose sight of it.

"Diane, you have to stop," Todd said. "Storm's close."

Finally, Diane looked up. Nicole was near, twisting her blond hair. Nicole's lips trembled. "We need to go."

Todd exited the lab, motioning for them to follow.

"The muster station is right outside our lab," Diane said, turning off the scope.

Nicole started pacing. "I'm scared. I need to get out of here." She rushed out of the lab and headed toward the deck.

Diane caught up with her. "This is the last place we should be."

Nicole clutched the rail, her knuckles as pale as her face.

Diane pointed toward the muster station. "We have to return to the rec area."

Nicole watched the dark clouds. "Out here, I can see the storm. Hiding from it inside the ship is like hiding from an invisible monster. Scarier."

Diane couldn't understand why Nicole didn't want to be near lifeboats. "Now you see it. Let's go in. We're not safe here."

Under the shadowy, ominous sky, waves broke into white foam, different from the frothy pinks of the Gulf and the rest of the Atlantic. The whitecaps on the churning waters were reminiscent of a time when people could turn on the faucet and not worry about ingesting toxins or releasing poisons into their homes. Yet, there were other dangers closing in on them.

Lightning strikes flashed off the ocean. Their vessel could handle strong winds and rough seas, but it was small compared to the enormous storm with roiling, bruised clouds edging its way toward them.

CHAPTER 37

Diane and Nicole returned to the lab and ensured instruments and bottles of samples were fastened and protected. Many people were wearing life jackets and stood in the recreation area adjacent to their lab. Crew members scrambled in and out of the muster station, securing large equipment and bringing in smaller gear. There was no sign of Brandon, Todd, or OSCF's cofounders.

Nicole sat on the steps that led up to the lab and called her mom. Diane thought Nicole appeared more relaxed, so she went to the cabin to text Uncle Bo. After three texts, she didn't receive a reply. This worried her as much as the storm did. The thunder sounded even closer. The gentle sway of the ship turned into a constant rocking.

She left a voicemail, trying to sound as calm as possible. "Hi, Uncle Bo! We're running into bad weather at sea but things should be okay. On an incredible research vessel. Have so much to tell you. Please call me. Love you!"

The thunder clapped right before Diane heard a loud knock at the door. She jumped and ran to open it. Brandon stood outside the cabin door, wearing a life jacket and holding out another for her. "Everyone has to put one on . . . just in case."

Putting on the vest, she mumbled, "I'd die from hypothermia before drowning."

Brandon's eyes darted between her cabin and the hallway. "Do you know where Nicole and Todd are?"

"Nicole was sitting on the steps to the lab. Not sure about Todd."

Bizarre whooshing sounds came out of nowhere. Straight winds and intense rains bombarded the ship. The rocking motion accelerated. A jolt caused her to grab hold of the doorway. Increasing winds turned into a high-pitched, howling screech. The ship strained against the force of the storm. Diane began feeling lightheaded and nauseous.

Her cabin's port hole darkened. Deafening scream of wind and rain rocketed all around them. She tried to cover her ears with both hands, but Brandon grabbed her arm and pulled her toward the muster station.

The ship violently rolled from port to starboard. Suddenly, the bow rose high in front of them; the deck went nearly vertical under their feet. They lunged towards the laboratory steps and desperately clung to the railing to avoid being hurled backward and crashing into a distant bulkhead.

Her eyes tightly shut, Diane tensed, preparing for the unknown. Memories returned of going to the beach with high school friends and jumping into waves created by a distant storm on the Gulf. The ship's sudden movement from vertical to horizontal brought her back to reality.

The deck below their feet was going vertical again, but this time in the opposite direction. Feeling a great force pull her forward, Diane tightened her grip.

Books, shoes, equipment…everything was flying everywhere.

Loud pops. Cracking noises. Diane feared the ship would fall apart.

People screamed.

It seemed to go on forever, though the incident lasted only a few seconds.

Bursts of seawater streamed into the recreation area, sloshing on the floor and splashing against the walls. Within seconds, a deluge of frothy water rushed toward Diane. The wall of water smashed into her, knocking her down, and pushing her to the floor. Frigid water covered her like shards of glass pricking her skin. She struggled to get her bearings, submerged in the icy liquid. The water's force made it impossible to move. Her body went numb.

Arms wrapped around her and jerked her up onto the steps.

Brandon. His skin was wet and cold.

Her body shivering, she clung to him and waited for the freezing waters to recede.

The ship continued to heave up and down the tremendous swells. She spotted Todd, half-crouched in the far corner, missing his eyeglasses.

"Todd!" Brandon yelled.

Todd seemed unable to hear Brandon over the commotion. He kept squinting, looking down at his feet.

Diane couldn't find Nicole.

Her legs felt weak and shaky as she tried to stand up on the rolling ship. Some people staggered, checking on others who were crying or not moving. Grabbing onto anything for balance, she leaned to her left and put one foot in front of the other. Slowly, she made her way to the cabins and then to the galley, which was empty except for dishes strewn across the wet floor. No Nicole.

She heard Todd shouting, "Nicole!"

Prior to the ambush of winds and rains, Nicole had gone outside to calm her nerves. If Nicole had returned to the deck outside, the chance of finding her, alive or dead, was slim.

CHAPTER 38

The ship had reached calmer seas when Diane joined Brandon and Todd in the recreation area.

Todd threw up both hands. "We can't find her."

Jenson and Landry were checking on people when Brandon got their attention. "Nicole's missing," he said.

Landry gasped. "No!"

"Where did you last see her?" Jenson asked.

Diane pointed to the lab. "She was sitting on the steps. We haven't checked outside."

Jenson whistled to get everyone's attention. "I need everyone available to look for Nicole, a petite blond woman, who's missing." He furrowed his brow, watching the crew split up to search for the young lab tech.

"We've got to find her," Landry pleaded in a weepy voice before joining Todd and Brandon to search the onboard laboratories. Brandon motioned for Diane to follow them, but she stopped when Jenson pointed to a couple of male technicians and shouted, "Need your help outside to search for Nicole! I'll check starboard! Both of you check port side!"

The ship's rocking had slowed, but they hadn't completely cleared the storm, and the ocean still churned. Not wanting Jenson to be alone on deck, Diane followed him. After noticing her, he barked, "You stay inside."

Diane took a step back. "You shouldn't be out there alone."

He frowned and fidgeted a bit. "Fine. Stay close."

Balancing while moving forward required great concentration on a swaying ship. Water sloshed across the slippery deck, and every so often, a swell of seawater spilled over the rails. The rain drenching them felt warmer than the subarctic ocean.

Between the crush of the storm and a missing person search, no one had not suited up with the breathers.

The water underneath the ship was clear and perhaps free of red algae. Maybe protective gear wasn't necessary.

Diane slipped as she caught up with Jenson. He grabbed her around the waist to keep her from falling against the rail. He held her close and asked, "Are you okay?" When she nodded, he released her and moved quickly, shouting, "Nicole!" Even though he was no longer a star athlete, he had the agility of a big cat.

Diane panicked when she spotted an empty life jacket drifting between the waves near the ship. Cold chills surged through her body. She shook uncontrollably while studying the rolling sea, fearing she may soon find a lifeless body.

Jenson lifted a hanging canvas and stooped to the deck.

Diane screamed when she saw Nicole leaning against the rosette under the tarp. She was unconscious, her skin gray, lips blue, her hair matted with slivers of ice. The threaded belts of her life jacket were entangled with cables from equipment partially covered by the tarp.

Jenson unraveled the ropes, then carried Nicole's limp body to the recreation area and began CPR.

After a few heart-stopping seconds, Nicole coughed up seawater, bubbles streaming out of both sides of her mouth. The crew started shouting.

"We need blankets!"

"Where are the mylar covers?!"

The ship's doctor yelled, "Move her to sick bay! We need to treat her for hypothermia!"

Diane followed Jenson, who carried Nicole to the medical room and placed her on a cot. Two crewmen entered and covered Nicole in a silver emergency blanket and white quilts. Nicole was as pale as the covers.

"How can I help?" Diane asked.

The doctor carefully lifted the blankets and listened to Nicole's heartbeat with his stethoscope. He asked, "Do you have any medical training besides CPR?"

"No," Diane and Jenson answered in unison.

The sick bay wasn't tiny like their cabins, but it was too small for more than three people.

The doctor nodded at the door. "You both need to leave."

Outside the sick bay, Diane leaned against the bulkhead and slid to the floor. She closed her eyes and prayed as Nicole had done when Matt had destroyed the lab. The news had been showing people gathered in churches along the coast, begging the Almighty for clean water. She thought of her childhood prayers before bedtime and her mom taking her to church enough times to ensure she was baptized.

When she opened her tear-filled eyes, Jenson was watching her. "Nicole will be fine. Are you okay?" he asked softly.

She wiped her eyes and nodded. Forcing her voice to not sound weepy, she blurted out, "I'm fine."

Jenson's gaze softened, revealing a gentler side of him. The regret and guilt for leaving Uncle Bo in a poisonous environment and not staying with a fearful Nicole had her on edge, but Jenson's warm regard comforted her. Still, she thought he should know that his experimental treatment of wastewater could be a problem, and she couldn't help but to ask, even at a time like this, "Do you think OSCF's pilot plant has something to do with the toxic bloom?"

Jenson's relaxed posture went rigid. He took a step back, his eyes narrowing. He growled, "Why would you ask that?"

Diane realized she'd entered a different storm. "Well . . . th-the report I sent you showed the River 10 site is only, uh, ten miles downstream from the pilot plant. I was just . . . curious if you thought there could be a connection."

Jenson massaged his temple. "We've closely monitored the process *and* the treated water. We have staff managing the plant, meeting the required standards. Waters leaving our pilot facility are clean." He stepped forward, looking down at her. His voice deepened. "There's no connection."

She considered the disruption of operations resulting in a raw sewage spill and Landry's husband with contacts to the state, but she said nothing. Jenson was a man of high caliber and intellect. She couldn't understand why he wasn't even considering the possibility of an association between the bloom and his exploratory process located only miles from where the red dino originated. Was it denial or that he didn't have all the facts? How much did he *really* know about the plant? His knowledge of it could be based on half truths provided by someone who had access to people cleaning up their mess.

Jenson crossed his arms. "Have you been to the pilot plant?"

She didn't hesitate to answer. "I heard great things about the new process. I was measuring sediments around River 10 and heard it was near. Just wanted to see if you had any concerns. Your experimental treatment of wastewater with no emissions sounds promising." She forced a smile, hoping he believed her newfound enthusiasm.

For a few seconds, they looked at each other in silence. Finally, Jenson lowered his eyes, taking a big breath and exhaling slowly. He stared at the sick bay door. "Many have accepted that the bloom originated from nutrient spikes we discovered in the Gulf basin. It's possible your resting cyst in River 10 was carried out to the Gulf, where salinity and runoff exacerbated by floods caused it to develop into the red dinoflagellate."

He paused for a second to wipe the sweat off his brow, then continued. "Right now, our focus is on getting rid of the bloom. The scientists you shared samples with are reporting an unusual blue copepod that's feeding on the algae. They believe it can neutralize the toxin, making the dinoflagellate safe for the copepod to consume."

Jenson gazed at her with a rare softness, almost fatherly like her uncle. "When we get back, I want you to work on the purple water samples. You'll be in the lab, not in the field. We need to have a better idea of what's going on here."

Have to get back to Uncle Bo. "I need to get some things I left at my family's place. Is that okay?"

"I want you in the lab when we get back. Get the analyses done. In a few days, you can go home and get your stuff."

Uncle Bo had not responded to her messages. Not hearing from him worried her, but she couldn't get to him until Jenson was satisfied with her work.

CHAPTER 39

Diane sat outside the sick bay for hours, waiting for an update on Nicole. She texted her uncle. *I'm getting worried. I need to know you're okay or I'm calling Mom.*

She looked up from her phone and saw Brandon, Todd, and Jenson talking at the end of the corridor. Diane was too far away to hear their conversation, but when it was over, Todd followed Jenson. Brandon walked toward Diane. He sat down on the floor beside her. The dark circles under his eyes were fading. Perhaps he had taken a nap since he had nothing to do after losing his bots.

"Nicole's a fighter," he said, touching her arm. "She'll be fine." He scooted close, his shoulder touching hers. "Your colleagues have been working with the samples since we moved out of the storm. A blue bug is making mincemeat of our red parasite." He put his arm around her shoulders. "I'm sure when Nicole is feeling better, the two of you could work on growing a culture of them."

She didn't know what to say other than Jenson had just clipped her wings and she felt responsible for Nicole. *I convinced Jenson to sample.* That decision had cost them extra time that could have been used to move the ship farther away from the storm.

"Was anyone else hurt?" she asked.

"Some have cuts and bruises. Nicole would've been okay if she'd stayed inside the rec area. What the hell was she doing out on the deck?"

The sick bay door opened, and Diane shot up from the floor. The doctor stuck his head out. "She wants to see Diane."

Nicole smiled when Diane entered the room. Nicole's color had returned; her hair had dried into tangles. Her voice was grainy and strained. "There you are."

"So glad you're okay," Diane said, kneeling beside the cot. "We found you near the rosette. What were you doing?"

"I was looking for you. Couldn't find you. Guessed you might have gone to the deck to get more samples from the rosette."

"Why would I do that in a storm?"

"Didn't think a squall would stop you. Besides, it was just starting, and I went for a quick look. Water hit me. Lost my balance. That's all I remember."

"The life jacket saved your life."

Nicole blinked slowly. "I went into the water?"

"The straps on your vest were twisted with hanging cables. I have no idea how that happened, but it kept you from falling off the ship. I'm sure you were underwater at times, but you remained on board."

Nicole was silent for a second, then muttered, "It was so fast."

Diane took Nicole's hand and squeezed it. "Unless you have a death wish, don't go out on deck during a storm."

Nicole stared off into the distance and mumbled something Diane couldn't make out.

"What did you say?" Diane asked.

Nicole blinked hard. "Oh, nothing. So . . . what did you find in the samples?"

Diane updated her on the copepod and what the other scientists had found.

Nicole's eyes brightened. "Thank you for being here, but you need to be in the lab. Figure out the conditions required to grow it. We've got a lot of culturing to do back in Florida."

"You're right. I'll get back to it. I hope you return to the lab soon," she said, giving her a big smile.

As Diane left the sick bay, Landry walked in and thanked the doctor. She overheard Landry say, "I told him not to stop. He never listens to me."

Recalling that Landry had witnessed her encouraging Jenson to stop the ship, Diane guessed she had found another reason to dislike her.

A loud grinding noise that sounded like something ripping through the hull startled her. The ship was breaking ice, sailing closer to Nuuk Port.

• • •

Diane found Brandon and Todd unhooking instruments in the lab.

"We're expected to arrive at the docks in a couple of hours," Todd said. "That should give you enough time to get your things and pack samples to carry on the plane."

While putting supplies and equipment into large shipping boxes, Brandon said, "The ship's crew has been in contact with the port for the vessel's repairs and maintenance. Jenson said an airport shuttle would wait at the dock. All this stuff will be sent later."

"Are you guys flying back with me?" she asked.

Todd shook his head. "Staying behind to ship out these boxes."

"What about Nicole?" Diane asked, taking out ice packs from a portable freezer and placing them in the container holding the purple water samples.

"She'll be transported to a local hospital," Brandon said, taping up a box. "A doctor has to release her for travel back to the States."

Two hours later, after she'd said goodbye to Todd, Brandon walked her to the shuttle, carrying her duffel bag and the cold container with small bottles of purple water.

"What about the bots?" she asked.

"Jenson is getting satellite pictures of where many of them were lost. We'll head back out and retrieve what we can."

Diane watched him place her things in the shuttle. His arms were firm without the crazy overly muscular look. When they had slept together, he'd held her close, and she could feel his well-toned muscles, conditioned from hard work on the seas. He embraced her tightly. "I know we haven't known each other long, but when the water was pulling you down on the ship, all I could do was get in and pull you out. Like a reflex. No hesitation. It was the same instinct I had when you were floating in the Gulf. You have an unusual effect on me." He kissed her, his heart pounding against her chest.

"Thank you for saving me from the red water . . . and the icy water."

He held up two fingers and mouthed the word *twice*, then laughed. "I meant what I said about going away together. Time to enjoy each other instead of fighting for our lives."

"Before we plan vacations, tell me why you were glaring at me after Jenson warned us about the storm."

"What are you talking about?"

She mimicked his scowl from that day. Brandon's smile wavered. "I might have gotten three hours of sleep on this cruise. I don't recall doing that. Probably dozed off with my eyes open. I'm so tired. I could be walking and talking in my sleep right now."

His explanation seemed reasonable, and he sounded genuine. If he knew about her trip to the discharge pipes and disapproved of her actions, she was certain he would have mentioned it, and probably wouldn't want to spend time with her. She asked, "Where would we go for a getaway?"

"The Mojave Desert." A smile lit up his face. "We can set up a tent and cuddle in the cool night air."

"Why the desert?"

He leaned in and pecked her on the lips. "I'm tired of this damn water."

CHAPTER 40

In Fort Lauderdale, Diane finally reached Uncle Bo on the phone.

"Well, if it ain't Miss Know-Noth—"

"Are you okay? How come you haven't returned my texts or calls?"

"I answered your first twenty texts. I'm as healthy as a horse." He paused, then asked, "What'd you find?"

"A predator chowing down on red algae. Blue copepods."

"That's great, but I thought Cocoa Puffs were brown." Bo let out a playful laugh that turned into a coughing fit.

"Geez! You need to leave right now," Diane demanded.

He waited a few seconds before responding. "Before you go off on a tangent, I have bad news. I bumped into the table, and the jar holding the preservative fell on the ground. Everything spilled out. I have a container full of red algae, but no way to preserve it."

"It's not like you to run into things. Appreciate your help, but please stop, go back to Atlanta, and see a doctor."

"I've been helping the last of our neighbors move." Bo chuckled. "Someone needs to tell them to wear deodorant on packing day. Shoo-wee. I could smell it through the respirator."

Diane tried suppressing the anger in her voice. "You're going to end up in the hospital."

"I'm wearin' the mask, changin' cartridge filters like you told me. Got plenty of bottled water." He paused, clearing his throat. "Feel bad for them. They finally found a place to rent in Missouri on Vrbo, then the damn property owner canceled their booking a day ago, saying they asked too many questions. Ain't that a kick in the—"

"Please leave."

"I'm gonna stay and help them. Can't imagine packin' up and leavin' with no place to go. I'll head out in a day or two."

She knew her uncle would not refuse people who asked for help. "I'm going to hold you to that. I'll talk to you soon."

"Okay, goodb—" He began coughing and hung up.

She closed her eyes and took a deep breath. *How can I get the analyses done to appease Jenson and get back to Uncle Bo sooner than a few days?*

She needed to record the results from the shed experiment. If the River 10 dino morphed into the species with the thick armor, then the treated water contained enough chemical to cause the mutation. She would send the treated water sample she'd hidden in the lab to Yan, who would determine the amount of reduction fluid released into the tributary. It was a perfect plan.

• • •

Diane returned to OSCF and began analyses of the purple water. She walked into the chamber and looked behind the yellow containers.

What?!

The sample of treated water was gone.

Tossing out the yellow flasks, her heart raced, her body shook. She searched every shelf and corner. She hurried out of the chamber and searched the lab, flinging open every cabinet and looking under tables. Her limbs trembled as she spun toward the lab door, opened it, and glanced down the hallway. No one was there.

She searched the chamber again.

Nothing.

She collapsed into a chair and grasped the sides of her head, trying to regain her thoughts.

Dead river dino culture, missing treated water sample. Accidents? No!

Nicole had said OSCF directors, biochemists, Landry, and Jenson had access to the chamber. Her labmates were unlikely suspects because they had been busy getting ready for the cruise. Brandon had been in the Gulf retrieving and repairing bots. She felt a powerful urge to drop everything and run back to her uncle.

I need help!

She recalled the email from Matt's family. Airports had been packed with people trying to escape the Gulf Coast and the Eastern Seaboard. She wondered if she could get an airline ticket, doubting her stamina to keep the Jeep operable from Florida to Kentucky. Besides, she was unsure if Matt's family had any inkling of what he knew regarding the bloom or the pilot plant. It seemed like a wild goose chase.

Diane worked into the night, analyzing the purple waters, and hoped the mysterious origin of the toxic bloom was in her family's shed, where a river dino swam in treated water from a pilot plant.

CHAPTER 41

Diane was glad to see Nicole return the next day. Her color had returned to normal. "I'm ready to grow some blueberry-colored copepods," she said with a big smile.

"Welcome back. Glad to see you're feeling better." Diane would wait until she was alone with Nicole to discuss the missing sample of treated water. She wondered if Nicole had told someone.

Their analyses of the purple water showed minimal to zero toxins.

Nicole checked on the number of blue copepods in her culture. "They're like the red dino, super easy to grow. And what an appetite these blue babies have! Devouring everything in the dish."

Diane exposed the blue copepods to seawater similar to the Gulf. "It's unbelievable. This organism does better in warm water than in cold water. Our cultures of it have grown exponentially in a short amount of time."

Nicole nodded. "It'll wipe out the bloom in no time."

The rapid growth and adjustment to environmental changes bothered Diane. The copepod's ability to thrive in a different location was likely related to where it came from, the cold blob. She said, "I think it has adapted to changes in salinity and temperature because it came from an environment where fresh water is mixed with salt water. Perhaps the slowed movement of water in that area affects temperature. They had to acclimate."

"How are they able to neutralize the toxins?"

"I don't know. Maybe Earth's last-ditch effort to bring balance?" She remembered Uncle Bo's words: "Mother Nature will rid herself of these vermin."

OSCF scientists visited the lab to watch the bioluminescence of the blue copepod and the red dino. After the copepod fed on the dino, an iridescent purple color was emitted from its round, transparent body. Even Jenson stopped by the lab. "I'm here to see the light show."

Diane set up the scope for him. He looked through the lens, grinning like a little kid, then glanced up at her. "Glad I decided to stay in the purple waters to take samples. I know we had some trouble at sea, but this . . ."—he pointed at the microscope—"is incredible. Scientists from academia who took part in the cruise are having great success growing it. We have a meeting to discuss releasing it in large quantities throughout the Gulf of Mexico and the Atlantic."

Diane's mouth dropped open. She knew the oceans were in terrible shape, but the blue copepod was an invasive species to southern waters. They belonged in the subarctic ocean.

Jenson, who must have noticed Diane's trepidation, moved toward her. "This is the greatest chance we have to make things right." His choice of words was interesting. No mention of why the bloom had occurred in the first place.

"The growth of this copepod in warm water is off the charts," Diane said, pointing to a cultured sample. "It'll take over."

"Yes," Jenson exclaimed. "It'll eat the algae in record time, and the waters will be clear. That's what we want. Fish and other animals will return. They'll have a feast of copepods."

"I suppose," she said, drawing out the phrase and shrugging. "What harm could an invasive organism inflict on an ecosystem that's already destroyed?"

Releasing massive numbers of the subarctic copepod into warm Gulf waters that would incur exponential growth of the organism felt wrong, but she couldn't argue with him.

That evening, Diane called to check on Uncle Bo. His cough sounded worse, and he had not returned to Atlanta. She'd had enough of his refusals to leave and planned to tell Jenson she needed to return to her Gulf home.

• • •

The next morning, OSCF physical oceanographers showed a satellite image of the Gulf of Mexico taken at night. Breathtaking swirls and streaks of sparkling dinos were shown on a large screen. Bioluminescence from enormous populations of a resistant parasite revealed the Gulf's strongest currents and eddies. It reminded Diane of spiral galaxies, where stars followed circular patterns.

A scientist pointed at different places along the eddies and said, "Locations with the strongest water circulation have high concentrations of red dinoflagellates. We believe placing the copepods in these points along the currents will transport and increase the copepod population throughout the Gulf." The images reminded Diane of newsfeeds spotlighting the Gulf of Mexico as the "Gulf on Fire" with its far-reaching bright red waters and brilliant lights at night.

Jenson stood up. "OSCF, as well as academic and government institutions, have obtained funding and resources for releasing the copepods into the Gulf and into the Atlantic along the Eastern Seaboard. Our primary focus will be on culturing the copepods for release throughout the Gulf because it was the hardest hit." He pointed out Diane and Nicole in the audience. "Our bio-lab staff will participate on the Gulf cruise, which leaves in two days."

Diane had learned that Brandon and Todd were transporting bots to Canada and were scheduled to return that evening. She wanted to see Brandon but needed to get back to her uncle. Besides, she would get to spend time with Brandon on the cruise.

She strode up to Jenson. "Before the cruise leaves, I need to visit my family's home. You said I could go there after I completed my analyses."

"Be back soon," he said, studying his phone. "Ship departs in two days."

Diane found Nicole alone, walking to her car after work. After some small talk, Diane cleared her throat and asked, "You know the sample of treated water I hid in the walk-in?"

"Yeah, what about it?"

"It's gone. Someone took it."

Nicole stumbled a bit, then found her balance. "Someone probably mistook the bottle for an old, dated sample and threw it out. There could be other reasons besides someone sabotaging your work."

"It's possible the person who took the treated water from the plant is the same person who destroyed the River 10 dino culture."

Nicole scrunched her nose. "I can't imagine anyone at OSCF purposely destroying our work. It doesn't make sense."

"You were the only one I told about putting samples into the walk-in chamber. Did you mention it to anyone?"

"No. I didn't even tell my goldfish. Honestly, I think you're overreacting. I'm sure it's just a mistake. I can ask around."

"Don't do that."

"I'm so sorry, Diane." Nicole rested her hand on Diane's shoulder. "Would you like to come to my apartment? We'll order pizza and play Minecraft. Take your mind off things."

"Thanks. Maybe another time. I need to head back home."

After she'd left Nicole, Diane texted Yan. *No sample of treated water from the plant for your analysis. Had it. Now it's gone. Thanks anyway.*

Yan responded, *Did it grow legs and walk away?*

Diane stared at the text then answered, *Thrown out? On purpose? Accident? Don't know.*

A minute passed before Yan replied, *No mistakes. No coincidences. Be careful!*

Right now her focus was on getting to Uncle Bo and checking on the experiment in the shed. Figuring out who was interrupting her work would have to wait.

CHAPTER 42

Diane arrived home to find the shed door open. Uncle Bo had always closed it to keep out strays. "Uncle Bo!" She shouted through the respirator.

No response.

Inside the shed, the experimental container was on its side. Bright red contents were spilled on the table, dripping onto the floor.

Her heart raced. She threw off her respirator and screamed "Uncle Bo!"

She hurried through the shed. He was nowhere to be found. Sprinting to the house, she yelled out to him. She flung the door open and dashed from room to room.

And then she saw him, face down on the kitchen floor. "Uncle Bo, no! Wake up!" she cried, shaking his shoulders.

She turned him over, took off his respirator, and found his face covered in drool and vomit. She dialed 9-1-1.

"Nine-one-one, where is your emergency?"

Diane rambled off the address, her voice jittery. "We need an ambulance. My uncle is on the floor unconscious!"

"Due to the loss of staff, we have a limited number of teams ready to respond," the operator said in a subdued tone that infuriated Diane. "It could be an hour before we can send an ambulance."

Resisting the impulse to scream into the phone, she grabbed Bo under his arms and dragged him to the Jeep. Her body was wet from the sweltering heat and the physical strain of getting him into the vehicle. She blasted the AC and raced to the hospital.

Thirty minutes later, she came to a screeching halt in front of the ER and yelled at a passerby wearing green scrubs for help. Within seconds, a team of masked hospital workers was outside with a gurney. Bo was wheeled back to a room and lifted onto a table. Diane chewed her bottom lip as she watched a medical team in full-body protective gear work on him.

A physician asked her, "When did you last speak to him?"

Diane wrung her shaky hands, holding back tears. "On my way home. Around four hours ago."

The doctor jotted in his notebook as the team frantically worked on Bo. A tech handed the physician a chart. After perusing it, the doctor asked, "Was he wearing a respirator with a filter?"

"He had it on when I found him. He said he wore it all the time."

"Toxins are so thick around the Florida Panhandle. The point of entry could've been through the skin. High humidity can make dermal entry plausible. The only real protection is a full biohazard suit."

Her heart sank. "Will he be okay?"

The doctor made more notes. "There's a medication that works well with his level of contamination. It's difficult to get because of the high demand. We'll treat him with fluids and other methods. Try to stabilize him. The medication should arrive in one to two days."

"That could be too late!"

She moved toward her uncle, but the doctor stopped her. "Sorry, he is considered a biohazard."

Her mouth dropped open. "He's not radioactive. He's *sick*."

"He's contaminated. The neurotoxins in his system are extremely high."

Uncle Bo was placed back on the gurney and wheeled through a set of doors. Tears streamed down her face as she watched the physician head toward the same doors.

She called out after him, "I need to know. Will he recover?"

The physician turned, his shoulders slumped. "We're doing all we can."

Diane dropped into a chair and bawled. If she hadn't asked Bo for help, he'd be in Atlanta surrounded by family. She had been forced to make the toughest decision of her life: continue the search for answers and rescue the whole region from a terrible scourge or focus on the safety of the few family members she had in the entire world. Knowing the dangers and the possibility of death, she had left her uncle just as she had left the young woman on the ship. She sunk deeper into the chair, gazed down at the white floor, and wondered how cold and inhuman she had to be to succeed. How many other breakthroughs in science have required difficult choices and sacrifices?

She reached for her phone and called her mom. When Mom answered, Diane blurted out, "Listen—"

"I was thinking ab—"

"Uncle Bo's in the hospital." Diane gave her a rundown of what she knew.

"I'll be there as soon as I can," Mom said, sounding as scared as Diane felt.

Diane texted Jenson. *My uncle is in the ICU. Family needs me. I won't be going to the Gulf.* No longer caring about the bloom or if someone was working against her at OSCF, she turned off the phone ringer. In a few seconds, the phone vibrated, and the screen lit up. Jenson. She let it go to voicemail, but he didn't leave a message. After a brief moment, the screen illuminated again. Jenson had sent a text. She closed her eyes, took a deep breath, and read it. *I'll take your place on the ship. What hospital? Take care of your family.*

She blinked a few times and reread the text. Every time she had expected Jenson to terminate her from OSCF, he had reacted with understanding. A numbness found its way through her body as she read his words. The thought of abandoning her uncle again was unimaginable. She'd stay forever to ensure he received the best care. Minutes later, she responded, *Pensacola Baptist Hospital.*

When her mom arrived six hours later, Uncle Bo was on life support. Through the ICU window, mother and daughter watched the man who had constantly sacrificed his needs to meet theirs. Diane recalled as a child believing her uncle was the strongest, wisest man in the world. Now, connected to a machine and hanging tubes, he appeared small, frail, and helpless.

"This is my fault," Diane said in a raspy voice.

Mom wiped her eyes with a tissue and vehemently shook her head. "No. It's not."

Diane stared at her. "I was so consumed with finding the reason behind the oceans turning red that I put him in danger. I sacrificed Uncle Bo."

Shaking her head, Mom cried. "You didn't do this. I spoke to him and tried to get him to leave. He said you wanted him to leave."

Her body trembling, Diane dropped her chin to her chest and chewed her bottom lip.

Mom rubbed Diane's shoulder. "No one is to blame."

Diane looked up with watery eyes. "At sea, I found a very sick woman around my age. She wanted me to stay with her. I should've . . ." She glanced at the floor. "She died."

Mom tilted her head, studying her daughter. "You didn't know tha—"

"I knew she could've died," Diane snapped, stepping back from her mom. "Just like I knew leaving Uncle Bo at the house put him in danger."

Mom reached out to hug her. "No—"

Diane rushed toward the door leading out of the ICU and yelled, "Don't make me feel better! I don't deserve it!" Outside the ICU, Diane balled up onto a chair and sobbed into her folded arms. Mom found her and gently patted her back. Diane whimpered, "I'm sorry."

Mom squinted her tired eyes. "There's only one person you need forgiveness from."

Diane nodded. "Yeah, Uncle Bo."

Mom let out a heavy sigh. "You need to forgive yourself."

They stayed the night in the hospital, sleeping on chairs outside the ICU. In the middle of the night, Diane heard someone whispering. Mom was on her knees, elbows on a chair, hands folded in prayer position. Whatever her mom was asking for, Diane hoped she would receive quickly. The exhausted postdoc drifted back to sleep.

• • •

Diane and her mom were awakened by footsteps the next morning. They sprang up from their chairs, expecting to see the physician. It was Brandon, carrying a bouquet of yellow daffodils. "Got in late last night. Dr. Jenson said your uncle was here."

She glanced at her mom. "Mom, this is Brandon. We work together at OSCF."

Mom smiled at him. "You can call me Vera."

Brandon extended the flowers to Vera. "Sorry we're meeting under these circumstances. I hope he improves soon."

Mom took the flowers, thanked him, and moved a few feet away, dabbing her eyes with a tissue.

Brandon turned to Diane. "I'll be heading out to the Gulf tomorrow. I really wanted to see you before I left."

She grinned. "That's sweet, but you could've just called."

Brandon's face reddened. "I don't know how long the cruise will last. Calling and texting are so impersonal. I want to sit with you for a while."

Strange, but Diane just wanted to be alone with her suffering family. Maybe it was that her work had been destroyed by someone in the lab or that she had returned home to find Uncle Bo near death. She cared for Brandon but needed this time to herself. "We're okay. You should probably get back on the road."

"Well, um, I can—"

"If they work you like they did on the last cruise, you should head back. Rest before getting on the ship."

Fidgeting with his phone, Brandon glanced at Vera, then back at Diane. "I'm sorry. You're right. I should've called. Hope your uncle recovers soon." He hugged her lightly with one arm and nodded at Vera as he left.

Vera returned to her daughter's side. "A nice-looking man going out to sea tomorrow drives most of the night from Fort Lauderdale with flowers to see you and wish your uncle well. You literally tell him to hit the road. If Bo were awake, he'd say, 'Kid's got no lick a' sense.'"

"Unbelievable. I have to repeat what I say at the kitchen table, but I have a conversation with a guy halfway across the room and you hear everything," Diane said.

"Why were you cold to him?"

Diane sighed. "I just want to be alone. So much has happened."

Mom sat down and patted the chair next to her. "Tell me about it."

Diane took a slow, long breath and told her mom everything. She described events from the time Brandon jumped into the red water to save her, right up to sitting in the hospital. The destroyed river dinos, the missing sample of treated water from the pilot plant, and all her doubts.

She expected her mom to be upset that she hadn't shared her allergic reaction to the red water or that she had dangerously hung over a large pipe discharging water that was possibly hazardous. Instead, Mom walked into the ICU. Diane followed her. They looked through the window separating them from Bo.

Vera watched her brother, who was surrounded by large beeping machines. "As your mom, I want to say leave the job; it's not worth it. But if you're right, a danger continues to exist in the waters. Is there anyone else who could take this on? What about the EPA?"

"I think they're provided measurements from the state. I no longer have the samples of treated water from the plant. The experiment is done, so I don't have a mutated dinoflagellate as evidence. I have nothing other than destroyed dino cultures, a missing sample, and a hunch."

"Maybe in time OSCF could fix the process so the hazard no longer exists. But if your suspicions are true, they would get away with all this death and destruction—ruined oceans, tainted air and water. Are you okay walking away from that?"

"I don't know what else to do short of dredging the Mississippi hoping to find the exact resting cyst to grow the dino, then sneaking around again to get more treated water from the pilot plant and repeating the test." Diane took a ragged breath and dropped onto a nearby chair. "Besides, I want to stay here with Uncle Bo."

"If Bo knew everything you told me, what do you think he'd say?"

"Whoever's responsible should be tarred and feathered."

"There's nothing you can do here except worry. I'll let you know if his condition changes. Is there anyone who could help you?"

Diane rubbed her face and thought of Matt, who'd engineered the chemical process. "Maybe," she answered, remembering Matt's family and their open invitation. As her mother kept a worried eye on Bo, Diane searched on her phone for airline tickets to Louisville, Kentucky. Most airlines were sold out, but she found one ticket and quickly purchased it. "Thanks, Mom. You gave me an idea."

She kissed her mom on the cheek and emailed Matt's family. *Thanks again for the open invite. If it's okay, may I visit tomorrow*?

Minutes later, Carla Toft replied. *We'll be here.*

Uncle Bo had to get better. She didn't want to live without him and wondered if her mom could.

Returning to her Gulf home to pack, she replayed the look on Brandon's face when she told him to leave. Maybe she made a hasty reaction without taking his feelings into account. Perhaps she'd been too quick to cast doubt on OSCF. It didn't seem possible that someone had mistakenly cleaned out the bottles containing the treated water discharged from the pilot plant. Life would be easier if her misgivings could be dismissed as misunderstandings.

But who killed my river dinos?

While packing, she saw an envelope on her bed she hadn't noticed when she'd arrived. Inside was a check for one thousand dollars and a note. "Buy yourself a new radiator! Love, Uncle Bo."

The tears flowed down her cheeks under the respirator as she set the check and card on her nightstand. She reserved a hotel room in Akers, Kentucky, an hour's drive from Louisville. Her flight departed from Pensacola in two hours. It was a long shot and her last chance to discover what had created a parasite that caused the seas to bleed.

CHAPTER 43

Diane sat in a rental car outside of a one-story, white vinyl-sided house in Akers, Kentucky. A woman, probably in her fifties, maskless, shaded her eyes with one hand and had the other hand on her hip.

Diane felt awkward and took off her mask. She raised her hand as she stepped out of the car. “Hi, I’m Diane Nelson from OSCF. Are you Carla Toft?”

“Yes, I’m Matt’s mom. You’re the only one from that place that’s reached out to us.” Carla ran a hand over her short silver-gray hair. Her puffy eyes had tiny red streaks crowding out the white. Diane wasn’t sure if the redness of her eyes was from exposure to the toxin or from crying.

“I’m sorry about your loss,” Diane said. “I started at OSCF after Matt. Everyone says he was a great chemist.”

“He got his first chemistry set when he turned eleven.” The corners of her lips rose into a small grin. “Played with that thing forever. I loved watching him.” Her sad smile disappeared.

Diane wanted to hug the grieving mother and tell her it was okay to enjoy memories of her son.

“Fred, Matt’s dad, is out of town,” Carla said. “He’s a trucker. On a long haul this week.”

Behind their house, they had at least ten acres of land with cattle and a barn. The smell of cow manure was a relief compared to the stench of putrefaction on the coast.

Diane followed Carla into the house, which was warm and smelled like someone had been baking. She glanced at the bread-shaped mounds covered in aluminum foil on the kitchen counter and noticed a small boy, around eight or so, sitting at a little desk with flasks. He was pouring liquid from one beaker to another.

Carla said something about a church bake sale and stopped to motion at the boy. "That's Robby, Matt's nephew. Matt got him interested in chemistry." Carla leaned close to her and whispered, "Robby's autistic. Loved his Uncle Matt. During the police investigation, he started throwing things, violently rocking back and forth. We thought he'd hurt himself. He stayed with his dad until the investigation ended. My son, his dad, has a fiancée with no patience. Sent him back here as soon as possible."

Robby noticed Diane watching him. "What the hell are you looking at?"

Carla clapped her hands and blurted, "Language!" She set a pitcher of lemonade on the kitchen table and poured each of them a glass. "Robby doesn't acknowledge most people. He likes you."

Diane smiled, not sure what to say. "I was wondering if Matt shared anything about what he was working on at OSCF. Something about a wastewater treatment plant in Louisiana?"

Carla shook her head. "When he went off to Fort Lauderdale, we didn't see him much. I'd get a few short calls. He'd rush off the phone, saying he had to go somewhere or that he was busy." She stopped and gazed at Robby. "Every so often, he'd come and visit. Robby was always so happy to see him. They'd take nature walks and play with the chemistry set. After spending time with Robby, he'd . . ." Carla paused, took a drink of her lemonade. "He'd say he was busy and had to go back to Florida." Her voice trembled and took on a different tone. She was clearly fighting back tears. "We . . . never knew." She looked at Diane, her eyes watery. "He was kind. Never got into trouble. We have relatives I wouldn't be surprised if they got into a shoot-out with anyone. Matt wasn't that way. Something must've happened to him." The glass in

Carla's hands shook as she sat it down on the table. "He should've stayed close to home."

"I'm truly sorry for you and your family," Diane said, looking back at the boy, who glared at her. She quickly turned to Carla. "Did you get Matt's belongings?"

Carla led Diane to a room with an aquarium containing an orange starfish. "Matt got into starfish after a family trip to the beach. He kept this aquarium full of them. I don't know much about how to care for them. That's the last survivor." She pointed at four boxes in the corner. "That's what we got back of Matt's. I should go through his things. I just . . . don't know."

"Do you mind if I look?"

"Not at all. That's why I answered your email. The police said Matt attacked OSCF because he was fired. I feel like there's more to it."

"What else did the police say?"

"They constantly asked if he'd ever been diagnosed with a mental illness. He hadn't, and I told them so. Because I don't understand what Matt was working on, I'm hoping someone like you can make sense of it. I want to know what happened to my son."

Carla left her in the small, plain room with a poster of the periodic table hanging on the wall and a twin-sized bed covered with a baby blue quilt. The boxes contained mostly personal items, but she found a hard hat, yellow vest, ID badge to the wastewater treatment plant, and a laptop, which she could start without a password. Maybe the police had altered it for easy access.

Diane looked through the folders and found documents describing the review of new chemicals under the Toxic Substances Control Act. The reduction fluid had passed the ninety-day review at the wastewater plant. There were MSDSs and information on a National Pollutant Discharge Elimination System permit for pilot plants. Nothing about abnormal measures of treated water discharged from the facility, adverse environmental effects, or the toxic bloom.

She searched drawers, closets, and dresser tops. Nothing.

"Why are you in Matt's room?" Diane lurched in surprise and turned. Robby stood in the doorway, rocking from side to side.

"Just looking for information about his work."

Robby stopped swaying and squinted. "Matt and I used to go for walks along the cow paths. You wanna go?"

She surveyed the room and found nothing new to search.

He inched closer and whispered, "I know secrets."

Diane's eyes widened. She nodded, then followed him. On the way out, she passed Carla. "We're going on a nature walk."

Robby, already ten feet ahead, yelled back, "No, it's a walk on cow paths."

Carla shouted, "Don't be gone long."

Robby scampered along the narrow dirt trails, jumping in a zigzag over piles of cow manure. Diane kept up with him, though once she misstepped and came up with stinky greenish-black muck in the tread of her shoes. *Ugh, cow shit.*

Robby laughed while bounding toward a barbed wire fence. "Gotta watch those stink bombs." He plopped down on a spot of bare grass and started tunneling out a hole in the dirt with his hands. "We're at the secret spot."

Diane's phone vibrated with a text message from Brandon. She ignored it and sat down beside Robby. "What are you digging for?"

"Our boxes of secrets. It's fun. We put things in the box no one knows about. You can put your secrets in."

He handed her a dark metal container the size of a shoebox. Inside were notes from Robby's teachers and tests with failing grades. She removed a set of baseball cards and held them up.

"Those aren't secrets. I just like putting something in the box."

"Do your grandparents know about your secret spot?"

He shrugged. "Dunno." He pulled out another box and held it on his lap. "This is Matt's."

She guessed Robby had taken her there because she'd been searching Matt's room, wanting to know more about his uncle. "May I look at it?"

"These are Matt's secrets. He only shares with me." Robby started to rock back and forth. A teardrop fell, staining his dirty cheek. "No one shares anything with me. Not like Matt."

She reached out to comfort him, but he jerked away.

Recalling his fluid-filled beakers, she asked, "Did Matt show you the walking water experiment?"

Robby's rocking slowed. Shaking his head, his wet eyes got big.

After Diane described how to use food coloring, paper towels, and cups of water to create a walking rainbow, Robby grinned. He hesitated for a second, then handed her the box. "Matt would've liked you."

"Thanks, Robby."

He found a stick and poked it at the ground, walking along the fence line.

Diane opened the box and saw a USB stick and a schematic of the wastewater treatment plant. While Robby leaped after a frog, she shoved the flash drive into her pocket. Then she took pictures of the diagram marking locations of the treatment plant's detectors. Matt's detailed drawing of the pilot plant revealed that near the discharge pipe were sensors monitoring abnormalities in treated water before it entered the tributary.

A few minutes after he'd left, Robby got bored with the frog and returned to the secret spot. They buried the boxes and walked back to the house.

Diane found Carla and asked, "Okay if I take the hard hat, vest, and ID badge I found in Matt's things?"

"Why do you want them?"

"I suspect Matt might have discovered something important at a wastewater plant. His things may help me gain entry to it. I'm sure his access is gone, but I have nothing right now. Everything's worth a try."

"Yes, please take them."

"I enjoyed the memory you shared of Matt playing with his chemistry set as a kid. I wished I'd known him."

Carla's eyes started to water.

Robby stopped Diane in front of the door. "Will I see you again?"

"I hope so."

Robby was quiet but began to sway.

"We'll see each other again. When the oceans clear, you can visit me and my family on the Gulf."

Robby jumped up and down, looking back at Carla. "Yes, please. I've never been to the ocean."

Diane's childhood memories of the Gulf were beautiful waters free of poison and teeming with life. Would Robby ever get to experience the sea the way she had?

CHAPTER 44

Back at her hotel room, Diane read Brandon's text as she booted up her laptop. *Sorry for showing up at the hospital. Just wanted to be there for you.*

She couldn't deny that her heart beat a little faster with thoughts of him. His warm smile and the feel of his strong arms caused unfamiliar emotions of romance mixed with excitement. How could she be sure of anyone other than her family? She typed, *I'm sorry. I was upset about my uncle.*

Brandon responded. *I care for you. Thought you felt the same.*

I've been hurt in the past. My guard goes up. I think of you often. Have a good cruise.

Wish you were here. Still on for a desert trip?

Absolutely. Need to call Mom. Talk later.

Mom said that Bo's condition hadn't changed. They continued to wait for the medication used to treat high levels of toxicity. When she ended the call, she inserted the flash drive into her laptop. It contained a spreadsheet and two email chains from OSCF accounts between Matt and Landry. The first chain of emails occurred on February 22nd and 23rd.

> *Dr. Landry, to burn off residual from the reduction fluid we'd have to increase the temperature of the heating process. It's highly flammable and could cause an explosion. It can't be done. We need*

to let the state know the accurate measures of residuals in the treated water.

Matt, you know my husband has worked very hard to ensure OSCF reports the concentrations to the state. We do the measurements. All we need to do is tweak the process. Dr. Jenson is proud of your work. He has several buyers in another country interested in applying the new process to their wastewater treatment.

Dr. Landry, I hate to bring this up again, but I can't change the process. Preliminary tests showed larger organisms were not affected by trace amounts of the reduction fluid. The test failed to detect changes in unicellular organisms. I redid the test. The results showed abnormalities in freshwater microorganisms. This needs to end.

The second chain of emails occurred on March 5.
Dr. Landry, I've been trying to reach you. I tried tweaking the amount of reduction fluid in the system. The treated water continues to have high concentrations of fluid. A young girl died swimming in the river. I fear our process may be responsible for her death. I admit I was the one who tripped the plant's system. But why didn't the backup system work? Why were men sent out with barrels of reduction fluid to the river? What's going on there? The system at the plant has to stop. We can think of another way.

Matt, I've been busy. Never text me. Email me using my OSCF email address. The plant engineers were upset that the backup system didn't work. Idiots poured the fluid directly into raw sewage floating in the river. That company lost the contract rebid.
I don't know about a swimmer's death. What you did was wrong. Either get the process to work or reimburse OSCF and my husband for the costly clean-up. If anyone finds out it was you that caused that mess, you could end up in jail. I want to protect you. We should meet with Dr. Jenson.

Diane was shocked by the deception and ruthlessness of Landry's emails. She opened the spreadsheet. Matt had entered concentrations of reduction fluid left over in the treated water. If the measurement was too high, it was highlighted in yellow. From January 10 through May 20, every measurement exceeded standard levels.

Senator Landry had set up OSCF to regulate themselves by handing over measurements to the state. Todd had mentioned the senator had once worked for the EPA, but that didn't mean he had influence over the federal agency. She wondered why Matt hadn't reached out to them. Perhaps he didn't want to disappoint Landry, or he was afraid of going to prison.

She guessed Matt had buried his shameful secrets in a box, hoping someone else would find them. If he hadn't killed himself, then he could have confessed. The plant would have been shut down. Diane recalled the numerous bullet holes in the walls of the OSCF building. Matt's choice to take his own life and leave his nephew behind revealed the severity of his mental state.

Did Jenson know about the fraud?

Her last encounter with Jenson about OSCF's pilot plant causing the bloom hadn't gone well. She needed to find someone who could help her reveal the truth. Even if it meant losing her career, those who destroyed the ocean had to be brought to justice.

CHAPTER 45

Diane sat in an airline terminal the next morning, rummaging through her backpack. She pulled out a couple of business cards. One was from the police officer who had taken her witness statement the day of Matt's attack. The other was for the journalist, Isabelle Corzo. She knew reaching out to the police or the media would be a breach of the NDA and could cause her termination. Her first call was to the EPA's regional office. When a woman answered, Diane told her about the high chemical concentrations in the treated water measured at the pilot facility.

When the employee asked her name, Diane answered, "I'd like to remain anonymous."

"I've looked up state reports from the pilot plant. Treated water leaving the facility shows normal concentrations. The amounts of residuals listed are within limits. We can contact the state and confirm the measurements," the woman said.

Diane sighed. "That won't work. The state's receiving false data."

"We'd have to contact the plant. Our agents are bombarded with high alerts associated with toxic air and water. We'll try to get someone out there soon to do measurements."

Matt's schematic of the plant had shown the location of digital sensors monitoring water leaving the plant. "I could go to the plant and take pictures of the sensors monitoring the treated water. If the digital display on the monitors reveals illegal concentrations going into the tributary, what would be your response?"

She could hear the woman typing as she answered, "Our technicians would need to confirm the readings. We'd take steps to shut down the process and be forced to institute a backup system to clean wastewater."

Diane's voice rose to a high, angry pitch. "If I show this plant is discharging illegal amounts of hazardous chemicals into public waters, that information should be sent to the highest person in charge, and the plant should be shut down immediately."

The background sound of clicks on a keyboard stopped. "We are exercising due diligence for every emergency possible. Right now, most of the eastern U.S. has become an environmental hazard. I understand your concern, and we will address it."

Though EPA and other federal agencies were overwhelmed with public health emergencies related to the bloom, the employee's lack of urgency when people and animals continued to die was mind-numbing. The river was full of unicellular organisms. The reduction fluid could trigger mutations in them, too.

Diane went to the ticket counter, changed her destination to New Orleans, and reserved a rental car. Usually, she'd call the police to report someone breaking the law, but her instincts said to reach out to a journalist. Isabelle had blamed the toxic bloom for her grandmother's death and was eager for information.

She dialed Isabelle's number. A woman answered after the first ring. "Isabelle Corzo here."

"Hello, Ms. Corzo. My name is Diane Nelson. We met at OSCF the day after the attack."

"I remember you," Corzo said in a curious tone.

Diane hesitated for a second. "You wanted to know what started the bloom."

Isabelle shushed someone in the background. "Yes."

"I discovered emails between Matt Toft and Susan Landry. It seems Dr. Landry and her husband falsified data to the state about chemicals measured in the water coming out of OSCF's pilot plant. I have files that show this."

Isabelle's Cuban accent was more pronounced as she spoke in a rush. "Could you email the files to me?"

"Absolutely. I believe the experimental agents released in the treated water are responsible for the anomaly causing the bloom."

Diane could hear Isabelle clicking on computer keys, and she wondered if she'd done the right thing. "I wasn't sure if I should report this to the police since they're investigating the attack or—"

"No, no," Isabelle sputtered. "We've heard the Louisiana police are primed not to believe anything against the Landrys."

"Just got off the phone with EPA. A woman there basically said they'll get around to it."

"A person on our staff has contacts inside EPA. I'll call him immediately."

"I'm going to fly to the plant today and use Matt's old ID. Maybe I can get pictures of the sensors showing concentrations of chemicals in the discharge."

"How did you get his ID and the files?"

"Flew to Kentucky and visited his family."

"Wow. Maybe you should be an investigative reporter."

"I may need a job after this."

"I'm going to contact the Clean-It-Up environmental group. They have an amazing team of legal eagles who'll help you navigate those waters. I'm glad you called. Anything you learn, Diane, you send to me. We'll get the truth out."

"Thank you."

"The day of the attack when I first saw you, I knew you were a fearless woman."

"If I'm so brave, why am I scared shitless?"

Isabelle laughed. "Because you're smart. Please call or text me as soon as you leave the plant."

They said goodbye. Diane watched the TV in the airline terminal show Florida's Lake Okeechobee covered with floating remains of fish, alligators, and turtles. Other pictures showed empty streets near waterways choked with rotting masses of dead frogs and snakes, attracting vast amounts of flies. Most buildings were vacant along the Gulf Coast and the Eastern Seaboard. It was horrifying to witness the destruction of an entire coastline.

The reporters switched to Jenson in a yellow hazmat suit, his mask dangling from the portable breather. The ship was close enough for the network to send out a drone that displayed images of the purple seawater.

Jenson was back on the screen. "We've introduced a subarctic copepod that can consume the red algae while neutralizing the toxins. We believe the oceans will be free of the bloom after the purple waters have cleared. It's difficult to know how long the toxins will remain in the environment. It may take years for marine life to return."

She looked around the terminal and envied people watching the news with horrified expressions, because they knew only what was presented on TV or online. It was maddening to know what had caused the toxic bloom yet have no influence to stop it. Jenson was a powerful force. People listened to him. Thoughts of sharing the flash drive with him stayed with her. The secret email had mentioned how he was planning to sell the process to another country, but that didn't mean he was part of the deal to falsify data. Todd had said Landry obeyed Jenson. Nicole had mentioned Matt's meeting with Jenson and Landry. Jenson might have already known that his plant was poisoning the water. She decided not to share the contents of the flash drive with him. The realization that she had the daunting task of linking OSCF's pilot plant to the fatal bloom was truly terrifying.

• • •

A group of second-shift workers stood at the gate when Diane arrived at the pilot plant in Louisiana. She put on Matt's hard hat, vest, full-face respirator, and badge. As the gate to the facility opened, she merged with the group and slid past the guard station. No one seemed to notice her making a beeline for the locked gate leading to the discharge pipes. Matt's badge might no longer provide access to secured areas, but sometimes it took a while for permissions to disappear.

She ran Matt's badge through the scanner. Nothing happened. Maybe it was like those hotel key cards, where it took a couple of tries to gain entry. Her limbs trembled and her face perspired. The sweltering summer heat mixed with anxiety caused her to double over for a second.

Forcing herself upright, she scanned the badge twice. Beads of sweat rolled into her eyes. She removed her respirator to get a closer look at the badge strip and the scanner, then tried a few more times. After wiping her forehead with the back of her sleeve, she slid the respirator over her face.

Now what?

A person in bulky protective gear walked up to her, and a man's voice boomed from behind the mask. "Having problems?"

"Oh, no, I'm fine. I can do this later."

She tried to leave, but the man in the bulky suit grabbed her shoulder. "Aren't you the OSCF scientist who took a tour of the plant not too long ago?"

Taking off her respirator had been a mistake.

CHAPTER 46

The bulky-suited man and Diane stared at each other beside the steel gated entry to the discharge pipes. He moved closer and leaned in to view her badge. "I knew Matt Toft when he came around here. You don't look like him. And he's dead." His voice sounded older than Diane, but not as old as Uncle Bo.

Her heart pounded as a drop of perspiration ran down her forehead.

"Don't worry," he said. "I won't tell anyone. You should be more careful. I saw your face. You have the same expression Matt had before he tripped the system."

"You were here? The lead operator said none of the workers returned."

"Don't believe everything you hear. I'll never understand why Matt didn't set fire to the system. Sensors would've detected too much heat. Screens would've come down, and the backup process would've started."

He spoke to her so easily. She couldn't make out his facial features behind the hood's thick mask. His ID badge hung with the name CHET way below his hood. No last name.

"Did we meet during the tour?" she asked.

"No. I was heading to the warehouse to move fluid." He gestured toward the area where the underground compartments held reduction fluid. "You were over there with the lead operator."

"I'm sorry, who are you?"

"Just another hard hat who moves flammable fluid from one place to another."

Walk away! "Well, I should be—"

"Look, I hate this place. It's a paycheck. I knew Matt. He told me about the chemicals in the treated water."

Diane was nervous, but she was also intrigued.

He motioned southward. "I live in a shabby apartment about nine miles downstream. Every other weekend, my thirteen-year-old daughter would visit. She loved to jump in the river and swim—even when it was freezing. Months ago, right before the heavy floods began, she jumped into the river and a few hours later complained that her head hurt." His voice broke, and he stopped talking for a few seconds, his facial expression hidden. Diane waited.

"I figured she was getting a cold from swimming," he said, his words forced. "Later, she developed a fever. I took her to the doctor's office, where she passed out. They admitted her to the hospital. No one knew what was wrong with her."

He looked up, his hood tilting upward. "Next day, she died," he said quietly before staring at Diane. "Autopsy showed she died from a brain-eating amoeba. Doctors said it was a freak occurrence because this amoeba wasn't like the ones they usually see. When I returned to work, Matt told me about the high levels of reduction fluid in the treated water. He actually said that he'd done tests showing the chemicals discharged from this damn process could alter the DNA of an amoeba." Chet breathed heavily behind his mask. "All I could see was a man who poisoned the waters. He killed my little girl!"

He stopped for a second and turned toward the main building. "All I had left was rage. I punched him. The next day he tripped the system."

Diane recalled Matt's email linking a young swimmer's death to the pilot process. Landry's response had been apathetic.

Chet kicked at the ground. "I called everyone: my boss, the state, the feds. Everyone said the treated waters were clean, plant was meeting the standards."

Surprised he hadn't been fired, she asked, "Why are you still here?"

"Nowhere to go. I have no one. No purpose. Then I see you. That look on your face as you kept working with the badge. It reminded me of Matt on the day he tripped the system. You both have a faraway determination as if you're on a mission."

Diane studied his hood, wishing she could see his face.

Chet pointed to four surveillance cameras mounted at different angles on the main building. "I know the security guard in charge of those. You see that green light on the cameras? When it stops blinking, it's no longer recording."

She couldn't believe he was giving her advice. "Do you have a badge that works?"

He laughed, causing his suit to shake. "Not to that gate. That's only for important people."

His advice was helpful, but she still couldn't get to the sensor near the treated water.

She scanned the grounds and noticed they were alone. "Where is everyone?"

"Mandatory meeting. I'm heading there, but first I'll visit my buddy in the security guard station. Don't forget. no blinking, no recording." He turned to walk away and said, "I'd like to put a match to it. Set it all on fire."

She watched Chet disappear into the main building.

The cameras were blinking.

She investigated the gate. It was too high to climb. The perimeter of the gate extended into the woods, leading down to the tributary. She followed the path along the metal fence, stopping when her phone beeped twice. Texts from Brandon and Nicole.

Quickly, she glanced at the phone to clear the messages and noticed she had missed a call from her mom. No voicemail. Diane called her back immediately.

Mom was weepy; her words were incoherent. Diane trembled, her stomach a tight knot. Her words tumbled out. "What's wrong? How's Uncle Bo?"

Her mom sobbed and cried out the words while gasping for breath. "He's having convulsions. Shaking uncontrollably. He may not make it. You need to get back!" Mom's cries turned to a shrill scream. And then the line went dead.

Diane slumped to the ground, her stomach churning, her head throbbing. She rocked back and forth on her knees and sobbed. *I shouldn't have left him!*

Feeling unsteady, she got to her feet and wobbled to the front of the warehouse containing the shiny barrels of reduction fluid. Underneath her were lines that fed the reduction fluid to the compartments. She stared at the warehouse.

Uncle Bo could die.

It was her fault.

Nothing mattered anymore.

She looked up at the main building. The camera lights had stopped blinking.

Rummaging through her backpack, she found her first aid kit with a small container of rubbing alcohol, a piece of paper, and the Dolphin Bar & Grill matchbook. After dousing the paper with alcohol, she looked toward the trees and spotted those with the largest trunks.

She looked again at the cameras. No blinking.

Her heart pounded, her face was wet under the mask, and perspiration soaked her body. She crept closer to the large warehouse door. The chemicals were highly combustible. Things could go wrong quickly.

Like throwing gasoline on a bonfire.

Looking back a final time at the trees, she scanned the surroundings. No one.

Diane bent down and spotted a barrel on the other side of the warehouse door. It was close enough to touch. She placed the wet paper in the space under the door next to the barrel and lit the match with trembling hands.

The unsteady spark grew to flames, consuming the barrel inside the warehouse.

She sprinted toward the largest trees, not stopping until her feet left the ground, landing her face down in a ditch.

Boom!

Her eardrums felt as if they'd burst. A wave of tremendous heat and wind swept through the trees. The hanging limbs above her were on fire. The warehouse and the grounds holding the compartment chambers were engulfed in orange fire and billowing grayish-black smoke.

Sounds were muffled as she raced through the trees toward the tributary, feeling a tremor underground. When she was a few feet from reaching the water, her eyes widened in shock at what she'd done. The enormous blast had rendered the plant inoperative. Gallons of raw sewage spilled into the water, like a bacteria-filled waterfall. A dark brown sludge headed toward the Mississippi River.

Employees ran out of the main building, shouting. "Fire!" "Call 9-1-1!" "What happened?!" They stayed near the main building. Most of the smaller buildings were spared from the blast, though some closer to the warehouse burned. The scorching black smoke curled toward a sky filled with toxins.

Diane headed toward the gate and glanced up at the cameras. No blinking.

She jumped into her Jeep and sped away. In the distance were muted echoes of sirens. She wasn't sure if the sounds were real or imagined.

Was Chet outside watching the flames with his mouth gaping? Or was he on the phone with the police describing an OSCF employee who'd just blown up the plant? OSCF was responsible for the plant, the chemicals in the river, and his daughter's death.

If the police were going to arrest her, they'd have to follow her to a tiny brick house near a rotting coast many hours away.

• • •

Diane thought of going to the hospital when she reached her Gulf home. She wanted to see Uncle Bo. *How would Mom feel if the police arrived to arrest me?*

Her legs trembled as she stumbled out of the Jeep. She dragged herself to her front porch, leaving behind her respirator. Her ears rang so loudly, she couldn't depend on them to hear approaching sirens. She plopped down on a step and watched for police cars.

She thought about Uncle Bo. Knowing she had killed the only light she'd ever known would make living unbearable. It would be better to be behind bars and wallow in shame than to be out in the world with constant reminders. She took a deep breath of thick toxic air, then laid her head in her lap.

Warm fur rubbed against her legs. A loud insistent meow. *Wily!* She gazed into the cat's amber eyes. *You're alive.* The cat meowed loudly and continued to rub against her. She petted his orange fur and expected tears, but none came. Every fiber in her body felt numb. Her brain couldn't even process grief.

The cat found a comfortable place on her lap and stayed with her for the longest time. Eventually, he jumped down and ran into the crawl space under the shed. She followed him to the hollowed-out entrance covered with respirator filters and a hole big enough for Wily to enter. The cat drank from a water bowl being filled by a tube of water coming from inside the shed, where a series of large, enclosed containers continually fed a line of bottled water that filled several bowls. Her mom's large oval porcelain platter was filled with dry cat food.

Her phone beeped with a text from Mom. *Bo's convulsions have stopped. He's stable for now.*

Diane almost collapsed with relief. After a moment, she exhaled slowly and went inside. The check and card from her uncle were on the nightstand. She recalled news reports that showed people shooting, fighting, and stealing as an increasingly toxic environment made them sick and drove them away from their homes and livelihood. Then she imagined Uncle Bo helping neighbors move heavy furniture. She envisioned him walking in and out of the shed, surrounded by poisonous air, sweating in the heat from the sun and the respirator, setting up a haven with clean water and food for a stray cat.

The teardrops came and didn't stop until she had nothing left but an empty ache in her heart.

CHAPTER 47

Diane was jarred awake by banging at the front door and someone shouting her name. She pulled the covers over her head, terrified the police had come to arrest her.

They can break in.

More banging. Then a woman's voice yelled, "It's Dr. Bennett!"

Diane thought her director was still recovering in New York. She got out of bed and discovered Bennett standing outside. Bennett's color had returned, but the dark circles under her eyes remained. "I heard about your uncle," Bennett said, walking inside. "Brandon and Nicole have been trying to reach you since yesterday. I left OSCF this morning to make sure you're okay."

Definitely not okay.

Bennett furrowed her brow. "How's your uncle?"

Diane rubbed her temples. "He's in awful shape. On life support in the ICU."

"I'm so sorry to hear that."

"Thought you were in New York."

"I returned to work yesterday. I can drive you to the hospital."

Diane wasn't ready to face her family. Her shame and guilt were too overwhelming. Deafening sounds of the blast and Chet's raw, anguished description of his daughter's death stayed with her. Chet had been unaware of the threat to his daughter. But Diane had knowingly left her uncle in danger, and believed she deserved punishment. Total blackness consumed her like a gloomy warehouse full of combustibles and dark secrets ready to burst.

Brandon's mom had said Bennett was trustworthy. "She's good people." Not knowing what else to do, and no longer caring what happened to her, Diane blurted out what she'd done. "I blew up OSCF's warehouse of reduction fluid!" She took a deep breath and continued. "Some small buildings caught on fire. Everyone was supposed to be in the main building."

Bennett's eyes widened; her mouth gaped. She wobbled a bit while sitting down on the couch and muttered, "No one was hurt."

Diane plopped down beside her. "The blast destroyed the plant's function," she said flatly. "The Mississippi River is flooded with millions of gallons of raw sewage."

Bennett exhaled, burying her face in her hands. After a moment, she dropped her hands, and turned to Diane, her voice was unsteady, increasing in pitch. "Why would you do that?"

Diane began describing the emails between Landry and Matt, and Bennett held up a hand to stop her. The director's mouth hung open, her head moving slowly from side to side. Bennett sounded bewildered. "He did lab tests on macro and microorganisms." Her posture slumped. "How did I miss that?"

Diane had noticed Bennett distracted by her work in the lab. "Maybe you were preoccupied?"

Bennett rubbed her forehead and muttered, "Everything you're telling me . . . it's doesn't sound like Dr. Landry."

While Diane described the plant and the man who'd lost his daughter, Bennett continued shaking her head, blanching. Once, Bennett opened her mouth to say something. Diane waited a moment, giving her a chance to talk. But the director said nothing, so Diane continued. "When I heard Uncle Bo's condition had worsened, I just . . . snapped."

Bennett remained silent, her gaze unfocused. Finally she said, "I think we should go to the hospital. You need to be with your family."

"I trespassed and destroyed property. Isn't someone going to arrest me?."

"If there's evidence or a witness, yes. But from what you told me about the plant worker helping you, it doesn't sound likely."

"Aren't *you* going to turn me in?"

"Why? It's likely the plant's reduction fluid triggered the red dino to mutate and cause this global disaster. I say abolish that new technology. For good. Why should you have to pay the price for making things right?"

"But . . . what about the raw sewage in the river?"

"The explosion received a lot of media coverage. EPA is on the scene to work with the state on remediation. There's already talk that the plant will be rebuilt as a traditional facility."

Could this be happening? Will I really get away with it?

Diane slumped onto the sofa, relieved. "EPA's sampling waters in and around the facility?"

"Yes. Everyone's been trying to reach both Senator and Dr. Landry. She's OSCF's primary point of contact for the pilot plant. The Senator has been working with the state watershed management organization. EPA's communicating with Dr. Jenson."

"How badly is he taking all this?"

Bennett's eyes widened. "He hit the roof. Pulled a cabinet off the wall and smashed everything inside." She paused, rubbing her forehead. "I've never seen him so furious. Then he just sort of collapsed."

Diane didn't like the idea of a devastated Jenson. OSCF's secrets exposed worldwide could send him over the edge. She struggled to know if she was doing the right thing. If she'd gone this far with telling Bennett what she knew, then might as well let her know about working with a journalist. "There's something else. I met someone from a major newspaper who's interested in what I know." She squared her shoulders and continued. "It's important to show what caused the bloom."

Bennett blinked hard. "Shit. OSCF being responsible for the bloom will make a juicy headline. *Sun Sentinel*?"

"*Miami Herald*. The reporter has connections with the Clean-It-Up group and mentioned they had a strong legal team. I wonder if they can help me."

Bennett appeared to be mulling over Diane's interaction with a reporter. "Well, I think you should seek legal advice. You should share this with your family. Prepare them for the worst."

Mom's going to freak out! "I don't think the plant worker will turn me in."

Bennett rubbed the back of her neck. "Before your discovery in the shed, there was no talk about a mutation. Many, including me, believed the unusual dino was a new species unearthed by the floods, brought to life by runoffs exacerbated by the spring floods. We believed its abnormal outer shell was attributed to being a novel organism."

Bennett paused, taking a deep breath. "I didn't know about the accidental spill Matt caused. It makes sense the Landrys didn't want EPA or anyone else in those waters doing the cleanup. They knew the waters carried illegal concentrations of chemicals from the process."

Bennett's somber demeanor changed when she flashed a tired smile at Diane. "Dr. Jenson told me about your fresh-water-to-salt-water theory. You followed the problem of the toxic bloom back to a wastewater treatment plant. Impressive."

Diane shrugged. "Just followed my gut." She glanced down at her phone and saw a missed call from Isabelle. "You've had a long drive. Would you like something to eat or drink?"

"Do you have bottled water? The government has sent more tankers, but their water tastes weird."

Diane smiled. "We have cases of bottled water. I'll grab you some."

As soon as she reached the back room, she texted Isabelle. *Wasn't able to get evidence from the sensors. Plant explosion.*

Saw the news. Glad you're okay! The Clean-It-Up group has your info. I'll send their email and number. We're getting tomorrow's front-page cover! Reports on what you (anonymous OSCF insider) found.

Thanks, Isabelle. Returning to OSCF. Have to figure out who destroyed my work and is responsible for this disaster.

Keep me posted. Be careful!

Diane tucked her phone in her pocket, grabbed two bottled waters, and rejoined Bennett.

"Thanks," Bennett said, taking the bottles. "Let's get you to the hospital. You need to be with your family."

• • •

Diane dropped off her rental car, then rode with Bennett to the Pensacola Baptist Hospital in silence until Bennett finally spoke. "I knew Matt was working on a process to treat waste with no emissions. I had no idea about Senator Landry's involvement." After a few minutes of staring at the road, Bennett continued, "I don't understand why the police didn't locate the emails you found. There should be a digital trail. If anyone could get those emails, it would be Brandon."

Diane leaned forward, eyes widening. "That's not a good idea."

"You got only a couple of emails Matt saved. If Brandon could retrieve every email originating from the server, imagine the information we could get. Probably texts too."

Diane didn't like the idea of involving Brandon. "Dr. Landry told Matt to communicate using only OSCF's email. Why not use a third-party computer company to hack into the accounts?"

"That would need approval for acquisition of funds. I doubt the cofounders would sign off. My pockets don't go that deep."

Diane closed her eyes and sighed.

As she turned onto the main highway, Bennett shook her head. "The sad thing is I heard Dr. Landry's presentation on the experimental process. It was impressive, and if successful, OSCF would receive unlimited accolades for reducing greenhouse gas emissions . . . that in addition to providing a cleaner, easier way to sanitize wastewater. All of that translates to substantial funding from the government and donors. It had the support of Dr. Jenson, an exceptional scientist." Bennett paused and in an airy voice mumbled, "How could he have gone so far astray?"

Diane turned to Bennett. “You think Dr. Jenson knew everything?”

Bennett frowned and shrugged. The light from the windshield accentuated the discoloration of the puffiness under her eyes.

“Are feeling you okay?” Diane asked.

“Honestly, I’ve been burdened by Matt’s death.” Bennett took a deep breath. “As I’ve gotten older, somehow I’ve lost the will to fight.” She turned her head toward Diane and gave a sad smile. “I’m glad you’re a fighter. You’ve given me the motivation to stand up for what’s right. Even if it means losing everything.”

She wondered what Bennett, an esteemed scientist, meant by “losing everything.” Did it have something to do with the bloom? With Matt? Whatever it was, she was relieved that Bennett had shown up. She felt better, off-loading her problems to someone who understands the science, an OSCF insider who could watch out for her. “Thanks for listening and not turning me in.”

Bennett smiled, shaking her head. “On behalf of every creature great and small, I thank you for blasting that plant to hell, where it belongs.”

CHAPTER 48

Diane, fearing bad news, remained in the car parked in the hospital garage even as Bennett got out and motioned for her to follow. After a moment, Diane lowered her head and exited the car, then trudged through the hospital's sliding door entrance.

Once inside, they suited up to enter her uncle's ICU room. Mom sat near Uncle Bo, who was sitting up, still attached to tubes and monitors.

"The medication arrived late yesterday," the physician said, studying his notes. "Toxin levels have decreased, organ functions are normal, but recovery will be long. We've prescribed breathing treatments and supplementary oxygen along with his medication."

A cry escaped Diane as she rushed to her uncle and hugged him. "I'm so sorry, Uncle Bo," she said, sobbing.

The skin around his gray eyes sagged. He'd been a young fifty, and now he looked like an old man. Still, he grinned under the mask. Between breaths, he said, "Have . . . a joke . . . for you."

She shook her head and wiped away her tears. "You need to relax."

"Diatom asked dino . . . how business goin'? Dino says, 'It's really bloomin.'" He wanted to make her happy even though he was lying in the ICU.

She hugged him again and overheard Bennett introduce herself to Mom. Diane spun around. "Dr. Bennett, this is my Uncle Bo. Greatest man on Earth."

Bennett smiled a lot during the visit. She'd always seemed irritable and distracted at OSCF. Diane realized her responsibilities to maintain a lab of type A personalities and answering the demands of headstrong cofounders were enough to make anyone prickly.

Though Diane didn't want to leave her uncle, the medical staff insisted he needed rest. He was given more medication and was soon asleep.

As they walked out of the hospital, Bennett turned to Diane. "You need to take a few weeks off to help your family. Talk to your mom about reaching out to the environmental group's legal team."

Diane worried about Bennett, who stumbled a bit toward the car. Perhaps all of this was too much for a career scientist who had become accustomed to predictability. Bennett winced. "Sorry, I'm lost in thought of how anyone could think they could get away with spewing chemicals into a river. Eventually, it would kill off fish and amphibians. Their lies would've surfaced."

"The problem is the residual was too low to affect sexually reproductive animals like fish and frogs," said Diane. "In those animals, a gene could mutate in one parent, but most of the time, the good gene can be inherited from the other parent."

Bennett nodded. "Most mutations are recessive."

"But for asexual organisms like the red dino, dividing at a very high frequency, the mutated gene is copied and passed on to a large population of new cells. That's what Matt observed and told Dr. Landry. Either she didn't think the effect on a unicellular organism was a big deal or she didn't care."

"Sounds like they planned to keep the treatment plant going as an experimental facility until they came up with a way to reduce the residual. Who knows how long that would've taken?" Bennett stared at an empty space in the parking lot. "What happened to the shark? The one covered with algae and caught in a buoy line."

Diane remembered the bull shark thrashing in the red Atlantic. She lowered her eyes. "We cut it free; then it sank."

Bennett's eyes closed for a moment. "We'll work closely with government and academia to ensure the copepods eliminate the red dinos." She stopped before unlocking the car door and said in a low, steady voice, "Whoever's responsible for this deserves to be strapped to a buoy in the middle of the ocean and visited by a bull shark."

CHAPTER 49

When Uncle Bo returned home, Diane and her mom prepared meals and took turns watching him. Both tried to convince him to return to Atlanta. He huffed, "I ain't goin' back there."

Mom tightened her respirator. "You're ridiculous. Staying here puts us all at risk."

Diane remained silent. They were in this mess because of her. Whatever made Bo happy was what she wanted.

Over the next few days, they helped Bo sponge-bathe with jugs of water from the government tanks and drove him to medical appointments. They gave him breathing treatments at home under a full-face ventilator, which was attached to portable tanks of oxygen.

One evening while Bo slept, Diane watched the news with her mom. The TV showed the charred remains of the wastewater plant's warehouse and a couple of buildings. Federal workers stood near the discharge pipes.

"We've found chemicals in the water exceeding standards," said an EPA spokeswoman. "We're working to confirm initial tests. In the meantime, we're interviewing people connected to the plant and OSCF."

The screen filled with Jenson's face. A reporter asked him about the *Miami Herald* report alleging OSCF's responsibility and a cover-up. His answer, as always, was, "We can't comment on an ongoing investigation. We're fully cooperating with the authorities."

The cameras turned toward streets where people held up signs demanding an investigation of OSCF. Picket lines of protestors marched outside the foundation's gate in Fort Lauderdale. An advocate from the Clean-It-Up group shouted through a bullhorn, "OSCF's reign of chaos is through! Dismantle now or we'll dismantle you!"

A reporter interviewed police at the wastewater treatment plant. An officer said, "Someone set fire to the warehouse, causing the explosion. We're examining evidence and reviewing surveillance footage."

Mom shook her head at the TV. "Isn't that the plant you think made the bloom?"

Diane glimpsed at the text Isabelle had sent with contact information for Clean-It-Up and then thought of Bennett encouraging her to share with her family what had occurred at the plant.

Better to let sparks fly now than wait for bigger fireworks.

Diane cleared her throat. "Yes." She bit her lower lip, took a deep breath, and stood up. "It was me! I set fire to the warehouse and caused the explosion."

Mom tore off her mask, mouth gaping, her eyes unblinking. "What?"

"I set fire to—"

"Hush!" Mom's eyes darted around the room, then back to Diane. "Why?"

"I called the EPA. They were too busy to listen to me. I was trying to get pictures of the sensors that monitor the treated waters to send to them." She sat next to Mom. "That's when you called about Uncle Bo having convulsions, and you weren't sure if he was going to make it. I . . . lost control, lit a match, and ran away."

"Diane Nelson, you could've killed yourself or someone else!" Mom marched across the room, then plopped down on the couch. She covered her face with her hands, just like what Bennett had done.

Slowly moving her hands away from her face, Mom scooted to the edge of the sofa. "Police mentioned surveillance footage. Did you see cameras? Did anyone see you set the fire?" She bit her thumbnail, and before Diane could respond, her mother continued. "You need an attorney. Your cousin knows that stuff. She can find one."

Diane wanted to tell her mom everything but hesitated. Mom noticed her restlessness. "Heaven help me, what else, Diane?"

"Well . . . I'm the anonymous source who gave evidence to the *Miami Herald*. The journalist advised me to contact the Clean-It-Up environmental group. I have their number. They want to help."

Mom's eyes widened. "You spoke to the newspaper? The environmental wackos know who you are?" She threw up her hands. "Please tell me that's it."

Diane grimaced. "I talked to a worker at the plant that day, but he helped me. His daughter died from another sort of mutation that the plant probably caused." She lowered her eyes and muttered, "I also told Dr. Bennett that I destroyed the plant."

Mom gaped as she rocked her head. She let out a yelp, looked up, then returned her focus to Diane. "Give me that group's number."

Diane wrote the information and handed it to her. Mom paced back and forth while staring at the piece of paper. "In the morning, I'll call these people, find out if they can help." She fell into a chair. "Good grief. I know you're passionate about your job, but whatever possessed you to . . .?" Mom's voice trailed off. She wrung her hands and got up to pace again as she muttered incoherently.

Mom's unusual ferocity reminded Diane of a time in middle school when she had gotten into trouble for standing up to a classroom bully. In "mama bear" mode, Mom had confronted the principal and unleashed a rage that Diane had never witnessed in her before.

Mom, still mumbling, put on her respirator, then strayed into another room. Diane went into the bedroom where Bo was sleeping. His breathing was more regular now. She rested next to him, watching the rise and fall of his chest.

Diane's labmates had texted twice, inquiring about Bo's health. Nicole and Todd had brought up the plant explosion. Diane had only mentioned hearing about it.

Not wanting to say the wrong thing under pressure, Diane had not responded to any of Brandon's messages. Finally, she texted him. *Sorry for not replying sooner. Been busy taking care of Uncle Bo. Heard about the plant explosion.*

After rereading the message a few times, she pressed send. A second later, her phone beeped. Diane shot up from the bed.

Not Brandon.

Bennett had emailed.

Hope your uncle's feeling better.

Good news: Bot measurements in the Gulf show high numbers of blue copepods and decreasing concentrations of red dinos.

Bad news: OSCF has scheduled a cruise to leave Tampa Bay in four days to assess conditions in the Gulf. You need to return to OSCF in two days. You'll be trained in an atmospheric containment dive suit. We'll talk about that "other thing" when you return.

Diane trusted Bennett. But returning to an organization she had exposed for corruption and criminal wrongdoing frightened her. She was resolute in holding OSCF accountable for the destruction of the environment, the deaths of countless animals and people, and the near loss of Uncle Bo.

CHAPTER 50

The next day, Mom kept re-organizing Bo's medications in a seven-day pill container as if looking for something to keep her busy. Her voice sounded less stressed. "I spoke to Amanda Johnson with that environmental group. Her firm will represent you for free. And guess what? She's a scientist too. Smart as a whip."

Diane wasn't surprised. Clean-It-Up had powerful lobbyists.

Behind the respirator, Mom took a long breath and exhaled. "Ms. Johnson's advice is for you to just hush." She handed Diane the piece of paper with Johnson's number. "If the police come around, we should call her immediately!"

The TV stayed on the news channel for updates about the plant explosion. When cars drove by, Mom was the first to the window. Whenever she spotted an automobile resembling a patrol car, she would repeat, "Oh my goodness," until the vehicle was gone.

Most of the broadcasts showed images of the bloodred waters with swirls of purple. A reporter wearing a bulky hood and standing in front of a high-rise condominium near a North Carolina beach announced, "Beach workers were removing animal carcasses when they discovered a horrible odor coming from Sea Breeze, a retirement community."

The camera panned to black body bags covering a road.

A beach worker pointed at the building and yelled through his thick mask. "Damn stench was the worst I'd ever smelled, even though this filter."

The reporter turned toward a federal Commissioned Corps officer. “We’ve discovered hundreds of dead people who either couldn’t or didn’t want to leave their homes. All died of toxicity.” She took a labored breath behind her mask. “We’ll need to incinerate their bodies. Buildings near the coast should be deep cleaned or demolished.”

Trying to divert her mind away from the nonstop tragedies, Diane was studying her résumé when Mom sat beside her. Mom’s eyes were swollen from lack of sleep. “What job are you applying for?”

“When colleges reopen, I’ll apply for a teaching position.” *Giving up my dream job . . . if I’m not in prison.*

“Great idea. I also have a good plan.” She gave Diane a tired smile. “Cousin Marnie reached out to Bo’s physician. They’re moving his prescriptions and therapies to Atlanta. I’ve convinced him to leave. You need to come with us.”

“You think the police can’t find me in Atlanta?”

“I finally convinced my hardheaded brother he needs to leave this death trap. We should stay together.”

Diane looked at her phone, wondering why Brandon hadn’t texted. “OSCF is going out to the Gulf. It’ll probably be my last cruise.”

“I’m worried about you returning to that place. What if they find out it was you who blew up the plant and tipped off the reporter?”

Though fearful, Diane put on a brave face. “I have a powerful advocacy group, an incredible lawyer, a newspaper—and a mama bear on my side.” Her thoughts kept returning to Brandon. “Also, I want to see my labmates for one last time.”

Mom tilted her head. “You wanna see that good-looking fella who brought flowers to the hospital.”

Diane offered a small smile. “I’d like to see him.”

“You should enjoy the feeling of romance and excitement. Heaven knows they don’t come often.”

• • •

Their cousins were driving down from Atlanta to pick up Mom and Bo the next day. Diane split her time between her uncle and cleaning the shed. The small River 10 container was packaged and labeled "Persistent Organic Pollutant" and sent to a hazardous waste site for incineration.

Marnie was severely allergic to cat dander, so Diane made sure Wily had plenty of bottled water. As she reached in to refill the platter with dry food, the cat rubbed against her arm. "That'll last you until I get back."

Inside the house, Bo was on the couch with a tray of his medications. "Wish you were coming to Atlanta instead of going back to the place with that ex-football player," he said. "I don't care for him."

She scrunched her nose, frowning. "Why?"

"When he was here, I saw how he looked at us."

"He just has a forceful presence."

Bo studied her for a moment. "We don't have the nicest place to live in, and we probably don't sound too smart. But we're honest, decent people. Your boss may smile and sound nice, but he looks down on us. I really don't care what he thinks of me. I worry about you."

"He's nice to me."

"I don't fret about miserable people who want others to be unhappy. Their backstabbing is expected. I fear those who are always ready to put on a big smile. If they decide to rip me apart, I might never see it comin'."

Who can be trusted? Jenson? My labmates?

Diane believed the real enemy was the cruelly manipulative cofounder—Landry.

CHAPTER 51

Seconds after entering the OSCF building, Landry saw Diane and motioned her to follow. Diane's muscles stiffened as she entered Landry's office and watched Landry close the door.

Diane's heart sank to her stomach. She sat across from Landry, who sat behind a mahogany desk in a dark leather wing-backed chair that swiveled. The cofounder's light auburn highlights fell in cascading waves around her flawless skin. Her curvaceous frame was clad in a pink silk blouse and a fitted skirt. Landry pointed to a newspaper on her desk. "The *Miami Herald* published an interesting article. What I call a lot of misinformation from a nameless, malicious coward. Know anything about it?"

Diane fidgeted, her eyes wide. "No."

Landry leaned across the desk, narrowing her perfectly dark-lined eyes. "The treatment plant shared surveillance of everyone on the grounds the day of the explosion. Shows a young woman at the gate to the discharge pipes. Before the blast, the footage shows her walking toward the warehouse. Know anything about that?"

Diane's heart raced. Realizing she'd look guilty drenched in sweat, she tried to slow her breathing. "No."

Landry kept her eyes on her. Diane's muscles tensed; her mouth felt dry. Amanda Johnson, her attorney, believed if the police had recognized her on the surveillance tape, they would have already arrested her. Because she'd bent to scan Matt's badge, maybe that had made it impossible for them to make an identification.

The cofounder folded her arms on the desk. "OSCF's pilot was exploratory with a lot of potential. Our work going up in flames has caused a major upset for the entire community." Her eyes narrowed. "If you destroyed our plant, I'll make sure you're thrown in jail."

Diane swallowed a lump in her throat but remained silent. Landry's tone grew menacing. "Do you have any common sense? Does growing up poor white trash make you stupid?"

Staring into Landry's cold eyes, Diane's heart throbbed. Her voice trembled, then became stronger with anger. "At least I'm not a heartless person manipulating others while riding the coattails of a great scientist."

Landry's scowl turned to a palpable hatred. Even the air in the room felt cold. She flew out of her chair, stomped around the desk, and loomed over Diane. "You're nothing but a redneck. Get out of my sight! You're fired!"

The cofounder's insults, her manipulation of Matt, and her lies about the water the plant had been discharging—they all fueled Diane's anger. Todd had said Landry did whatever Jenson wanted.

Diane stood, her fists clenched, and returned Landry's stony glare. "If that's what Dr. Jenson wants, then I'll leave. But if he wants me to stay, then you'd better keep out of my way."

If a person could turn into fire, Landry would have made the transformation and engulfed Diane. Baring her perfect teeth in a growl, Landry turned to her phone and punched in numbers. The cofounder stiffened her posture and looked at the door.

Seconds later, Jenson, followed by Bennett, walked into the office. Bennett stopped when she saw Diane, who struggled to remain calm.

Landry staggered like an injured animal toward Jenson. She sounded wounded. "I don't believe this woman meets our high standards. She insulted me. I want her gone now!"

A wide-eyed Bennett glanced at Diane, then turned to Landry. "I don't know what happened here. Dr. Nelson's one of the best biologists

I've seen during my years at OSCF. I can't find a person better suited for her position."

Jenson's lips tightened. He started to say something but stopped. He led Landry out of the office and glanced back at Bennett. "Stay here."

Bennett rushed to Diane. "What happened?"

In a low voice, she told Bennett that the plant had shared a video that showed a young woman at the gates leading to the discharge pipes. The same person had been recorded in front of the warehouse before the explosion. "Maybe she doesn't like me, but that's no reason to think I was the one who spoke to the reporter or blew up the plant. She's the murderer, and she insulted me. I retaliated."

Bennett sat close to Diane. "Have you told anyone else about the flash drive?"

"I told my mom."

Bennett looked at the ceiling and then back down. "Brandon, Matt, and Nicole knew about the river dino cultures because they worked in the shed. Jenson knew because of your report."

"You think one of them killed the river dinos?"

"I'm not sure. Did any of them know about the treated water sample?"

"Only Nicole."

Bennett rubbed her chin. "It's possible that someone went in there, thought they found some old or unknown samples and just threw them out, thinking they were unusable. We clean out the walk-in chambers when they get bogged down with stuff."

Both scientists were silent and still for a few seconds.

"Either Landry is a great sleuth or someone's helping her," Bennett whispered.

"Nicole said that other divisions have access to the walk-in chamber. Do you think someone in another lab could be involved?"

Bennett squinted. "I think it's someone in our lab. From this point forward, keep everything to yourself."

"You still want to ask Brandon about recovering emails?"

"He's the only one I know who can do it. What we learn from the emails may be enough to put Landry and her husband in jail." Bennett hesitated, looking at the door. "Maybe even Jenson. I'm not sure if I can figure a way to contract IT consulting without Jenson or Landry finding out."

"We can trust Brandon, right?" Diane asked, hoping Bennett would agree.

Bennett shrugged. "I can't imagine any person in the lab sabotaging work. Then again, I never suspected what Matt had been up to. Let's wait and see what comes out of the EPA investigation."

Jenson returned without Landry, then closed the door behind him. He walked behind the desk and stood with a commanding posture. His dark eyes focused on Diane. "Do you want to work here?"

She thought about the question. "I've always wanted to work here."

His body relaxed as he sat in Landry's chair. He observed her for a few seconds, then said, "You remind me of my younger self. I don't want to discourage your determination, but as the leader of a foundation, I need to know that you value our work and mission. That includes respecting Dr. Landry."

"I admire OSCF, but Dr. Landry verbally attacked me."

Jenson's face reddened; his eyes darkened. Was he upset that Landry had insulted her or that she had spoken out against his cofounder? He was slow to respond. "If you're in a situation at work you're not sure how to handle, come to me."

She nodded. Jenson studied her until Bennett broke the silence. "Diane is scheduled to train in the containment suit today. She'll be a great asset on the Gulf cruise."

Jenson was quiet. Perhaps he had changed his mind about her participation on the ship. "I'm looking forward to the cruise," Diane said enthusiastically. "See what we find." *Uncover backstabbers responsible for this tragedy.*

Bennett added, "I'd like to have her out there."

He grinned. "That's why she's here."

Bennett turned to Diane. "Most machinery becomes inoperable in the red waters, especially in the Gulf where the bloom is the thickest. We've lost most of our bots in the subarctic. We're limited in obtaining accurate concentrations of dinos and copepods." She pointed to a map of the Gulf of Mexico hanging on the wall and used her fingers to trace an invisible line from Tampa toward the Panhandle. "Along this track, we'll send down divers in containment suits with advanced tech cameras to record color changes in the water column."

Diane blinked and asked, ""You want to record shades of water?"

Bennett nodded. "When the copepods feed on red dinos, the color of the water changes from crimson to purple. If you see grape-colored swirls at a specific depth and nothing but red water below that depth, we can roughly estimate the rate of predation."

Diane considered the opposite. "What if we find red shallow waters and purple waters in the deep?"

Bennett raised her eyebrows. "That would be great. Copepods are still feeding at the surface but have saturated the water column."

For a moment, Diane was quiet, considering the idea. "But the color red is invisible in deeper waters."

Jenson answered, "The camera has a bright white light to illuminate the red algae." He jotted something on a notepad. "We also want to record any form of life that has survived in the Gulf. Visual records of remaining organisms will help direct future assessments of the Gulf. Maybe collect a few specimens to determine their levels of toxicity."

Diane shook her head. "We can use water samples to identify plankton concentrations. I don't think we should sample fish or other sea creatures. Whatever has survived should be left alone. Give the ecosystem a chance to recover."

"That could be years," Bennett said in a hushed tone.

"A marine biologist not eager to dissect fish is a welcome change," Jenson said with a smile that seemed more relaxed. "I agree. Let's leave life alone." He nodded at Bennett. "We're running late for our meeting."

When Jenson got up and turned, Bennett flashed a quick look of relief to Diane, then said, "The containment suit training is at the indoor pool, heavily chlorinated with new filtration. You'll be breathing through a hose connected to a purifying air compressor, safe from airborne and waterborne toxins. Todd's already there."

Uncle Bo didn't care for Jenson, but Diane liked his determination. Probably a silly wish, but she wanted Landry and her husband to be the sole perpetrators of the pilot plant disaster. She realized that Jenson never brought up the chemical process behind the catastrophe. He never questioned how the bloom began. He was in the middle of an EPA investigation, the media hounding him, yet he pushed forward to answer the next big question: was anything alive in the Gulf of Mexico? The prospect of finding anything other than red dinos and blue copepods was as likely as Jenson being innocent.

CHAPTER 52

Diane, wearing her full-face respirator, walked toward a large white building containing a rectangular-shaped pool that reached a depth of forty feet and was about ten yards away from the Atlantic. The seawater was a dark crimson color with hues of purplish indigo scattered across the surface. Waves crashed into grayish-pink foam. Beaches remained closed. No dead animals were on the sand. Nothing moved, flew, or leaped out of the water. A vacant, discolored ocean. An eerie emptiness.

A glimpse of the Earth before humans evolved?

When Diane entered the natatorium, Todd came out of the pool and took off his containment suit, which was connected to what looked like a fire hose full of water. The instructor was a tall, thirty-something platinum blond. "If you're Diane, you're next. I'm Angie."

Todd smiled at Diane. "You're going to love this. It's awkward at first, but the filtered air coming from the compressor is the cleanest I've smelled in months."

Angie pulled out a dry containment suit. "Too bad we can't live in 'em." She motioned at Diane while pointing to a pair of built-in, flipper-shaped bottoms. "Put your hooves into those."

Diane took off her respirator. A strong smell of chlorine caused her eyes to water. She pushed her legs into the suit until her feet touched the bottom of each flipper.

Angie helped Diane drag up the bulky, thick fabric until it reached her chin. Angie pulled the attached hood with a large, clear shield over Diane's face and snapped it into place. "Like an astronaut," Diane mumbled, sweating under the heavy outfit. "I expected it to have a tough outer shell, like an exosuit."

"There's a hard layer under the thick material," Angie said, moving in front of Diane and pointing to the controls on the arm pad. "You'll use the up and down buttons to control buoyancy. It adjusts the amount of air going in and out of the exterior layer. A digital gauge inside the mask displays your depth and air levels."

Diane raised her voice to be heard through the thick head cover. "How far down can I dive?"

"The suit can maintain normal atmospheric pressure inside. OSCF tested it in over a thousand feet of water. The air hose is strong enough to withstand a Mack truck." Angie pointed to a drinking straw-like tube fitted in the hood near the face. "If for some reason the air compressor fails, the suits are fitted with a backup supply of air, which is released when you pull on the tube with your mouth."

Diane examined the reddish-orange tube. "Bite and pull?"

"Yep. That will trigger the air, disconnect the hose, and shut the valve to the hose connector built into your suit."

"How much auxiliary air will I have?"

"About an hour's worth. Plenty of time to scramble back to the ship."

"Anyone else trained on these suits besides me and Todd?"

"Two researchers from a local college."

Angie guided her to the stairs leading down into the pool. The mammoth-sized suit and built-in flippers caused her to stumble, landing on her side. Angie struggled to get her upright.

On the last step, Diane took a deep breath, then dropped into the water. The heaviness caused her to sink quickly. Inside, the air was clean, lacking the usual tainted smells. The clear hood gave her better peripheral vision than her dive mask. She practiced moving around, enjoying the water.

When she returned to the surface, Brandon, Nicole, and Todd were watching her as Angie grabbed her arm and led her out of the pool.

Diane took off the suit and glanced at Brandon. He hadn't responded to her last text. Hoping to get his attention, she walked toward her labmates and chirped, "That was amazing. I can't wait to try it out in the Gulf."

With a lopsided grin, Nicole said, "You looked like the Michelin Man going for a swim."

Todd laughed. "Don't knock it till you've tried it."

Brandon just stared at his phone.

Diane knew she'd been hard on him, making him leave the hospital and not replying to his texts. "Brandon, will you be working on this cruise?"

Without looking up from his phone, he responded flatly, "The few remaining bots are dysfunctional."

She didn't know what to say, but after a few seconds of awkward silence, Brandon slid the phone into his pocket and smiled at her. "I've been told my job is to assist on the ship. I'd like to think of it as a pleasure cruise." He started humming a tune that Diane didn't know.

"I'm taking off before he sings," Todd said.

"Me too," Nicole said, giggling. "Good luck, Diane."

Todd and Nicole walked away, each looking back with a friendly wave and a wide grin. All Diane could think was that one of them could be working against her and helping Landry.

Uncle Bo warned me about the big smiles.

Brandon whispered, "I did that so we can be alone."

"Sorry I pushed you away at the hospital. I was worried and under a lot of stress."

He waved his hands in a "no big deal" motion. "I get it. Workday's over." Brandon moved closer to her and dipped his head. "How about dinner at my place?"

Diane smiled. "Sure. Are you cooking?"

"Does ordering pizza count?"

He flashed a charming smile, then hugged her. As she melted into his arms, Mom's advice returned to her: "Enjoy the feeling." Holding him, she thought of nothing else, relishing the warm embrace. His actions could prove that he had always been on her side. Or maybe she was looking for a way to convince herself of his sincerity.

CHAPTER 53

When Diane arrived at Brandon's spacious three-bedroom apartment, he had cold beer and warm pizza on the coffee table next to the couch. "I promise to cook next time," he said with a sheepish grin.

Next time?

"Who decorated your apartment?" she asked, noticing a shelf of neatly stacked books, potted plants lining the window, and color-coordinated rugs.

"My mom. She loves to embellish."

"Looks great. And amazingly clean. Don't tell me you have a cleaning lady."

"I won't," he said, suppressing a laugh.

A small digital piano sat in the corner. "I'd love to hear you play."

"After dinner."

Clean, smart, and talented.

He gave her a tour. The three bedrooms were not as well kept as the rest of his place. Piles of computers and electronics were stacked on the floor and desks. Maybe he wasn't flawless, but he came close to perfection.

They ate the pizza and drank most of the beer. She felt lightheaded, laughing more than she had in months. As the evening progressed, her guard fell and she asked, "Do you have any concerns about OSCF? I mean, what do you think about working there?"

He groaned. "No talk about work." He placed his hand over hers and led her to the piano. "I want to concentrate on us."

She sat close to him on the stool, watching his hands move with a hypnotic grace to "Moonlight Sonata." Memories of that night on the ship flooded her mind, sitting side by side on a bench, adrift on a glistening sea infected by a parasite. She had felt safe with him then. Now she felt something wonderfully different and unfamiliar.

At the end of the piece, he put an arm around her and held her close. As she rested her head against his chest, every part of her body relaxed. He gently lifted her face until their lips were inches apart. "For many, this is the worst summer. For me, it's the best because I met you."

Wish I could stay in this moment forever.

Over the past few weeks, the nights she'd spent with Brandon had been the only times her concerns and responsibilities seemed to melt away. Lightheaded and a bit shaky, she hugged him and whispered, "I always look forward to being with you, seeing your smile. You mean a lot to me."

They kissed passionately and stumbled to the bedroom, ripping off their clothes along the way.

Lying under him with his gaze trained on her, Diane felt like she was the only woman in the world. He lowered himself, laced his fingers through her hair. She stroked his strong back. That familiar rush of excitement came over her as his body pressed against hers, and soon all thoughts of a plant explosion, toxic red waters, and the contaminated dead faded far away.

• • •

A few hours later, Diane awoke in Brandon's bed to the sounds of him taking a shower. She shut her eyes, recalling the sensation of his touch. Propped up against his pillow, which still had his light vanilla scent, she scanned the room and saw cases of flash drives on a desk. Cables were draped over a chair. She rolled off the plush mattress and stumbled over a dismantled Xbox. Slim hard drives and CDs were stacked on a cluttered desk. At the bottom of the pile were several disks held together by a rubber band and a piece of paper that read “OSCF Accounts.”

Emails!

The water from the shower stopped. Diane snatched the top CD under the rubber binding and stuffed it into her shorts. Brandon walked out of the bathroom wearing a big smile and a towel around his waist. As he pulled her close to kiss, she felt the CD and backed away. She stammered, “We’ll get our cruise itinerary today. I need to go to my apartment since I haven’t been there for a while.”

He stepped back, his brow furrowed in confusion. “Did I do somethi—?”

“No, you were wonderful . . . *are* wonderful. I just need to get some things before we leave for the Gulf. And I want to talk to my family before heading out to sea.”

Brandon frowned and grabbed his clothes. When his back was turned, she slipped the CD into her backpack.

When they were dressed, they held hands and walked to her Jeep. After they shared a long kiss, he said, “We’re taking one sleeping bag to the desert.”

“I can’t wait.” The sweet sensation of butterflies in her stomach that had started last night stayed with her. *I’ll go anywhere with you.*

Fifteen minutes later, she rushed into her apartment, ran to her laptop, and inserted the CD. A folder labeled “emails.” Files dated over a year ago. She searched for Matt’s name. None of the emails were connected to Landry. A search for Landry turned up nothing related to Matt. No mention of the pilot plant. The emails were too old. More CDs were in the stack in Brandon’s room. Maybe those would have more recent emails. She leaned back in her chair and wondered what else she could learn from emails sent over a year ago.

Brandon had been at OSCF for several years. She searched for his name. Many of the emails had the subject line “AUV.” *Autonomous underwater vehicles.* Scrolling through the list, she discovered an email from Landry.

My niece is coming to town this weekend. I'll be able to get her a position in the bio-lab after she graduates. Are you available for lunch?

He had responded within seconds.

Sure. What's her name?

She replied.

Nicole.

Diane flopped in the chair, her mind spinning as she stared at the name of the friendly lab tech. Nicole had cultured the river dinos and knew about the sample in the walk-in chamber and Diane's suspicions of the pilot plant. Nicole had mentioned her aunt was a scientist but had given Diane a bogus name.

Suddenly, she felt alone and disconnected from everyone in the lab. This morning she had awoken with a desire for Brandon that she'd never felt for anyone else. But now the tenderness of their night together vanished.

CHAPTER 54

Diane drove along Hollywood Beach, remembering Nicole staying at her home and their late-night talks. The young, amicable labmate had ruined her work to appease a crazed relative. She cranked up Taylor Swift's "Bad Blood" on her iTunes, blasting the song loud enough to stop a few masked pedestrians on the street lined with signs saying, "For Sale" and "Beach Closed."

When Diane arrived at OSCF, Bennett was meeting with Todd, Brandon, and Nicole. Diane entered the lab and apologized for being late. She could feel Brandon and Nicole watching her.

"We're reviewing information about the upcoming cruise," Bennett said. "Two OSCF ships are heading to the Gulf. I will be with Dr. Jenson on *Mariner One*. All of you will be on *Mariner Two*. On deck, you'll breathe using the portable machine. Contained rooms have an air filtration system to remove toxins. As an FYI, three government-owned ships with remote-controlled deep-sea submersibles are going to the Atlantic."

Todd's hand shot up. "Why aren't we using submersibles?"

Brandon answered, "Gulf has way more dinos than the Atlantic, enough algae to cause problems for large submersibles with electronics that can't be hosed down with powerful algaecides."

Bennett pointed to two digital cameras. "Todd and Diane, you'll be trained to use these for recording and taking pictures. Two other divers from the university will do the same in containment suits."

Todd motioned at the equipment. "Who's videotaping off *Mariner One*?"

Bennett glanced at Brandon. "A new underwater robot camera with remarkable clarity—and can be doused in algaecide." She gave them a brief grin. "The *Mariner One* also has technology enhanced by OSCF engineers that can identify macroorganisms at a depth of at least 800 meters."

That's not fair! The *Mariner One* would get to use cutting-edge technology to make interesting discoveries while she had to wear a bulky suit and float around in murky water. She'd already worn OSCF's dry suit and almost died in toxic water.

Bennett wrapped up the meeting, then left for another. Diane studied the itinerary. Both ships would depart from Tampa Bay. *Mariner One* would sail to Corpus Christi, Texas. *Mariner Two* would sail to Mobile, Alabama. On the passenger list for *Mariner Two*, she found her name, her labmates' names, and Dr. Susan Landry. Her stomach twisted into knots. She rushed out of the lab to find Jenson, who had told her to seek him out if she had a problem.

Bennett was entering a conference room when Diane stopped her and huffed, "Me and Dr. Landry on *Mariner Two*. Huge mistake!"

Bennett sighed. "I know you're afraid of what she might know about you, but there will be many technicians and researchers on board. She won't do anything. What could she do?"

"Throw me overboard."

Bennett's eyes widened, and she stepped closer to Diane. "I don't think so. I'll skip this meeting. Let's talk to Dr. Jenson."

They found Jenson in the hallway, surrounded by physical oceanographers. "Could we speak privately?" Bennett asked him.

When the three scientists walked into a nearby office and closed the door, Diane spoke, her words rushing out. "Please don't put me at sea with Dr. Landry."

Jenson rubbed his brow as if to ward off a headache. "She wants to make amends with you."

"I could go on *Mariner Two*," Bennett said. "You'll have plenty of help on—"

"No," Jenson snapped.

"I'm begging you," Diane said, "please don't leave me on Dr. Landry's boat."

He took a deep breath. "What are you afraid of?"

"Her hurting me."

Jenson sighed. "If you want a career at OSCF, you need to learn to work with Dr. Landry, who wants a good working relationship with you. From what I gather, you both said things you shouldn't have." And without another word, he left the room, shaking his head.

Bennett touched Diane's shoulder. "I understand you're frightened. Maybe she's a liar, but that's a long way from drowning you."

Diane vehemently shook her head. "She's the devil, corrupting people with her lies. I think she's poisoned Jenson's mind."

"I've known her for years. She's been great for OSCF. Recruits the best talent and makes generous donations. We need to learn the details of her dealings with Matt and what was going on with the plant. There's a lot we don't know."

"Did you know Nicole is her niece?"

Bennett's mouth fell open. "I . . . did not." She started to say something else, then stopped. "Even if they're related, that doesn't mean—"

A man opened the door and motioned at Bennett. "We're waiting."

Bennett hesitated before leaving the room. "The dive instructor is at the pool today. You have about three more hours of training required for the certification." She forced a smile. "In a short while, you'll be in a protective dive suit submerged in seawater mixed with red dinos and blue copepods. Imagine what that'll look like. After seven days, the cruise will end. You'll be fine."

Diane went to the pool, which was a relief because she didn't trust herself not to go off on Nicole. No wonder Landry suspected her. She felt certain that Landry had lied to Jenson about wanting to make amends. Diane trusted Bennett, who had insisted she was safe. Then again, Bennett had been clueless this whole time. Brandon could be innocent, but something about the emails bothered her.

• • •

After completing tests for certification on the containment suit, Diane avoided the lab and went to her apartment.

Nicole texted her repeatedly. She ignored Nicole's messages. She received texts from Brandon almost hourly. He wanted to know if he could see her that evening. Consumed with worry and afraid of choosing the wrong words, she didn't respond. Instead, she texted Isabelle. *Landry gave me a beatdown about the article.*

Isabelle responded, *Say nothing! Hold your ground.*

She replied, *Heading out to sea with her. If anything happens to me, cover the story. She's the main suspect!*

Isabelle texted immediately: *Got it! Stay alert!*

Frustrated and confused, Diane tried to distract herself with social media. She grimaced at the posts of more dead bodies discovered in buildings near coastal towns. Some people had returned to their homes and were stocking up on masks and filters. Government tankers, using an updated filtration system, continued to supply water. Someone posted a time-lapse video that revealed fewer dead animals were washing onshore, with the caption, "Nothing Alive for Toxins to Kill."

She turned on the TV. When a reporter covering the plant explosion said the investigation had no suspects, she perked up.

Absorbed in the news, she jumped when the phone rang. Her mom was on the line, sounding less stressed. "Ms. Johnson said that Clean-It-Up has contacts inside the EPA. I think OSCF's in for a rough ride." Diane recalled Isabelle mentioning the newspaper had also communicated with the federal agency.

Mom's worried tone kicked in. "I don't think you should go into the Gulf. It's too dangerous."

"It's only for a week. I'll be okay."

Mom was quiet for a moment then said, "Bo wants to talk to you."

It was a relief to hear her uncle's upbeat voice. He sounded more like himself, laughing at something on TV. "Little Miss Know-Nothin', whatcha up to?"

"I'll be diving in a special suit and using an underwater camera. Not like the ones we used to get where the pictures come out fuzzy."

He hesitated for a second. "You sound jittery. Like when I used to tell you ghost stories when you were little."

"I'm just tired," she said, but the truth was Diane didn't know how to handle Nicole or Brandon. And she definitely didn't feel safe around Landry.

CHAPTER 55

While driving to Tampa Bay, Diane listened to the NPR station. An EPA spokesperson provided a statement. "The exploratory process at the pilot facility used a regulated chemical mixture considered safe at minimal concentrations. The levels we found in the waters near the discharge pipes violated our standards. We believe the state was provided false information."

Diane exhaled; her muscles relaxed. Hopefully, the authorities would arrest Landry before *Mariner Two* left the dock.

The next person interviewed was a police officer investigating the plant explosion. "Prior to the blast, a technician observed a suspicious person on the grounds but didn't know the suspect's name. This witness admitted to being a smoker and suggested a cigarette might not have been completely put out near the warehouse. That would be unusual, yet a cigarette butt was in the ashes. We're looking into that as a possible origin of the fire."

The police must have interviewed Chet. He had told Diane, 'I have no one. No purpose.' He was helping Diane cover her tracks. Maybe he was now doing his part to share her mission, even if it meant drawing attention away from her and onto himself. The sacrifice he was willing to make—after losing his daughter—it made her heart sink.

A few minutes later, Diane entered the harbor and found OSCF's research vessels moored with long ropes to the dock. Everyone on board wore breathers and yellow suits with their name written on the back and front. Crew members carried medical supplies and boxes labeled "EPINEPHRINE" onto *Mariner One*. Jenson, who had lowered his mask, stood on the dock and spoke to reporters. His calm manner exuded confidence. He didn't look like someone under federal investigation.

A team of technicians were securing the cylindrical underwater robotic camera with its wide clear lens mounted on the front and its thick, stubby tripod legs that it sat upon. Its retractable arms were designed to dig up sections of sediment to capture video and still images of life beneath the ocean floor.

Diane donned her gear and boarded the smaller *Mariner Two*. Four containment dive suits hung by their attached hoses. All divers had their own individual suit labeled by name. As Diane examined the individual air compressors, Nicole yelled, "Hey, you don't return texts anymore?"

Diane rolled her eyes, took a slow breath, then turned to face Landry's niece. "I've been busy."

Nicole paused for a moment. "How's your uncle? I heard he's better."

"He's fine."

"Todd and I guessed you and Brandon wanted some alone time yesterday. How're things going with him?"

None of your damn business!

Diane moved, putting distance between them while shrugging her shoulders.

"Aw, that's too bad." Nicole moved closer and whispered, "I heard EPA is getting ready to make arrests."

"I know nothing about it."

Nicole pushed up her mask and moved the breather on her back. "You're not talking much."

"I'm tired."

"We're bunking together."

I'd rather sleep on the deck. "Okay."

Nicole studied her for a second. "Don't worry. I've learned my lesson. If we sail into a storm, I'll stay inside."

Todd, Brandon, and Landry stood on the bow. Brandon spotted her, lifted his mask, and smiled. She gave a half-hearted, clumsy wave.

Mariner One had at least twenty notable academics from top-rated oceanographic institutes. *Mariner Two* had four young male oceanographers from a local university, who quickly introduced themselves. One of them, a diver, shared a map of the Gulf, pointing out stops along the route. "We'll arrive at our first dive station in the morning."

Landry and Todd approached Diane. The cofounder glanced at her and sounded resigned when she said, "Our last encounter was not a productive one. I was upset about losing a process that had a lot of potential to help the environment."

The cofounder offered no apologies, just empty words followed by a fake smile.

Diane and Landry stood in awkward silence and watched the *Mariner One* sailing out of the harbor. Minutes later, the *Mariner Two* left the port and made a slight turn northward. As the others wandered the ship, Diane watched Tampa Bay slowly disappear from sight, resisting the urge to jump into the infested waters, which were streaked with iridescent purple copepods, and swim back to land.

CHAPTER 56

The next morning, Diane awoke to Nicole snoring loudly. Diane rolled out of her bunk, got dressed, and headed upstairs. She was surprised to find the deck empty and littered with beer bottles. OSCF banned alcohol on working ships, but someone obviously had a late-night get-together. *Mariner One*'s team was probably hard at work while this crew was sleeping it off. She went to the bridge to see if the navigator was awake and sober.

Captain Joey was a small, wide, shaggy man. Candy wrappers strewn everywhere revealed his weakness for junk food. After she took a couple of steps forward, he noticed her and jumped a little. She quickly took off her mask. "Sorry, didn't mean to scare you."

"Takes a lot more than a little lady to scare this big ol' seagoer's soul." He pointed at an electronic map. "We're about twenty miles from the first station. You a diver?"

She nodded and glanced at the empty deck. "Not sure who's joining me. Looks like folks had a party last night."

He huffed and mumbled, "Ship of fools."

She spent some time with him, learning about his adventures in the navy. He was the type of sailor who probably had more salt than blood in his veins. When they arrived at the coordinates for their first dive, she studied the deck, then turned to him. "I see Todd and some techs. Nobody else."

Captain Joey winked at her and blasted the horn ten times. The repetitive sounds echoed an obnoxious racket almost loud enough to wake up a dead ocean. While the captain bombarded the ship with noise, Diane joined Todd on the deck. They each checked the air hoses connected to their respective suits. Minutes later, the two other divers staggered onto the deck and groaned.

Todd slid off his mask and rolled his eyes. "I'm going to raise hell about this to Bennett."

Diane put on her bulky suit with the flippers and shuffled to the edge of the stern. A female technician monitoring the air hoses helped Diane onto the lower step and into the red seawater with bright purple swirls of copepods feasting on dinos. The air from the hose rushed into her suit. The heavy, cumbersome uniform felt more like a floating cocoon. Crimson bubbles surrounded Todd when he fell into the water. Diane adjusted the buoyancy of her suit and slowly descended. When she started recording with the camera strapped to her sleeve, a bright white light illuminated the water. Todd tugged her arm and pulled her down to fifty feet, where she found fewer strings of red algae and more purple strands that looked like floating grape licorice.

Down a hundred feet, there was less red water, fewer dinos, and more lacy purple strings of copepods. Though they had plenty of hose to descend to deeper waters, Todd and Bennett had agreed to limit dives to a hundred feet. Todd pointed toward the surface, and he and Diane ascended to about eighty feet. Her heart raced when a tiny octopus drifted in front of her.

She nudged Todd, and they took pictures of it. After a few minutes of finding nothing else, they ascended to the surface and awkwardly boarded the ship. Diane stripped off her suit and chirped, "Found an octopus!"

Two researchers in yellow suits wearing masks paused their work of collecting sea samples to glance at her before continuing.

Todd and Diane found a maskless Nicole sitting on the deck with her face in her hands. Diane thought she looked hungover. "What's going on?" Todd asked.

Nicole fumbled with her phone and handed it to Diane.

It was a newsfeed of EPA's investigation of the pilot plant. Senator Landry had been arrested and had made a statement. "I received measurements from OSCF and reported them to the state. It was a shock to me that the numbers were false."

Dr. Landry, the plant's primary contact for OSCF, was also interviewed. "We provided accurate data. My husband must have altered the information." She cited marital problems as a motivation for her husband's attempt to hurt her and the foundation.

Landry threw her husband under the bus.

Investigators planned to meet with Jenson upon his return from sea. Government officials provided several comments, but one stood out. "We believe the experimental mix of chemicals found near OSCF's pilot wastewater plant may be responsible for the dinoflagellate producing a resistant red tide."

Finally!

Ongoing vocal protests by the Clean-It-Up organization, Isabelle's front-page article, and connections between the newspaper, lobbyists, and the federal agency might have helped grease the wheels of justice.

Todd flung off his respirator. His voice shook with anger. "This is awful! We're busting our asses for what? What good can any of us do if that shithead is jeopardizing our work?" He seemed genuinely shocked, and, unfortunately, believed Senator Landry had been the one to sabotage their efforts. He hung his head and muttered, "No need to email Dr. Bennett about an inebriated crew. It's over."

Diane guessed Todd couldn't accept the idea that OSCF had caused this catastrophe. She reminded him of the job at hand. "We still have this mission."

He frowned but remained silent, his posture slumped as he walked away.

Nicole stared at her. "They're redirecting Jenson's ship to meet with the EPA. Dr. Landry's in tears."

Diane was tired of the charade. "I'm sure your aunt will be okay. Where's Brandon?"

Nicole's eyes widened. "Umm . . . I think he's helping Dr. Landry set up a virtual meeting with Dr. Jenson's ship."

Nicole was getting ready to say something else, but Diane walked away. Even if Nicole apologized, Diane wouldn't believe her.

Half an hour later, the ship stopped at the second station, and a scowling Todd returned to the deck. A researcher walked up behind him and said, "We were told not to dive."

Todd was fuming. "What the hell are you talking about?"

The technician who'd been helping Diane get into her suit stopped and said, "I'll get the captain."

Within seconds, Captain Joey, breathing heavily behind his mask, showed up. "We diving?"

Landry and Brandon walked onto the deck, and Captain Joey slid off his respirator to talk to them. After scrutinizing the captain's scruffy face, Landry took a step backward and said, "We're sailing to the New Orleans port. That's where Dr. Jenson's ship is heading."

Captain Joey gasped. "No one told me that."

"I'm the boss, and *I'm* telling you that." Landry turned on her heels and stormed off.

Brandon remained on the deck, watching Diane. She noticed his sad expression and hunched posture.

After a few minutes on the phone with Jenson, Captain Joey reported back to them. "Dr. Jenson said they're finishing up work on their track before heading to New Orleans. He said there's an area where their detector is pinging, detecting life."

Todd and Diane exchanged curious glances.

"It's on the way to the New Orleans port," Captain Joey said. "They're heading there tomorrow. We'll get to it before they do. In the meantime, he wants divers in the water." He made a sweeping motion with his hand. "People, do your jobs!"

Jenson was sailing toward an unpleasant meeting with EPA officials, yet he remained steadfast in the mission to record the copepods' progress and to find life. Maybe his persistence had manifested from feelings of remorse, needing the subarctic crustacean to be successful in eradicating the bloom and hoping for something organic to alleviate his guilt.

Brandon helped Diane into her suit. “I don’t understand you,” he said. “You’re warm one second then ghosting me the next. I tried reaching you all day yesterday. Is something wrong?”

The warmth in his soft expression made her feel guilty. “Let’s talk after the dive.”

He smiled and helped her shuffle to the stern’s edge.

As she slipped into the water, a scowling Landry, fists clenched, stalked the captain. Maneuvering inches below the surface, Diane looked up. Captain Joey leaned over the water, observing her progress. The swaying of the water caused the burly man to appear like a floating angel watching from above. She watched for a few seconds, worrying that Landry, in retaliation for disobeying her orders, would push him in. The deadly sea felt safer than the boat.

CHAPTER 57

In the Gulf, Diane turned on the recorder and floated alongside Todd. The ship sailed into deeper waters. From the surface to about fifty feet, the red algae dominated the water column. She followed Todd into clearer waters at a hundred feet. Suspended in red hues with streaks of purple that reminded her of Mom's berry jams, she gazed down and wondered if animals in the deepest part of the ocean had escaped the poison. Closing her eyes, she felt the weightlessness and stillness of her surroundings, different from the chaos on the boat. When she opened her eyes again, a sudden flash of silver streaked by her.

A fish?

Gliding toward the patch of cloudy water where the light had flickered, she squinted, searching. She drifted for about a minute.

Another flash appeared to the side of her. She swam toward it.

Nothing.

A gigantic mass of grape-colored strings and a small clump of red algae floated by her. She disturbed the surrounding water, causing the tufts of crimson to collide with the feeding copepods.

Eat up!

Seconds later, the bloodred strands were bright indigo. The gauge in her hood showed she was at 143 feet. Todd was nowhere to be found. She pushed a button to increase the air in the outer layer and made a slow ascent. She kept looking for anything shiny as she rose.

Had it been my imagination?

After reaching the surface, she used the air hose to pull herself back toward the ship and found Todd bobbing in the water. He shouted through his hood as he held up her hose. There was a knot in it. "Found this! Loosened it so you'd have air!"

"Thanks!" she yelled, staring at the mangled hose in disbelief.

Minutes later, a technician helped Todd climb onto the stern. Captain Joey hoisted Diane out of the water. While helping her out of the suit, he chuckled. "You were down there long enough to grow gills. Find anything?"

"Maybe a fish? I'm not sure." She called out to Todd, who was heading toward the showers. "Did you see a flash or anything shiny down there?"

Todd scratched his head. "I saw algae and copepods feeding on it."

The captain pointed at her hose with the loosened knot. "How did that happen?"

She shrugged. "I didn't do it."

"Strange. I'll have the techs detach the hose and straighten it out."

Her stomach rumbled as a reminder that she hadn't eaten since last night. She headed to the galley and found Brandon, Nicole, and Landry leaning into each other, talking with grave, humorless faces. They didn't notice her, so she grabbed some food and escaped to her cabin.

While looking at her sandwich, Diane recalled a college counselor labeling her as a perfectionist in search of validation. She'd done everything possible to solve the mystery of what had destroyed the Gulf, and yet, while others gathered at a table, she felt insignificant and isolated. Being above the water always seemed lonelier than being under it. Months had gone by since her last swim in the ocean, feeling the way it enveloped her body, soothing her senses. Memories of the Gulf with an abundance of life caused her eyes to water. She thought of the small octopus wandering the waters, finding no food or another of its kind, doomed to die like everything else.

Grief gave way to anger at the thought of Landry getting away with her crimes: manipulating Matt, deceiving her husband, and perhaps lying to Jenson. There had to be a way to reveal the truth about what had happened. Bennett had said emails from OSCF's server could provide evidence. She believed Brandon had those emails. He could provide proof of Landry's guilt from files originating from OSCF's network. But would he do it?

CHAPTER 58

The next morning, Diane found a sunny spot on the bow to rest before the ship reached the place where *Mariner One* had detected life. She took off the breather, closed her eyes, and enjoyed the warm winds hitting her face.

Soon, someone sat down beside her, pulling her out of a trance.

Brandon.

He removed his respirator and sat close enough that their arms touched. The winds from the quick-moving ship blew back his thick, dark hair. They gazed at each other for what seemed like forever until he broke the silence. "No matter how many times you ignore me, I can't wait to see you." His hand cupping her face, he lightly kissed her lips.

Diane melted. "I care about you too."

She didn't want to break the spell, but asking about the emails was too important. She felt queasy. "I need to ask a favor."

Brandon stared into her eyes and in a smoky tone whispered, "Anything."

I don't want to do this!

Looking out at the dead Gulf, she believed this was the only way to uncover the truth. She took a deep breath, bracing herself. "Could you locate emails from the time when Matt worked on the experimental process at the pilot plant? The information could support the investigation and help Matt's family understand what happened to him."

Brandon's eyes narrowed, and he pulled away from her. "I can't access emails on the network," he said gruffly.

Diane's stomach was in knots. This would not end well. "You have CDs with OSCF accounts in your apartment."

Brandon stood; his posture stiffened. "You went through my stuff?"

"I didn't realize things sitting in your room were top secret."

After glaring at her for a few seconds, Brandon punched the ship's wall and stormed off. Before he rounded the corner of the ship, he turned, revealing a menacing scowl, then stomped toward her. She scrambled to her feet.

Brandon's voice quivered with anger when he said, "Why are you doing this?" He pointed to the Gulf. "We've loaded the oceans with a miracle copepod. The bloom is disappearing. OSCF's pilot plant is gone. The EPA's cleaning up." He paused, taking a breath, and lowered his voice. "Why can't you let this go?"

"This is a huge tragedy! The sea may never be the same. Someone has to be held accountable. If not, they'll do it again. Can't you see that?" Diane reached for him, but he pulled away.

Brandon took a jagged breath, keeping his distance from her. His posture softened but his eyes were dark and cold. "I'm begging you to stop," he said in a shaky voice. "I care for you. I want us to be together. If you don't stop . . ." He closed his eyes and let his words trail.

Diane realized something she had not thought of before. Not only did he have the capability of recovering files, but he could also make electronic information disappear. A computer genius who could destroy a digital trail, making it undetectable to law enforcement and computer experts. Communications that would have shown Matt was trying to do the right thing were gone. No proof existed to show that Landry and her husband had rigged the system.

Her legs trembled as she took a step back. Teetering between anger and heartache, she tried to calm herself and gain control. "You helped people get away with murdering the oceans, which could've ultimately killed everything. It still could."

Brandon didn't look at her, focusing on the red Gulf instead. "The bloom is Matt's fault. He broke into the plant and released tons of raw sewage into the river."

He believes a lie.

She imagined the final meeting between Jenson, Landry, and Matt. The cofounders had probably accused Matt of starting the bloom. Landry had ignored Matt's warnings. The guilt from the young swimmer's death and being punched by the girl's father had instigated his desperate attempt to stop the pilot plant. Matt's actions had caused raw sewage to spill into the river, which led to OSCF terminating his job—the last swipe at his sanity.

Diane positioned herself in front of Brandon and looked him in the eye. "No, the illegal amounts of chemicals from the reduction fluid in the river caused the bloom. The raw sewage gave the dino a jump start. But if the treated water hadn't altered the species' DNA, it would have died after reaching the ocean."

Brandon didn't move or respond.

Her voice trembled when she continued. "Why would you destroy communications that show who's responsible for this catastrophe?" Her mind raced with ideas about what could have motivated him. "Countless people and animals have died, lives shattered—an ecosystem *completely* destroyed!"

Her body shook; tears welled in her eyes. She realized the ship's engine had slowed. They had reached the place where life had been detected by Jenson's tracker.

Was Brandon a victim of twisted lies, believing his actions had preserved OSCF's ingenuity? Or had he known the truth and willingly destroyed evidence? She hoped he was like Matt, a victim of fabrications and manipulation.

They stared at each other as the ship slowed to a standstill.

Teardrops ran down her cheeks. "Why?"

"I could say I did it to protect a process my family believed in and to secure my position with OSCF. No answer would be enough." He pulled her toward him and hugged her. They held each other for a few seconds. A part of Diane wished she'd never brought up the emails.

Then he let her go and walked away.

She wanted to go back to her bunk and cry, but she had to get ready for the dive. The tracker from *Mariner One* indicated something was alive below them. All her training had been to prepare her for this moment so she could find sea life and protect it.

CHAPTER 59

Diane checked her air hose. The knot was gone. She waited for Todd and the two other divers to lower themselves off the stern. When it was her turn, she turned toward the deck and lowered herself onto the bottom step.

Nicole sat with her head in her hands. Landry glared at her. Brandon leaned against the bulkhead, his head tilted, his stare blank, reminding her of his expression on the North Atlantic.

I know all their secrets.

The thought of one of them hurting her made her shiver. Unsure about going under, she glanced at the technician guarding the hoses. Todd's hood disappearing under a crimson eddy made her set her fears aside. He was her diving partner, and it would be too dangerous for him to be alone in these waters. Leaving behind her uncle in a toxic wasteland and the young woman who had died alone were mistakes she would not repeat with Todd.

I have to go.

Similar to the other dive spots, algae dominated the surface, but the waters became more purple as they dove deeper to a hundred feet and drifted for a few minutes. Todd nudged her and pointed downward.

Something was moving a lot farther down—a long, billowy silhouette.

She strained her eyes and saw something like film floating above the blurred motion. It didn't look like algae or seaweed. Blinking, she tried to improve her focus. The obscure shapes were too far away.

The two other divers were ten feet to her and Todd's right, pointing their cameras toward the deep shadows. Knowing the images would be difficult to view on tape, she dove deeper and started recording again.

Suddenly, the air in her suit changed.

A loud whoosh followed by a powerful force shot her downward. Sharp pains struck her back, like electrical bolts radiating from her spine down to the bottom of her feet. Every nerve ending fired wildly.

Her body slowed. She clenched her teeth as the pain took over her body.

The gauge moved erratically. She pushed the button to inflate the suit to ascend, but the suit only got heavier. Diane continued to sink.

Water was permeating the suit. Her skin felt wet and clammy. She tried to propel herself upward. The pain crippled her back and legs. The suit allowed no freedom, like a rock heading to the bottom of the ocean.

She flailed her arms, searching for the air hose. Finding it, she frantically pulled on her connection to the boat. But the more she pulled, the deeper she went. With her teeth, she pulled the lever to initiate the backup air. The hose disconnected, and the connector to the hose shut. Her lifeline to the ship was gone. The dark coldness crept in as her body sank.

As Diane began feeling her body giving in to the cold, all-consuming darkness, she heard a strange sound. She passed through a clear substance.

Thick like molasses.

Her body ached as the cold, bulky suit tightened its grip. The electric shocks of pain worsened. Then Diane lost consciousness, her body slipping into darkness.

• • •

Lying on the seafloor, Diane heard tapping. She opened her eyes to the frigid darkness. Some snaggletooth dragonfish were investigating her hood. Their sharp, fang-like teeth made tiny pecking sounds.

She reached out, and an unbearable wave of pain surged through the back of her body. The curious fish dispersed quickly. Her headlamp no longer worked, but she could see a slimy substance on her suit. She scratched some off and brought it close to her mask. It looked like gelatin.

Did I fall through a swarm of jellyfish?

A few inches of water remained in her suit. Perhaps the knot in the air hose from the earlier dive had caused something to malfunction.

Instead of wondering how she got there, she became mesmerized by a majestic octopus hovering above her. The graceful rhythmic movement of its long tentacles was hypnotic.

An hour of oxygen was in the backup system. Having no idea how long she'd been lying on the seabed, she tried to slow her breathing. The thought of escaping her suit and swimming to the surface crossed her mind, but she knew without it, the pressure would crush her. With the drop in body temperature and depletion of air, sleep was inevitable.

Stay awake. Do something!

Carefully, she rolled to her right. Electric shockwaves assaulted her back. She froze on her side, clenching her teeth, praying the stabbing pains would stop. A few inches from her were grayish-blue sponges scattered on the surface of a protruding rock. A painful jolt shot down her leg. She fell over, crashing onto her back. Paralyzing pain coursed down her spine and legs.

Diane scanned the waters. A tiny squid floated nearby. Over the past several weeks, other deep-sea creatures had drifted to the water's surface as victims of the toxic bloom. But somehow these lucky survivors had been spared.

She shivered, and the involuntary movement caused another wave of piercing tremors to travel down her spine. Slowly, her body numbed; her eyes shut. The image of the young woman returned to her again, reeking of vomit on that doomed death ship, and wanting to see her mother.

Diane tried to remember every detail of her mom and uncle: Mom's shy grin, Uncle Bo standing on a trawler waving at her, his stories of catching big fish. Her thoughts faltered. *Gotta find . . . six-foot snook.*

When shivers racked her body again, she cried out in agony, opening her eyes. Only inches away, the little squid hovered, its dark eye watching her. Far above the curious cephalopod was a blurry movement of fluid that served as a border between life and purple clouds of subarctic copepods devouring river dinos.

Another small figure floated down toward her. An orange starfish. *Matt.*

Uncle Bo's laughter and Mom's warm hugs lingered. Frozen stiff, she closed her weary eyes.

CHAPTER 60

A roaring hiss awakened Diane. The ocean floor moved. Her mouth opened to scream, but she couldn't make a sound. A sudden pain stabbed her chest. The underwater robot camera hovered over her; its arms used for excavating the soil had dug under her. She gazed at the large lens, wondering who was looking back from the other side.

Flat on top of the extended mechanical arms, she didn't move a muscle. The pain was excruciating. She wanted to cling to the machine but feared the motion would cause the robot to lose balance. The motor started to grind, lifting her off the seafloor. The machine wobbled a bit while taking on her weight in the heavy, waterlogged suit. When the noisy orb ascended with her in its arms, the fish scattered.

The machine moved through the clear, thick fluid, making an odd sound like her old Jeep losing power. The robot dropped, then rose again. Its engine made a scraping noise, then quickly sputtered out of the syrupy mixture.

The persistent force of the engine propelled her upward. Rushing into warmer waters, her tremors increased. She felt dizzy; everything seemed to spin around her. As she ascended rapidly towards the light, an odd tingling in her arms and legs caused her body to ache. The pain was a small price to pay if it meant feeling the air on her face again.

• • •

The next time Diane woke up, she was inside a clear, elongated tube. She hadn't seen a hyperbaric chamber on the smaller ship. The tethered underwater camera had brought her to *Mariner One*.

She moved and winced in pain. A man she assumed was the physician was standing outside of the chamber. He picked up the connected phone. "Stay still," he ordered. "You just received an injection of powerful opioids. We're decreasing nitrogen bubbles in your tissue and increasing oxygen."

A wooziness, almost like a feeling of floating, overcame her. Her speech slowed. "Something . . . happened. My suit. Electricity . . . in my back."

"We've got an ambulance waiting at the port to transport you to a New Orleans hospital."

Within seconds, Diane fell asleep. About an hour later, she awoke outside the chamber on a stretcher, her hand connected to an intravenous line. Her body was sore, but she was more rested and alert.

Bennett, who was sitting next to her, stood up. The lab director's face was pale, full bags under the eyes. Her soft, concerned tone sounded strained. "You tried to warn me. I'm so sorry."

Remembering the deep-sea animals, Diane felt a rush of adrenaline. Her excitement caused her words to rush out. "I found life! An octopus, fish!"

Bennett shook her head, brows drawn together, and lowered her voice. "The underwater camera recorded no images of life."

Diane gaped. "I saw them!"

Bennett had an incredulous, almost fearful expression. "You were over eight hundred feet down in a damaged containment suit that by some miracle not only maintained atmospheric pressure but also kept pinging, so we could find you. At that depth, gases at high pressure cause an anesthetic effect, triggering hallucinations."

"It was cold and dark, but I saw them!" She remembered the robot sputtering out of the thick fluid. "Something happened to the camera. It went through a syrupy liquid. Maybe the reduction fluid poured into the river made its way to the Gulf? Or maybe it's a part of something else?" The incredulous look on Bennett's face made Diane stop. Closing her eyes, she mumbled, "I dunno."

"You rest." Bennett started walking toward the door. "I'll be—"

"Please stay." *Don't leave me.*

Bennett nodded and sat next to her. Diane studied the dark circles under Bennett's eyes. "You okay?"

Bennett stared at the floor. "After we dock, the ambulance will whisk you off to the hospital. With all you've been through, you deserve to know what happened." She hesitated, studying Diane. "Maybe we should wait."

Her breath hitched. "Tell me now."

"It's about Matt's death." Bennett rubbed her temples. "I saw Dr. Jenson crawl around the bench. I knew he was going to try to stop the attack. I went in the opposite direction, thinking maybe I could help if he ran into trouble. When Matt got closer to our hiding spot, Dr. Jenson lunged at him and grabbed the gun." Bennett lowered her eyes. "Matt said he was sorry. Then Dr. Jenson shot him in the face."

Diane gasped. "What?!"

"I stayed where Dr. Jenson couldn't see me. He laid the gun near Matt. When the police came, he said Matt shot himself. Hoping the investigation would show he was the shooter, I said nothing." She wrung her hands. "I plan to get an attorney and go to the police. Matt deserves justice."

Diane's mouth hung open. She narrowed her eyes. "You kept that to yourself all this time?"

"I was scared. Maybe if I'd gone to the police when it happened, details would have surfaced about the plant. Information learned earlier could've helped."

"Why did he kill Matt?"

"Matt knew too much. The police would've arrested him. In his fragile state of mind, he would've told the police everything. I don't think Dr. Jenson planned to kill him, but the opportunity presented itself, and he took it."

Diane swallowed hard, remembering Matt's bloody face. Thoughts of escaping her own death returned. "Who got me out of the water using the robot?"

Bennett moved forward in the chair. "Four technicians and I tried and failed. We were burning up the engine using mechanical arms to lift you off the ground. When we slowed the motor, there wasn't enough power to raise you." She straightened and studied her hands. "Dr. Jenson took over. He found the right balance to lift you without burning up the machine. He maintained control, guiding the robot to the surface with you in its arms."

Jenson had been nice to Diane, giving her second chances. Why did he have to be the one who had killed Matt? The image of her idol, who had inspired her years ago, was tarnished. He had always seemed like the perfect mix of scientist and adventurer. The man in charge of a research facility and a public image. How could he be so flawed and allow himself to become entangled in the steps leading to this horrible environmental disaster? None of it made sense—especially now, when she considered how it would have been so easy for him to sit back and let her die. But he was the one who saved her. *Why?*

Diane had another nagging question. "What happened to me? Did my air hose malfunction?"

Bennett cradled her face in her hands and sighed heavily. "A technician saw what happened. She went to the captain and told him everything. We were ten minutes away when he called us." Bennett stopped talking.

"I need to know."

"When you went into the water, the only people who remained on the stern were Dr. Landry, Brandon, Nicole, and the technician monitoring the air hoses. Dr. Landry told the tech she'd received an emergency message from *Mariner One* and convinced the tech that she could monitor the air hoses. She then ordered the tech to go to the bridge and inform the captain."

Diane's heart sank, thinking of Landry supervising her lifeline.

Bennett's hands were trembling. "When the tech returned to the stern, Dr. Landry, Brandon, and Nicole were standing near the air compressors. A hose flew up violently, hitting the stern, then flew off the ship and into the water."

Diane tilted her head. "I'm confused."

Bennett wiped her eyes, then continued. "When we arrived, Jenson sent down the underwater camera. After you surfaced, I boarded *Mariner Two* and found the crew examining Dr. Landry and Brandon. Both were sprawled on the deck, bleeding and unresponsive. Nicole was conscious, looking at everyone, her eyes wild. She broke down and told me everything."

Diane silently waited for Bennett to collect her thoughts. Bennett hesitated for a second, frowning. "Brandon and Nicole told Dr. Landry that you believed the residual in the treated water caused the mutation and was responsible for the bloom. Dr. Landry instructed Nicole to incinerate the river dinoflagellate cultures. She also got rid of the hidden treated water sample. Brandon told them you'd figured out that he'd destroyed digital communications. They decided something needed to be done."

Diane froze, her heart pounding.

Bennett fidgeted with her shirtsleeve then said, "When you went down, Nicole stood guard while Landry helped Brandon jimmy the compressor connected to your hose. He knew how to blast out a burst of air that would . . ." Bennett paused, taking a deep breath. "They sent out too much, causing the hose to detach from the generator. The hose flew off with a good amount of pressure."

"Brandon wanted to kill me." Diane's insides felt like jelly. She tried not to shudder. Movement caused too much pain, but she couldn't control the tears streaming down her cheeks.

He tried to drown me.

"Is he dead?" Diane asked.

"He sustained a large wound to his chest and remains unconscious. They've airlifted him to the hospital. Landry was knocked out with abrasions on her head. She's since regained consciousness. Nicole suffered minor scrapes."

Through the sobs, Diane whimpered, "I cared for him. I'm so stupid."

Bennett shook her head. "I'm the idiot and a coward for not going to the police about Shaun shooting Matt. You're smart and courageous."

Diane's crying turned into full-body heaves, sending shock waves to every nerve ending along her spine down to her feet. She thrashed in pain and cried, "I'm not smart! He used me!" She rolled onto her face. Sharp pains seared her back. Her screams escalated to a high-pitched shriek. Through the pain, all Diane could hear was Bennett shouting for someone to help.

CHAPTER 61

The next morning, Diane awoke in a hospital bed. A physician spoke to her mom and uncle. Bo had his portable oxygen. His color looked normal. The lines on Mom's face had deepened. Diane realized she hadn't heard Mom wheeze or cough for several weeks. Having to care for and support their family in a crisis had brought out her mom's strength.

Uncle Bo noticed Diane's eyes were open. He beamed. "There's my girl. How ya feel?"

She squinted at him and, in a cracked voice, quipped, "I'm not in today's obituaries."

Bo kissed her on the forehead. Mom, who had a caring but worried smile, reached over the bed rail and grabbed her daughter's hand.

The physician smiled at Diane. "You were heavily sedated upon arrival. We took x-rays and did an MRI. That surge of air sent an incredible amount of force into your dive suit and ruptured several disks in your back. You're lucky. It could've damaged your spinal cord."

Mom squeezed her hand. "So blessed."

Really? A man I was sleeping with tried to kill me.

Diane stayed in the hospital for two weeks. For physical therapy, she did back-strengthening exercises in a treatment pool of warm chlorinated water. The sharp shocks of pain had slowly eased to a dull throb. It still hurt too much when she sat on a chair or tried to lie flat on her back. She felt comfortable only when she was walking or lying on her side, supported by pillows.

The night before Diane was released from the hospital, Mom, who continually worried about her daughter getting arrested, turned on the news. A reporter, standing in front of OSCF headquarters, delivered the latest developments: "Renowned scientist, Dr. Shaun Jenson has just admitted he shot his former employee, Matthew Toft, during Toft's rampage at this location. Through his legal team, Dr. Jenson made a statement asserting that he acted to protect himself and his employees on the day of the attack. The state's Stand Your Ground Law allows use of deadly force when there's a threat of death or bodily harm. OSCF's cofounder did not explain why he waited until now to confess."

Jenson's admission of guilt was surprising. Perhaps Bennett had spoken to the authorities and information had reached Jenson, who was well-connected to powerful people.

The screen switched to a reporter standing in front of the EPA building. "OSCF has been connected to an ongoing EPA investigation of illegal discharges from an experimental wastewater treatment plant in Louisiana. Investigators say they want to determine the involvement of Senator Landry and the staff of the scientific foundation. Dr. Jenson's legal team says he is cooperating fully with the EPA. Officials have said that they have not found any evidence that Dr. Jenson is involved personally in this incident. "

From Matt's saved emails, Diane remembered reading about potential sales of the reduction fluid process to another country. No mention of that in the news. Those deals must have quickly dissolved.

An anchorwoman read from a teleprompter. "Congressional hearings are in the works for the beleaguered foundation regarding false information provided to state officials. On top of that, the deadly incident at sea has resulted in multiple—"

Diane snatched the remote and flipped to another channel that showed images of the dark red waters streaked with violet hues in the Atlantic. The caption scrolled across the screen: "Toxin levels in the air and water have not changed. Public water systems are mandated to install filtration systems to eliminate toxins."

Mom turned off the TV and patted Diane's hand. "Perhaps you should talk to somebody. You know, like a counselor, to help you deal with all that you've been going through."

Diane's response was flat. "Why rehash everything? What's done is done."

An on-staff psychologist had visited her yesterday. He had asked a lot of questions, and she had provided curt yes and no responses. Her anger and humiliation from the betrayal were difficult to put into words and made her uncomfortable.

Mom let out a haggard breath, appearing to dislike her daughter's refusal of help.

Diane moved the pillows, rolled off the bed, and started pacing the floor. "Toxins are still high. Guess we can't return home."

"Cousin Marnie has a furnished bungalow just outside of Atlanta. We can stay there as long as we need to."

Just then, Bo walked in with bags of fast food tucked under his jacket. Mom shook her head at him, then went to get coffee. He watched Diane walk in circles and scratched his head. "A lotta walkin' to go nowhere." He turned the TV back on, just at the start of a commercial for cat food.

Diane stopped moving. "Wily! We need to get him out of the crawl space. Marnie won't be living with us, up in that Atlanta bungalow. We can take him, right?"

"It's not Marnie I'm worried about. It's crammin' a big stray cat into a box."

Diane returned to pacing. "I could use the steel crate in the back of the shed."

Her phone beeped. It was a text from Isabelle: *Glad you're getting out of the hospital. Call me soon. Need to talk about Jenson.*

When no one would listen to her, Isabelle had published the truth about the pilot plant, and connected Diane and her family to a powerful environmental group with some strong legal counsel. Now the journalist wanted to talk about the man who had killed Matt, the same person who had maneuvered a robot through the vast depths to save her. Isabelle was determined to uncover the entire story. She wanted to catch the big fish that got away. The secret was finding the right bait.

CHAPTER 62

After Diane was released from the hospital, her family traveled to their Gulf home, packed a few things, and collected Wily. They moved into a three-bedroom bungalow in a suburb twenty miles south of Atlanta.

After the first day of settling in, she received a text from Todd, who had accepted a position with NOAA in California. *A diatom bloom off San Francisco. Interested in moving?*

I'm a Gulf girl. Good luck!

She looked at Isabelle's name on the list of contacts on her phone. Her back ached, and she was tired from a long day of cleaning, unpacking, and trying to comfort a frenzied tabby. For a conversation about Jenson, she needed to be alert. Instead of calling Isabelle, she wandered into the kitchen. Mom was at the table, googling for updates about the plant explosion.

Diane had tried to find online information about Chet, the worker who had lost his daughter and whose ruse about some careless smoking sent investigators down the wrong path. Without a last name, she'd been unable to find anything and had asked Mom if she should reach out to the plant to get his information. Mom had said, "Thank Chet in your prayers. Don't even think about calling the plant or trying to contact him. Too risky."

Though contacting Chet could draw unwanted suspicion, Diane wanted to see him again. *He protected me, and I don't even know what he looks like.*

Thinking of the plant brought back thoughts of Matt and his family. She wondered how they were doing with the news of Jenson shooting their son. “I told you about Carla and Robby, Matt’s family in Kentucky,” she said, turning to face her mother.

Mom nodded, rubbing her eyes.

“I told Robby I’d see him again. He’s never seen the ocean. When we return to our home, maybe we could invite them to stay with us.”

With downcast eyes, Mom shook her head. “We may never . . .” She stopped and studied Diane. “Our little house doesn’t have much room, but we’ll make do.”

Diane positioned herself flat on the floor with a pillow under her legs and tuned in to an interview with medical experts on TV.

An expert studied her notes then said, “When patients quickly presented with symptoms of contamination, we had medicine to neutralize and eliminate its effects. What we’re seeing now is delayed contamination.”

Mom let out a heavy sigh. “What now?”

The other expert presented a picture of a healthy cell as a perfect circle next to a damaged cell with withered edges. “Delayed contamination occurs when toxins enter the body in small amounts. Over time, poisons accumulate and assimilate with cells, particularly in the lungs and intestines, resulting in complete organ failure. Currently, there’s no treatment or cure.”

Diane’s mouth hung open. She had almost lost her life to discover what had caused the parasite. Many at sea had risked everything to bring back a miraculous blue copepod to save them. But even if it was being brought under control by the tiny predator, the bloom was still devastating. Because they had been exposed to the toxins for such a long time, Diane and her family were still at high risk. They were caught in this never-ending nightmare.

CHAPTER 63

Diane emailed her resignation to Bennett and Jenson the next morning. Bennett replied quickly.

Sorry to see you leave. Hope you and your uncle continue to recover. Please stay in touch.

A few hours later, she received an email from Jenson.

Would you be willing to meet with me? If so, when would it be convenient?

Staring at the message, she wondered why he wanted to see her. Before sending a response, her phone rang. She recognized the number, took a deep breath, and then answered, "Hi Isabelle."

"How you feeling?"

"Doing better. I know you want to talk about Jenson but—"

Isabelle cleared her throat. "We need to let everyone know what that asshole has been up to. All the death and destruction that he's responsible for."

Diane paused for a second. "Why are you reaching out to me?"

"From my sources, I'm convinced that Jenson used and manipulated the Landrys, your labmates, and the deceased postdoc who attacked OSCF. He's too clever to leave evidence pointing to him."

Diane recalled Todd telling her that Landry did whatever Jenson wanted. She stopped chewing her bottom lip and asked, "Why not use your sources if they know so much?"

"Only strong suspicions. What we need is a confession."

A laugh escaped Diane. "You think he's going to pour his heart out to me?"

Isabelle got quiet. Diane heard a soft, muffled cry, and then Isabelle tearily said, "You and your family survived. Many did not." Her tone escalated into an angry high pitch. "My grandmother is dead because of him!"

For so long, Diane had admired Jenson's scientific contributions and inspiring words. She figured in time that she could forgive herself for trusting Brandon. But the duplicity of Jenson felt like something else. It went beyond treachery. *Shaun Jenson killed the ocean.*

Isabelle sobbed. "I'm sorry, it's just . . ."

"You don't have to apologize. I resigned from OSCF."

Isabelle sniffled. Diane hesitated, considering if she should tell Isabelle that Jenson wanted a meeting. "I'll be coming down in a few days to move out of my apartment." She chewed on her bottom lip for a second and decided to share his request. "Dr. Jenson wants to see me."

Isabelle stopped crying. Her voice cracked with shaky excitement. "Perfect! We have mini recording devices that'll fit into a pin, a ring. I can set you up with one inside a bracelet. You can wear it to the meeting."

The idea of Jenson confessing his involvement in the environmental disaster made Diane uncomfortable. "Why would he reveal a secret like that to me?"

"He doesn't view you as a threat. If he did, you'd be dead."

Diane pondered that thought in silence.

Isabelle softened her tone. "Let me know when you're coming. I'll book a round-trip airline ticket and pick you up at the airport."

"I have to bring my stuff back."

"Hell, I'll hire movers and have them move your belongings to anywhere you want."

"You're doing all this and you don't know that he'll say anything. Chances are he won't."

"I have faith in you. You're an intelligent person who always tries to do the right thing."

Diane thought of being used by Brandon and let out a heavy sigh. "I'm not smart, especially when it comes to people."

"Lita, my grandmother, once told me a story about a rich man who gave everything he had to the poor. He ended up penniless on the streets of Cuba. People thought he was stupid, but he was always smiling. Maybe giving all his riches to the destitute wasn't smart. He did what was needed . . . what was right."

"Perhaps *you* should meet Jenson."

Isabelle laughed. "He wants to see you."

Diane couldn't refuse a paid round-trip ticket and moving expenses. She emailed Jenson a meeting invitation, which he accepted, and sent Isabelle and Bennett her plans to visit OSCF.

Isabelle responded with a thumbs-up icon.

Bennett wrote, *Wonderful. Have lots to share!*

Diane didn't fear returning to the foundation, especially since Dr. Landry and her posse were gone. What bothered her most was Jenson's request to see her in person. He could have virtually communicated farewells and good wishes. He had rescued her, so the idea of him physically harming her made little sense. Her experience at OSCF had taught her an invaluable lesson: trust no one.

CHAPTER 64

Three days later, Diane arrived at the Fort Lauderdale airport and found Isabelle inside a silver Subaru. As they drove to OSCF, Isabelle handed her a bracelet and pointed at the onyx gemstone. "Before you enter the room with Jenson, press down on the stone until you feel it vibrate. The sensation will be the instrument clicking on to record."

Diane gave her a sly smile and slipped on the bangle. "Like a James Bond movie. Is it a digital recorder that saves onto a file or YouTube?"

"No. The recording is saved only to the device." Isabelle pointed at the digital clock on the dashboard. "Your meeting with Jenson isn't for another hour. We could grab some food."

"Sounds nice, but I told Dr. Bennett I'd visit with her."

Isabelle drove up to OSCF's gate and showed the guard her press pass. After they pulled into the parking lot, Diane got out of the car and waved at Isabelle.

Isabelle gave her a thumbs-up. "Meet you back here in a couple of hours."

Diane watched the silver car disappear. With so much adrenaline flowing, she paid little attention to the pain gnawing at her back. Her wobbly legs and jittery nerves were reminiscent of her first day at the foundation when she had been full of ideas and excitement. Her head throbbed with the thought of having to enter the white-block building.

While walking toward the front doors, she stopped and stood in the same spot where Matt had been in his truck, gazing at a starfish.

Wanting to unveil their horrible truths, Diane and Matt had snapped. Matt had blown up a laboratory. Diane had destroyed a wastewater treatment plant. Now she was preparing to meet with the man who had taken Matt's life but had saved hers.

The guard at the front entrance nodded at Diane. Some workers stared at her while others gave curious glances. She found Bennett in the newly restored bio-lab that had fresh paint, new furniture, and shiny equipment.

Bennett had a radiant smile. Her bright blue eyes looked well rested. No dark circles, no beeping phone, and no stacks of paper in front of her.

Diane gaped. "My goodness, you look great, and so does the lab."

"Thank you. Please, have a seat." Once she was seated, Bennett jumped right in. "I told the authorities everything I knew. Of course, Shaun beat me to it. Still, it felt good to tell them what I had witnessed."

"What a relief."

"I called Matt's family, something I should've done a long time ago but didn't because of my guilt. I told them I thought Matt was a wonderful young man and a gifted chemist."

"Are you moving to another place, a different job?"

Bennett relaxed in a chair and beamed. "I have several offers in the works. I promised to help get the bio-lab organized in the meantime. It'll be another month before I leave."

Diane was amazed at Bennett's transformation from overburdened to joyful.

"How's your back?" Bennett asked.

"Better. I keep up with my exercises."

Bennett turned to her computer. "An oceanographic institute sent down a remote-controlled submersible in the same area of the Gulf where we pulled you out. OSCF's underwater robot camera must've malfunctioned. The institute recorded deep-sea life just as you said, except there's no floating thick substance."

On the computer screen were images of dragonfish with jagged teeth, cephalopods, schools of red fish with bulging eyes, and an orange starfish splayed on the seafloor. Diane was curious, but she was satisfied with not understanding how these creatures survived. The most important thing was that they were alive.

While Diane scrolled through the pictures, Bennett stood and said, "Maybe you and I could collaborate on a proposal for monitoring phytoplankton growth in the Gulf."

Diane stopped viewing the photos. "I'm going to look for a teaching position at a small college."

"Research. Asking questions. They're what you do. And who you really are."

Diane felt as if something inside her had broken after plummeting into the deep waters, some part of herself had been left behind on a cold, dark ocean floor. "Maybe slipping through a phantom chemical changed my DNA."

"We needed to harvest the blue copepod for our survival," Bennett said, furrowing her brows. "It could have been our biggest mistake."

Diane recalled being unnerved at Jenson's idea of harvesting the seas with an invasive organism. "We didn't have a choice."

"The blue copepod is now part of the food web throughout the Gulf and the Atlantic. It will most likely out-compete naturally occurring copepods that provide a normal balance."

"An invasive organism. Let's ask our alligators what they think about sharing a swamp with Burmese pythons."

"Exactly."

"I hope that our little blue crustacean provides a strong base for the food chain. We're going to need it."

Bennett tilted her head. "Meaning?"

"At the height of the bloom, I'd guess trillions—hell, probably zillions—of red dinos were in the ocean. What does the red dino do in an inhospitable environment?"

"It goes dormant, transitioning to a resting cyst."

"One sleeping cell, waiting for conditions to improve."

"You think we've delayed the inevitable? This will happen again?"

Diane paused, wanting to give a positive response. "Not necessarily. I've heard other researchers are finding some phytoplankton in the Gulf. Hopefully, the blue copepod will flourish and support the ocean. Without it, we're dead."

Bennett nodded, gazing at the picture of a starfish on her computer screen. "Other researchers and I are proposing a ten-year research grant to monitor and study the blue copepod and recovery of the ecosystem. I'd love to have you as a collaborator."

Diane stood, stretching her back. "Appreciate that, but I'm out. Gonna teach."

Bennett took a step back, studying her. "Do you know why I hired you?"

She shrugged. "My look of desperation?"

Bennett smiled. "You told me about finding a slick of fuel on the water, a disregard for sea life. You became a marine biologist to improve your understanding of an ecosystem that needs protection."

Diane snapped, "They're dead! I failed!"

Bennett moved toward the monitor and pointed at the starfish. "That's life! I'm giving you an opportunity to study what is happening and help our oceans recover."

Diane glanced at the clock on the wall. Five minutes remained before her meeting with Jenson. She stammered, "I'll think about it."

Bennett's voice softened. "I hope so. You're going to meet Dr. Jenson?"

Diane jokingly asked, "Should I wear a bulletproof vest?"

Bennett shook her head. "You'll be fine."

That's what you said about my boarding the ship with Landry.

CHAPTER 65

Jenson's office door was closed. After waiting several minutes, Diane's back ached. Just as she was getting up to stretch, Jenson walked out with a group of visitors thanking him for his time. He saw Diane and gave her a wide smile, his dimples on full display. "Dr. Nelson, glad you're here. Please come in."

She pressed the smooth black stone on her bracelet and felt a slight vibration. A hollow feeling grew in the pit of her stomach, and she chewed on her bottom lip.

Her back ached as she tried to find a comfortable position in the chair across from his large desk stacked with paperwork and journals. His oversized office smelled like lemon furniture polish and displayed several pictures of him with prominent personalities. When he passed her, a musky cologne scent lingered. He looked relaxed in a gray Dior suit with a lavender-colored shirt.

His amiable tone was businesslike when he spoke again. "I wanted you to know how much I've enjoyed your work and tenacity. Your intuition and analytic skills are incredible. I'll miss you."

"Thanks for the opportunity. I learned a lot."

A lot I didn't want to know.

"Also, I wanted to apologize to you. I had no reason to believe that Dr. Landry would hurt you. I never meant to put you in harm's way."

She nodded slowly, questioning his veracity. "Thank you for getting me out of the Gulf. Dr. Bennett said it was you who got the robot to lift me to the surface."

His eyes brightened. "I would never abandon you."

She had deserted a dying young woman and had taken advantage of Uncle Bo's loyalty that almost resulted in his death. Jenson hadn't forsaken her. "You saved me. But you shot Matt."

He had a weariness about him. "I had to . . . for everyone in this building."

"Matt said he was sorry. You had the gun. It was over."

"When that imbecile blew up his files, he destroyed everything we had on the reduction fluid and wiped out all of our data for testing other methods. Everything—gone!"

Diane felt the bracelet against her skin and extended her arms on her lap. "So you—"

"I killed the bastard before he completely ruined us!" His eyes narrowed. "For two decades, I've been fighting to get funds, to build and strengthen our mission. I'm always competing against heavy-hitting lobbyists backed by big corporations and other federal departments positioning themselves with huge budgets. Those pots of money go fast and often to people who don't give a shit about the environment." He paused, his tone sounding husky. "But I've been successful. Our work promotes and protects this planet. I would never let a disturbed psychopath destroy it."

"Your experimental process at the plant killed the ocean. If the blue copepod hadn't been able to neutralize the toxins and consume the algae, where would we be now?"

Jenson sank into the chair, his fingertips pressed together, and studied her. His stare was reminiscent of Landry's glaring. Though no evidence linked him personally to the illegal chemical concentrations in the river, she knew Matt had a final meeting with him and Landry. She believed Matt had made sure Jenson was aware of the chemical's damaging effects. "If you or that hellhound Landry had listened to Matt, all of this destruction could've been avoided."

His face contorted into a scowl, his lips tightening. “You’re so inexperienced and don’t know what you’re talking about.”

No longer able to sit with her back aching, Diane stood up. “Please explain it to me. I always wanted to work here because of your ideas and OSCF’s mission.” She paused, taking a short breath. “Please tell me it’s not all a lie.”

“What it takes to keep a genuinely good idea moving forward is at times . . . unrealistic.”

He rose from his chair, hung his head, and lowered his voice. “I asked you here for another reason.” He walked to the front of the desk and leaned against it, facing forward with his arms crossed. “While maneuvering the robot holding you, I noticed it had lost power in the ascent. Dr. Bennett said you observed a thick, clear substance.”

Diane stood in front of him. “Yes. She said others had gone there and hadn’t seen it.”

“That’s true. But a hundred nautical miles south of that location, I sent down a submersible that lost power. Reminded me of how the robot camera lost control.” He pursed his lips. “We returned to the location a week later, and other underwater vehicles had no problem navigating the waters.”

“Maybe the substance drifted.”

Jenson narrowed his eyes. “What did you think it was?”

“Your reduction fluid.”

His manner didn’t change. Instead, he moved toward the door.

She followed and turned to him before exiting the office. “What chemicals were you using at the plant?”

He didn’t answer.

After a few seconds, she said, “If the clear substance floating in the Gulf came from your pilot process, you have to clean it up.”

“I promise to do whatever it takes.”

Jenson reminded her of sea sparkle. His beautiful, shiny exterior was sought by mass media, but under that well-dressed, handsome shell was a person who knew how to dominate, how to kill.

Before leaving the building, she examined the onyx stone. Jenson admitted that he'd killed Matt to protect OSCF. She could hand over the device to Isabelle. That information along with the mother at the low-income unit saying that she saw workers dumping the clear fluid in the river should be enough to charge Jenson with atrocious crimes. OSCF would lose its power and dissolve. Justice would prevail. A smart decision. What was the right thing to do?

Jenson was the type of person who wanted to do the impossible. Saving her from the Gulf was a display of his power. The right thing was to let him clean up his mess. If he didn't try or caused more harm, then she would hand over the recording. For now, she wasn't turning in the man who had saved her. She slipped the bracelet off and into her pocket.

• • •

A few minutes later, Diane climbed into a silver Subaru. The journalist's big brown eyes glistened. "Did he confess?" Isabelle asked in an anxious voice. "What'd he say?"

Diane took a shallow breath. "Nothing useful."

Isabelle's eyes dulled. "Thought his arrogant ass would've let something slip." She glanced at Diane's wrist. "Where's the bracelet?"

Isabelle's strong desire to avenge her grandmother's death and to be the first reporter to shed light on Jenson's crimes in a news story was evident. Diane didn't feel comfortable telling her the truth. "When I walked through the metal detector, the bangle set off the alarm. Guards confiscated it."

Isabelle gaped. "Employees don't go through the detector."

"I'm not an employee. I turned in my resignation."

Isabelle stared at her. "Something sounds off. Let's go get it."

"I asked for it when I left and learned that the guard who had taken it was gone for the day. The guard on duty couldn't find it."

Isabelle scratched her head. "Oh, hell with it. I can get dozens more of them."

Later on, if Diane turned over the recording, she'd deal with Isabelle's wrath.

They drove to the Hollywood Beach apartment, where Diane met the movers, grabbed a few of her things, and turned in the key. When they got to the airport, she was getting out of the car when Isabelle grabbed her arm, pulling her back in. "Diane, I would probably feel beholden to someone who saved me, especially if I knew the person had every reason to let me die. You've been through so much horror." Isabelle shook her head, staring at Diane. "I just got a message from our tech person. The device and the bracelet wouldn't set off a metal sensor."

Shit!

Her heart racing, Diane tried to think of a smart response.

Isabelle dropped her head. She sounded defeated when she said, "You'll tell me when you're ready to talk." She stared into Diane's eyes. "Right?"

Diane nodded, tears welling in her eyes. She shuffled out of the door and whimpered, "I'm trying to do the right thing."

CHAPTER 66

August 26

About a year after leaving OSCF, Diane and her family moved back to the Panhandle. The Atlantic had returned to a beautiful blue color while the Gulf of Mexico had shades of indigo with swirls of purple. With each passing day, the sea breeze had transitioned from foul smells of decay to breezy salty air. Concentrations of neurotoxins had significantly declined in air and water. The news showed people celebrating as they returned to their homes, rebuilding businesses on the coast. Social media had pictures of Lake Ontario, no longer the color of bubblegum. Pensacola College had opened for the fall semester and had hired Diane as a biology instructor.

Diane had met with the prosecutor's office and given testimony regarding her assault and the resulting injuries. After hiring an expensive legal team, Dr. Landry had pleaded not guilty and was awaiting trial. Senator Landry had been found guilty of violating the Clean Water Act. He was fined two hundred fifty thousand dollars and sentenced to five years' imprisonment. Brandon and Nicole, individually represented by well-known lawyers, were cutting a deal with the district attorney by admitting guilt and providing evidence against Dr. Landry. The thought of these people receiving reduced sentences and the chance of getting out even earlier, thanks to parole, infuriated Diane. Mom had consoled her. "You get justice in the next world. In this world, you have the law."

Cable news televised congressional hearings used to obtain information about OSCF's pilot wastewater treatment plant. Members of Congress asked Jenson questions related to falsifying documents, then seconds later would praise the cofounder for discovering the blue copepod.

Government-owned ships on the Gulf were often highlighted in the news. Diane watched footage of Jenson inside a submersible being lowered into the purple waters. She had emailed Bennett and Isabelle and asked if they had learned anything new about OSCF's exploration of the Gulf. Neither was aware of any new discovery.

Diane had moved into an apartment close to Pensacola College. Regular exercises had strengthened her back, and she could go days without pain. Over the past week, her muscles ached, and she had lost her appetite. In the mornings, she awoke restless and fatigued. She worried it could be something serious. Medical experts continued to report findings of people with toxins remaining in their lungs or intestines. Thousands of patients had been diagnosed with delayed contamination. All of them had died.

• • •

The next morning, Diane visited the campus health center before driving to her Gulf home to spend the weekend with her family. Carla and Robby were driving from Kentucky to visit them.

"You've been repeatedly exposed to high levels of toxins," said the physician while she examined Diane's eyes. "We'll do a panel of tests."

Diane chewed on her bottom lip, thinking of what she would do if they diagnosed her with delayed contamination. "When will I know if I have it?"

"You'll receive an email with test results later today."

Diane scooted off the exam table and massaged her lower back. "If it comes back positive, what's the next step?"

"I'd refer you to a specialist."

After supplying blood and urine specimens, she thanked the doctor and drove to her family's house. No sense in worrying her family until she knew for sure.

Minutes later, Diane arrived at her Gulf home. The breezes felt brisk and free of putrid air. She spotted Uncle Bo walking toward the shed. His health had continued to improve. He no longer needed supplemental oxygen. Specialists monitored him and were vigilant about his lab work. Everything came back normal. He was feeling well enough to reignite his fish nursery after Henry had brought back juvenile snappers from the Atlantic. While stepping into the building, Bo almost tripped over Wily, who preferred being an outdoor cat. Diane had bought Wily a collar and noticed a tiny bell attached to it.

She called out to Bo. "Why does Wily sound like Tinkerbell?"

Bo took off his baseball cap and scratched his head. "That cat's got a bad habit of fishin' in the tanks. Thinks I can't see him slinking out with wet paws and a wiggly prize in his mouth."

Diane knelt and gave Wily a treat from her pocket. Shielding her eyes from the sunlight, she looked up at Bo. "Close the door behind you. Don't let him in."

"Well, he likes to watch me work."

Mom joined them. "It's more like your uncle enjoys the cat's company."

They heard a car door slam and turned to find Robby, holding a metal box, running toward them.

"Slow down!" Carla yelled and waved at them.

Robby rushed toward Diane, stopping a few inches in front of her.

Carla caught up, sounding out of breath. "Sorry, he's got ants in his pants."

Henry's truck pulled into the driveway. After Henry joined them, Mom introduced everyone.

Diane sat on the ground with Robby. He gave her the metal box. "This used to be Matt's secret box. Granny and Gramps took out all the stuff. I'm giving it to you . . . for your secrets."

"Do you still have your box?"

"Yep. It's not fun anymore. No one to share secrets with."

"How about Granny and Gramps?"

A shy smile lit up his face. He whispered, "That's who I keep secrets from."

She giggled. "Thanks for putting my name on the box. We could write to each other. You could share your secrets with me that way."

A large, toothy smile spread across his face with a look of pure joy.

Bo and Henry stood behind Robby. Bo studied the boy and said, "Heard you want to sail on the Gulf of Mexico."

Robby jumped to his feet. His eyes gleamed. "I'm ready."

Everyone laughed. Robby inched toward Carla.

"He has his swim trunks on," Carla said. "He can swim, but Diane told us it may not be safe enough."

"Beaches are full," Henry said, glancing at Bo.

Bo chuckled. "Hell, beaches are full when there are riptide warnings."

Mom smiled at Carla. "We haven't heard of anyone getting sick. Local reports show little to no toxins." She gave Bo and Henry a stern look. "They'll keep him safe—on the boat."

Bo nodded. "Sure we will. Me and Henry will anchor close to shore and use the smaller boat to sail to our picnic spot on the beach."

Robby skipped behind Bo and Henry toward the truck.

After packing sandwiches and potato salad, Diane walked with Mom and Carla to the beach. She asked Carla to share more memories about Matt. At times, Carla would get a little weepy but would regain her composure and smile. No discussion of trials, just nice stories of Matt.

They spread out a blanket and put out food and drinks. Carla gazed at the water and said, "Fred and I went to the beach many years back. I remember birds looking for a handout. Every so often something would leap out of the water far from the shore. Looks so different now."

The Gulf of Mexico wasn't the same. Though fish and other organisms would eventually start migrating into these waters from the

Atlantic, there were species found only in the Gulf that were gone forever.

"How's the orange starfish in Matt's tank?" Diane asked.

Carla covered her eyes with both hands, shaking her head. "Surviving, barely."

Diane handed her a book. "This shows how to maintain a saltwater aquarium. It has a section about starfish. You and Robby could read it together."

"Thank you," Carla beamed. "I need all the help I can get."

They heard the *Mississippi Queen*'s loud anthem and watched Bo and Henry anchor the ship. The men helped Robby onto a smaller boat, then motored to the beach. While everyone ate, Bo and Henry told jokes. Diane and Carla took turns tossing a Frisbee with Robby until almost sunset.

"Robby, we need to get goin'," Bo said. "Gotta get Henry's ship back to the harbor before dark."

After cleaning up, Diane returned to the house with Mom and Carla. Diane went to her old room and pulled out the onyx bracelet hidden in the closet. She slipped it on her wrist, then grabbed a pen, paper, and the secret box.

"It's dark outside," Carla said, looking through the window at the driveway, waiting for Robby to return with Bo and Henry.

"You want company?" Mom asked Diane.

"You and Carla stay and take it easy. Robby will be back soon. I won't be long."

Diane walked to the beach and sat on a stone wall close enough to see the small white breakers against the darkness. She checked her phone. No email with her test results. She took out the pen and paper from the box and wrote funny things to put in the box to share with Robby.

Jingle, jingle, jingle.

Wily had followed her. She rubbed his back. "You want more treats."

Staring at the Gulf, she wondered if the thick, clear substance had been a hallucination. A part of her wanted Jenson to find the anomaly and remove it, a heroic act to save the seas that he had destroyed. He was not the person she had wanted him to be. He'd killed the ocean, murdered Matt, and manipulated countless others.

He saved me.

Her phone beeped. An email with her lab results.

She hesitated to open it, staring at the screen. Steeling herself, she took a deep breath and read it.

Negative!

Bursting into laughter, she dropped everything. Her thoughts went to her grandma, who wrote personal verses. Diane picked up the pen and paper, then scribbled down her favorite passage.

Like the oceans, we can be calm, turbulent, and unpredictable, all while remaining a mysterious wonder full of infinite possibilities.

Diane slipped off the bracelet, stared at the onyx hiding Jenson's truth, then placed it with the verse inside the box. Rubbing the smooth metal exterior, she believed everything would be okay. Her family was well, and she was hopeful the oceans would recover, eventually.

She lifted Wily into her arms and gazed at the Gulf, the source of her inspiration and strength. The small sea that had provided for her family. In the surf, there was a silky light, faint enough that a passerby would not have noticed it. She knew it too well—the soft glow of sea sparkle.

THE END

ACKNOWLEDGEMENTS

Thank you to the Atlanta Writers Club for providing opportunities to learn more about the writing profession and to connect with other writers. The Roswell critique group played a crucial role in honing my writing and preparing this story for publication, and I owe them a great debt of gratitude for their support. A special thank-you to George Weinstein, Kim Conrey, and Daniel Burke for their review of the manuscript and encouragement.

The first person to read and critique an early draft of the manuscript was Marlene Adelstein. I am grateful to her for being so gracious and kind in her review, and for taking the time to answer questions about the business and art of writing.

Thank you, Elizabeth Zell. The excitement you had for wanting to read the manuscript lifted my spirit. Your friendship, feedback, and optimism helped me gain confidence as a writer.

Thank you, David Flegel. Your remarkable talent for editing, along with your fishing expertise, improved the manuscript.

To my amazing children, Anna, Isaac, and Michael Kirtland: You are the reason I strive to write a story with an important environmental message. Thank you for your unwavering love and support. Anna, thank you for creating an image of the fictional dinoflagellate. Your artistic skills brought the microorganism to life, solidifying its features in the story.

To my mom, Emma Joyce Roberts, an avid reader of fiction: You offered valuable input on the early version of the manuscript. When I shared your comments with other writers, they asked if you could be their beta reader. Your love of literature rubbed off on me. Thank you for nurturing my desire to read and write.

To my dad, Donnie Roberts: My world dimmed after your passing. The loss was an inspiration to create a character who encompassed your joy and love. Uncle Bo comes close to revealing your playful humor, wisdom, and devotion to family. Some of my fondest childhood memories revolve around you: water-skiing on the Green River, swimming in Lake Cumberland, and playing in the waves of the Atlantic Ocean.

ABOUT THE AUTHOR

With an M.S. in marine biology and a Ph.D. in environmental health sciences, K.A. Kirtland turned her love of writing and passion for life sciences into a page-turning eco-thriller. As a graduate student, she took part in research expeditions on the Gulf of Mexico and on the Weddell Sea in the Antarctic. In Atlanta, Georgia, she works as a public health professional and has published several journal articles. She is a member of the Atlanta Writers Club and has won awards from the Atlanta Writers Conference. She has three incredible children and a seven-foot-long Brazilian rainbow boa named Samara.

NOTE FROM K.A. KIRTLAND

Word-of-mouth is crucial for any author to succeed. If you enjoyed *Bleeding Sea*, please leave a review online—anywhere you are able. Even if it's just a sentence or two. It would make all the difference and would be very much appreciated.

Thanks!
K.A. Kirtland

www.ingramcontent.com/pod-product-compliance
Lightning Source LLC
LaVergne TN
LVHW091530060526
838200LV00036B/551
9781685134839